THE
MAGICIAN'S
TOMB

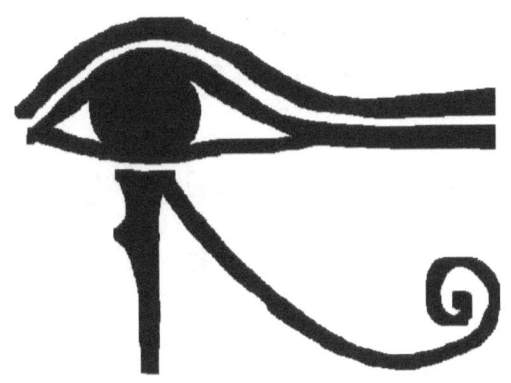

Also by W.J. Cherf

The Manuscripts of the Richards' Trust

Bow Tie

Recovery

Children of Ptah

Imhotep

Maat-ka-re. Memoires of a Time Traveler

The Adventures of J.J. Stone

The First Soul

The Lictor of Magic

I Am the Storm

THE MAGICIAN'S TOMB

ADVENTURES IN PARANORMAL ARCHAEOLOGY I

BY

W.J. CHERF

FOXBAT PUBLISHING

Foxbat Publishing
ISBN: 978-0-9989318-5-2

DEDICATION

Every author is indebted to those who offer their criticism. It is the process that makes a story better and often thick skin is required. To the august members of the Fiction Foundry of Colorado Springs, Colorado, I extend my deepest thanks for your time and many fine suggestions, which propelled this project into book-form. To Chris in particular, well, what can I say. Words cannot express my gratitude.

Bottom line: Sweet Sue liked this one. That's all that really matters.

CHAPTER 1

The season's Khamsin Winds had come and gone. As a consequence, the tawny desert plateau of Sakkara looked as if a vast broom had swept it smooth. Some ancient remains were choked with sand, while others tantalizingly peeked out from beneath their wind-blown overburden. Throughout, delicate though hellishly sharp Neolithic stone tools of black obsidian, tan flint, and brown chert lay on the surface waiting for a passerby to collect them. Gorgeous deep blue and green glazed faience fragments competed for similar attention. Such things the sharp-eyed Omar gathered, sometimes weighing down his cotton jellabiya's pockets as if filled with lead.

But on this day, from afar, Omar saw an odd depression marring the terrain's otherwise uniform contour. As he approached, the young lad found newly exposed bedrock and a long rectangular shape leading up to it. Next to one edge, Omar got down on all fours and brushed away some of the sand. Disregarding the sharp stone flakes cutting into his palms and knees, what Omar saw told the fourteen-year-old all he needed to know. He ran faster than his shadow to tell his father of his good fortune, while he loped down the ramp-like slope of the plateau toward the lush fields of the Nile Valley below.

Mere minutes later, the young man found his father who stood with a grimy wrench over a sputtering diesel pump. "Father! I have found something!"

Looking up to his son, Habib, the field foreman at the Temple of Ptah excavation, pulled out a rag from his back pocket and began wiping off his oil-covered tool. "So, my son, tell me of your many adventures."

That very day and only a scant ten meters away, a middle-aged Egyptologist named Dr. Erik Reissen was hard at work within the Temple of Ptah, located within the ancient site of Memphis. Perspiration streamed down the sides of his chiseled face and darkened his tan shirt in ever expanding areas that ended in dried salt stains. Reissen's personal devil was the Aswan High Dam and Lake Nasser, which conspired to raise the ground water of the valley. His trenches consequently had bilge pumps that fought off their transformation into deep buffalo mud wallows. Secretly, the Austrian yearned for the Egyptian government's permission to dig in a more suitable environment—like the one just above him on the Sakkara plateau. Then, at that moment, his last functioning water pump gave up in a shriek of metal and a plume of diesel smoke.

"*Scheisse!*" he cursed. "This ruins the budget.

Now, I have four pumps that need rebuilding. This accursed season is now total rubbish!" His nearby graduate students cringed while pretending not to hear.

The archaeologist stood over the sizzling hot, seized motor. Its ruined head gasket freely bled fuel. Disgusted, and with hands on hips, Reissen stared at it with a defeated look on his face as seeping ground water already inched in.

"Erik," his experienced field foreman, and long-time friend, said in Arabic, "things could be worse."

"How, Habib?"

"Everything is in the hands of Allah."

The frustrated archaeologist stared back with a tight jaw, while sweat dripped from the tip of his straight nose.

"My friend, fifteen minutes ago my ever-adventurous son came to me with some news. He found something on the plateau that he is very excited about. He wants to tell his Uncle Erik about it."

"Well I suppose now is about as good as any." The Austrian said with a kick. "This pump is worthless." He nodded to his foreman. "Okay then. I ready to hear what Omar has to say."

Habib waved his son over. "Alright, my son, tell Uncle Erik what you told me."

All excited and wringing his hands, Omar did, but Reissen only half listened as he eyed the boy's bulging jellabiya pockets.

Raising his hand to pause the jumbled narrative, "What's in your pockets, Omar?"

The blushing boy said, "Some things that I found in the desert."

"Let's see them," the archaeologist encouraged, as he took Habib's oily rag and laid it out on a flat foundation stone.

So Omar did, carefully laying out all of his new-found treasures. Seeing them transported Reissen back to his youthful home in the mountain village of Steinegg, Austria, where he too once scoured the countryside in search of stone tools. Carefully, touching each, the Austrian smiled and conspiratorially said, "Omar, these tools are beautiful. Now, please continue and tell me what you found."

After several minutes, Reissen decided, slapping his thighs. "Let's take the truck and go see Omar's find."

After a brief drive up from the valley to the Sakkara plateau, Reissen parked his tan Toyota pickup in the bus parking lot next to the massive Step Pyramid complex. There, the threesome got out.

"Omar," his father said, "take us to your discovery."

"Yes, father." And off the scamp went, heading north, his sandals leaving rooster tails of sand in the air. On and on he went, past the Pyramid of Userkaf, and the many flat-topped tombs of the Old Kingdom.

While Reissen and Habib tried to keep up, the Austrian remarked, "Must be nice to be so young."

On the windward side of a minor eminence, Omar stood impatiently waiting, unconsciously bouncing on his toes. An exposed bedrock outcrop and its all too regular adjacent depression then came into view. Reissen stopped and looked around to get his bearings. *I'm just west of the tombs of the First and Second Dynasty kings. I wonder ...*

Standing proudly over the narrow depression in the afternoon sun, Omar pointed, "Here, father. Here it is, Uncle Erik."

Reissen dropped to his knees and examined the very spot that Omar had cleared away. He allowed his fingers to follow along the exposed, chiseled edge. "This looks very promising."

Looking over at a grinning Omar who had squatted down opposite, the Austrian smiled, shook his head, and said, "Habib. Is it allowed to reward your son with a box of ice cream?"

Habib, seeing his friend's ploy, stroked his thick salt and pepper moustache in pretended consideration. "Well, I suppose. He is, after all, a good son."

At hearing this, Omar, still grinning ear-to-ear, squeezed his hands together in gleeful anticipation of the rare treat.

The Austrian sat back on his weathered boot heels, pulled out his smart phone, and called the Antiquities

Inspector of the Sakkara plateau, a man named Dr. Hussain Kama. To his mild surprise, he found that the bureaucrat was still at his desk.

"This is Kama," The man answered tersely.

"Inspector Kama, this is Dr. Erik Reissen of the Austrian archaeological mission. I apologize for this intrusion so late in the day, but I am calling to inform you of a new discovery in your district."

"Dr. Reissen, where in my district?"

"North Sakkara. Just north of the pyramid of Userkaf."

"Dr. Reissen, I was under the impression that you were in Memphis at the Temple of Ptah. How did you happen upon this news?"

"A tip, Inspector Kama."

"I see, and where are you now?"

"I am looking down at it right now."

"And what's its condition, Dr. Reissen?"

"I have no idea, inspector. It appears to be undisturbed. The recent sand storm must have exposed it."

"Where did you say you were again?"

*　　*　　*

Kama put down the receiver with a heavy sigh, pausing to think.

Yet another issue to address.

More paperwork.

Should I send out my assistant Ali Hassan to assess this? No. I'll go. I need the exercise. Besides, Reissen's voice was quite revealing. While still quite clipped and precise, it actually betrayed much more. That stiff-necked Austrian was actually excited about something.

*   *   *

Twenty minutes later, a white Toyota Corolla jounced along the secondary road that faced the massive tombs of the First and Second Dynasty kings. Kama had to admit that it was good to get out of the office. Besides, Reissen's poorly concealed excitement was contagious.

Parking his car on the side of the road, the Egyptian antiquities official got out, and saw Reissen waving his arms from high above on the plateau. As the thick man fought his way up the steep slope and its loose surface, each labored step reminded him why he no longer worked in the field.

Kama, heavily perspiring and puffing hard, said, upon reaching where Reissen and two others stood, "This had better be good, Dr. Reissen!"

"Look for yourself, Inspector Kama," the Austrian gestured. "This depression appears to be the entrance to something—perhaps even a tomb."

Accessing the length and width of the depression, Kama got down and felt along the exposed chiseled edge. Standing up and brushing off the knees of his pants, "It certainly does."

Now looking the Austrian in the eye, "Does your mission have the resources to look into this?"

Shrugging, Reissen said, "Yes, Inspector Kama, it does. We can provide you a preliminary assessment. But on one condition."

"Which is?"

"That next season this site is added to my current excavation permit."

Now Kama, shrugging, thought, *all of my archaeological resources are already stretched beyond their capacity. Reissen and his team represent a quick and ready fix.*

Mind made up, Kama answered, "That seems a reasonable request, Dr. Reissen. I will see to the amendment of your mission's permit myself. How quickly can you secure this site?"

"Immediately, Inspector Kama. Just inform your antiquities security detachment of our arrangement, and I'll see to the rest."

* * *

The next morning, Reissen held a meeting of his entire field staff. The group agreed that Habib and the bulk of the Austrian field crew would wrap up their season at the Temple of Ptah, record and secure their finds, and fill in their trenches three weeks early. Reason: no bilge pumps.

In the meantime, Reissen and three graduate students would begin their investigation of what had become the "Omar Find." Yes, there was lots of grumbling, but as soon as the temple team finished their duties to Habib's satisfaction, they too were to join Reissen up on the plateau. This carrot silenced the grousing.

By mid-morning of day one, Reissen and his band had loaded up their truck with all their gear, drove up to the plateau, and stood before the suspicious rectangular depression.

"Okay, everyone," Reissen said, "Time to get to work!" And they did, naturally falling into their practiced activities.

Jürgen Peters and Willim Franks busied themselves with the set up of their state-of-the-art base station—a laser surveying tool. This high-tech toy would provide the team with a versatile and state-of-the-art 3D plot of the entire site.

Else Wald, a willowy red-haired woman with freckles and wearing a cap with back and side flaps, wasted no time and began snapping photos. It was her task to capture the site while in its pristine state—to provide the needed imagery to establish an archaeological baseline.

Peters, a short, well-built, and shaggy-haired

Bavarian, made his measurements at the base station. Franks, like a lanky and hyperactive toad, hopped about from datum point to datum point with his surveyor's rod. All of this activity Wald photographed for posterity.

Before noon, the virgin site had been recorded, mapped, measured, and entered into Reissen's laptop. Satisfied with these preliminaries, the archaeologist announced, "The preliminary survey is encouraging. The width of this depression, from edge to edge, is precisely 4.57 meters, or ten Egyptian cubits. That number is not accidental. If this is a tomb, that measure would provide more than enough room for a stone sarcophagus."

Bright and wide grins shined all around.

"But as for the length of this depression, only one thing can provide that ..." Reissen turned to the truck and pulled out four, short-handled garden hoes and several rubber tire baskets.

"Alright everyone," Reissen said, "Let's clear out this depression."

Rather quickly, the Hollywood allure of Egyptian archaeology became serious work. The four-some spread themselves out along the depression's length, with each clearing away a side. Reissen chose the end nearest the bedrock outcropping, while Peters, the opposite.

The grueling drudgery of moving and lifting sand

and rock went on for the next seven days. From dawn until noon, Reissen and his team labored.

On day eight, Peters announced that he had exposed the beginning slope of a ramp in the native limestone bedrock. Work immediately stopped while the rest of his team examined his claim.

"Excellent, Jürgen!" Reissen beamed. "Else. Grab your camera and meter stick to record this moment! Meanwhile, let's take a water break. I must take some notes."

*   *   *

As it turned out, Jürgen's find marked only the beginning. The sharply chiseled edge along the depression's length quickly gave way to smoothed vertical limestone walls decorated with a long, raised relief of an undulating snake on each side. On day twelve, Jürgen was the first to note this detail when he uncovered the unpainted tip of a snake's tail at the ramp's entrance.

At this point, Habib and the rest of the Austrian field crew joined in. To Reissen's amazement, the cleared depression became a long descending entrance ramp that ended with a raised cobra deity on each side—in clear protection of the deceased. The cobra deity, *Wadjet*, was the royal insignia of Lower Egypt that usually appeared on a pharaoh's brow.

Is this an entrance to a royal's tomb?

The ramp ended at a decorated bedrock grotto partially shaded from the sun. The central image was a beautifully carved false door and lintel—an ancient Egyptian funerary device that provided a magical entrance to the underworld. Around this carved image of a door was arrayed the deceased's biographical data complete with a portrait front and center. Surrounding the false door proper, the smoothed limestone bedrock was covered in twelve registers or columns of delicate raised relief hieroglyphs. An offering slab before the false door completed the scene, where relatives could place funerary offerings of beer and food for the enjoyment of the deceased.

But there was more. Before the false door and its offering table a grotesque scene was preserved in the talcum powder-like sand. Five naturally mummified figures lay in preserved postures of exquisite agony. Their measles-like skin, dried to the consistency of brittle parchment, was peppered with bloody punctures. Four huddled individuals cowered before the false door and hid their heads in tight fetal positions. The fifth had attempted to escape by crawling away up the ramp, dragging behind him outstretched, apparently useless legs. His arm groped for something just beyond his grasp. *What was he reaching for?* Reissen wondered.

Found discarded near each grave robber lay a copper chisel and wooden mallet, once valuable objects dropped for some dire reason. The team also noted in the flooring before the false door five chisel marks in the bedrock. All matched the abandoned copper chisels. Whatever happened to the five, it occurred shortly after their first chisel strikes.

"A most horrible way to die." Habib concluded from his squatted position near the bodies. Reissen soberly nodded in agreement. "But of what? That's what I want to know."

As the Austrian stood up, he looked around, and then beckoned. "Else. I want tight shots on these individuals, especially their skin. While we can't do autopsies on them, perhaps someone back home can tell us what happened to them."

Returning his gaze to his foreman, "Once we record these remains, I'll call Inspector Kama for further instructions."

In the meantime, Else carefully picked her way between the fallen forms, placing metric scales and signage next to each before capturing their grisly images.

Reissen could tell that his field photographer was uncomfortable with the necessary process. In fact, the entire team just stood around and stared in disbelief.

Willi Franks summed it up best, "Grave robbing in Egypt is a high-risk business."

On the last day, Peters and Franks resurveyed the site. Wald painstakingly recorded its many details, totally oblivious to what her images would reveal. With the inscribed walls securely tarped and the hole filled in with the help of a borrowed bulldozer, the season came to a close for the Austrian archaeological mission. For Reissen and his team, they had made a herculean effort during those three weeks. Now, they had to wait until next season to continue.

CHAPTER 2

Like seeks out like. While prim ivory tower social engineers may pontificate and postulate otherwise, the desire to associate with those of shared interest cannot be deterred. In the end, it is the very nature of like things to congregate. For Hidden Folk enclaves of vampire, witch, werewolf, faith healer, succubus, wizard, revenant or ghoul, they do exist; and for that matter, so does any mix of them with gifted paranormals. While the existence of such gatherings might shock most humankind, they nonetheless convene on a regular basis throughout the world. For example, it is well documented that such associations can be found in every major city, and in larger urban metroplexes, often there are several to choose from.

So who are the Hidden Folk? A precise definition fails. But in general, they are the misunderstood outcasts of Western Civilization, the pagan remnant of the ancient world, the mythological creatures that modernity chooses to ignore, that humankind's *science* derisively labels as cryptids. In short, they are those which the Christian Church and Islam refused to embrace, declaring them unholy and unclean abominations worthy of persecution and even pious slaughter.

* * *

The monthly meeting of the International Cultural Studies Society of Cairo met within the pink neoclassical walls of the Egyptian Museum near Tahir Square. After sundown and when the museum was closed to the public, the society's twenty-six members filed in through the staff entrance on the right. Once inside, they made their way on the Ground Floor to the three-story tall northern hall. There, they sat around eight temporary tables arranged in a narrow rectangle, beneath the monumental statues of the heretic Pharaoh Akhenaton. Not that the membership particularly preferred this location, but it was the only configuration available amid a floor space cramped with Egypt's most ancient artifacts.

The First Chair, an appointed parliamentarian, rapped upon the wooden table's red linen surface with a smoothly carved stone, clearly of Neolithic origin, to convene, lead, and close the proceedings. The First Chair sat at one end of the rectangle. At the table's opposite end, sat the Senior Chair, a position held solely by seniority, and as was the case with this enclave—extreme longevity. The Senior Chair decided upon the society's monthly agenda, made comment when needed, embodied its spirit, and motivated the membership. By tradition more than inclination, the enclave was not a democratic institution; rather it was firmly autocratic as it consistently followed the Senior Chair's lead.

The First Chair, Shaheen, banged the stone twice to bring the meeting to order. He had done so without touching it. Of Persian origin, the name "Shaheen" roughly translated as "Royal White Falcon," which in this setting appropriately morphed into the "Royal White Horus." Impeccably turned out in a dark silk suit, the telepathic and telekinetic adept formally called the meeting to order with a deep voice that echoed in the large open space.

"Welcome, my brethren. It is good to see you once again. Our agenda today is full, so let us begin, forthwith. First off, dear colleagues, *Decorum*."

This request produced a rustling of clothing as the membership removed, shut down, and placed their personal handheld devices before them on the table.

"Thank you all." He bowed. "Next, I recognize the Second Chair."

The Second Chair, Fazilah Rahman, the chronographer of the society, was a tall, striking, and ageless blue-black woman much cherished for her extraordinary empathic and healing powers. Born in the northern Sudan, Rahman's age remained her own secret, but rumor placed her birth somewhere in the mid-seventh century, squarely in the midst of the Islamic Conquest.

Consulting her open laptop, Rahman reported, "This is rare. We have no anniversaries this month. However, next month will be a busy one as five of our membership will be celebrating." She concluded with a dazzling smile of perfect teeth. "That is all that I have to report, First Chair."

"Thank you for your report, Second Chair," Shaheen acknowledged with a bow of his head. "I next recognize, Dr. Hamid Gohar. Sir, the floor is yours."

An utterly unremarkable, dark-haired and mustached Egyptian fractionally bowed his head toward Shaheen in acknowledgment. A member of the Supreme Council of Egyptian Antiquities, his office had been recently moved to the newly constructed Grand Egyptian Museum in Giza. By trade, Gohar, whose Persian name meant "precious jewel," was a respected international linguist and papyrologist. His unique abilities ranged from telepathy to spell forensics—in other words, he was a crack "spell whisperer" who could identify all the particulars of a spell's casting. At the ripe old age of six hundred and five years, Gohar's seniority fell along this enclave's median age range.

"Thank you, First Chair. I wish to report upon an interesting development that has occurred within the

North Sakkaran necropolis." The membership naturally leaned in with interest. "The Austrian Archaeological Mission from the University of Vienna has uncovered the remains of a tomb that we may have to deal with in the near future. On the basis of a preliminary visit to the site, the tomb's owner appears to be named Djedi, a heretofore mythological magician dating back to the Egyptian Old Kingdom. My dear colleagues, *if* this is indeed the tomb of the master magician Djedi, then he was one of us—a distant member of the Hidden Folk. Consequently, this situation I will continue to monitor closely as the excavation by the Austrians progresses."

"Thank you, Dr. Gohar." Shaheen silkily said while his colleague opposite signaled to be recognized. "Next, I believe the Senior Chair, Tarek el-Marsy, wishes to share something."

"Thank you, First Chair," began Tarek el-Masry, "the Egyptian", who next month would be one of the five to celebrate his birthday. In his case, it was his two thousand and forty-eighth. Born as Wennofre in the year Cleopatra VII committed suicide, Tarek's abilities lay as a physician and magician. His extraordinary longevity he once quipped to a wise diet and healthy dose of magic. Things that he learned while holding an influential post as high priest of Isis in Alexandria.

"How can I say this without offending someone at this gathering?

"The truth is—I can't. Modern humankind is an

arrogant bunch. There, I said it, and I feel so much better for it.

"Where do I begin?" Tarek continued with hands waving theatrically in the air. "Humankind thinks they are the most wise, creative, and industrious species. Yet, they consistently get into pickles they cannot extract themselves from, lacking the intelligence, motivation, and patience to do so. That's where we come in," he pointed around the table—"the Hidden Folk. We do what we can, and with a bit of luck, another crisis is averted."

He then paused.

"But I'm not finished." The Egyptian leaned in.

"Without question, humankind is, and has always been, unnecessarily dangerous and warlike. With heads held haughtily high, they universally award themselves apex predator status, something that is far removed from reality.

"Don't believe me? Take our cousins the Forest Folk, considered a laughable fairy tale, a cryptid species by most of humankind. When in fact, they are the earth's premier hunters and have been so since the last glaciation. Ask any North American First Nation shaman, or for that matter, any Hindi, Pakistani, Russian, or Nepalese elder." He counted off on his fingers. "They all have given the Forest Folk fearsome names—cannibal demons, hairy savages, and devils of the forest. Remember: these names, and others, were given by those who know them up close and personal.

"Now we hear from Dr. Gohar about the possible discovery of one of our ancestors, of the magician Djedi himself. Humankind flat out considers him an Egyptian myth. But mark my words," now wagging his finger, "if humankind can attach bones to myth, it no longer is myth. For us Hidden Folk, such a result does not bode well. Even worse, if humankind comes into possession of Djedi's secrets, then the arrogant will indeed inherit the earth."

As usual, Tarek's words fell heavily upon his colleagues, seemed almost to suck the air out of their lungs. The potential ramifications seemed endless.

However, for one member, the most junior, he hadn't heard a word of the old Egyptian's rant. Instead, it was Gohar's words and thoughts about the Austrian mission's archaeological find that consumed him. The young one saw in Gohar's mind that the man had held quite a bit back. His fingers, when he touched the carved hieroglyphs of Djedi's name, had actually received a psychic shock of kinship. None of this did the papyrologist mention to the membership at large, but the young one read it nonetheless. As if necessary, Gohar's hard stare back at the young one's psychic intrusion spoke volumes.

* * *

The antecedents for the International Cultural Studies Society in Cairo reached back to the third century of our era with the Platonic revival by the Egyptian philosopher Plotinus. At the core of his philosophy rested three principles: the One; the Intellect; and the Soul. Radiating out from the Alexandrian School in Alexandria, the unquestioned academic nexus of the Eastern Mediterranean, these ideas would influence the ancient Classical world, Judaism, Christianity, Islam, and even the English Enlightenment.

Shortly thereafter, however, this intellectual primacy rapidly eroded with the ascendency of Christianity, the Christianization of the Roman emperors, and the closing of pagan temples and institutions under Constantine I. Later, the Emperor Theodosius I promulgated a series of anti-pagan Decrees during the 390s. These prohibitions included a complete ban on pagan sacrifice, oracles, pressure placed upon bureaucrats who did not enforce the emperor's constitutions, the breakup of pagan enclaves, the closing of temples, abolishment of pagan holidays, and punishment for the practice of witchcraft.

Finally, with the gruesome murder of the pagan mathematician Hypatia in 415 by a frenzied Christian mob, Classical antiquity in the Eastern Mediterranean winked out; outlawed paganism went underground. Their intellectual principles and religious tenants would later percolate to the surface here and there. In time, the pagan enclave in Egypt resurfaced during the rule of the Ottoman Empire.

This long hibernation intellectually stunted the sect in Egypt. Mystic elements had firmly taken hold. Its membership included pagans of all stripes, Christian heretics, the psychically gifted, and the *other* ones—the Hidden Folk. Acceptance of the strange and paranormal had replaced reasoned logic and common sense. Dark magic, witchcraft, and other latent mental talents were wholly embraced as legitimate methods of influence and control. While the outlawed enclave had many names over the centuries, and underwent numerous incarnations, it was during the Nassar administration that the International Cultural Studies Society in Cairo formally came into being as a corporate entity.

CHAPTER 3

Reissen sat in his Viennese university office surrounded by laboratory-pristine work surfaces and neatly shelved banks of books. The tight room did enjoy an open window, which allowed in the restful sounds of bird song. Breezes rustled an old oak's canopy. Blooming summer flowers added their sweet scents.

Reissen preferred simple functionality. His U-shaped Bauhaus-inspired blond desk provided that. To his left sat a state-of-the-art tabletop-sized flat screen and keyboard. On his right was his departmental land line. Before him, facing his office door, lay his father's old red leather writing pad, which still held the faint aroma of tobacco. Just fingering a worn corner brought back fond memories of a young boy scribbling on it.

At the moment, a collage of digital photographs populated the flat screen, which depicted the western-facing wall of the Sakkaran site. Reissen's immediate concern was to identify the name of the tomb's owner. Moving his cursor, while controlling the zoom feature, he scanned about searching for a name.

It didn't take long. But because he was so stunned at what he found, the incredulous Austrian continued to examine every inch, every row upon row of beautifully sculpted hieroglyphs with his cursor, just to make sure. In no less than six instances, the name of the monument's owner was the same—Djedi.

Mein Gott! The magician Djedi of Papyrus Westcar! A man who reportedly rejoined the decapitated heads of animals as an amusement for the Pharaoh Khufu—the builder of the Great Pyramid!

Sitting back into his high-tech office chair, Reissen's mind went into an intellectual spin.

This is big...no...really big. And then there were those five bodies.

Snapping out of it, the Egyptologist reached for a pad of paper and got to work on translating the inscription on the false-door. Rather quickly, Reissen identified that the text was a traditional magical offering known as the *ḥtp-dì-nsw* formula, or "the offering given by the king."

> An offering given by the king to Osiris, the lord of Busiris, the great god, the lord of Abydos.
>
> That Osiris may give a voice-offering of bread, beer, oxen, birds, alabaster, clothing, and every good and pure thing upon which a god lives.
>
> For the ka of the revered magician Djedi,

true of voice, son of the royal architect
and magician Imhotep and sorceress
Neferka.

The Egyptologist mentally gasped again. *Djedi is
not only the son of the famous architect and magician
Imhotep, but also the son of a sorceress! An Egyptian
legend is coming to life right before my very eyes!*

Djedi's birthright statement caused the man to
blink in thought as he translated the thirteen vertical
registers of the inscription that framed the false door.

Register 1: I am Djedi, magician, first oracle,
high priest of Thoth, and hereditary
guardian of the most sacred precincts of
the good god.

Register 2: I have seen numerous miracles
during my many inundations of
existence. I witnessed the erection of
many horizons (sc. pyramids) in the
West.

Register 3: One horizon (sc. pyramid) even
dared not to hold true to its form (sc. The
Bent Pyramid of Pharaoh Snefru). Year
1, third month of the third season, day
12, under the majesty of the

Register 4: King of Upper and Lower Egypt,
Sanakhte, Son of Re, Nebka. On this day,
I, Djedi was begotten of the royal
architect and magician Imhotep and
temple sorceress Neferka.

Given that Djedi is the offspring of magicians, Reissen speculated, *Could it be that a magician's powers were inheritable?* Taking a deep slug of coffee, the Egyptologist read on.

> Register 5: In the fullness of time I became my father's assistant in all things. At my majority I followed in his footsteps as magician, second oracle,

> Register 6: and *sem*-priest of Thoth. I, Djedi, inherited the responsibility for safeguarding the most sacred precincts of the god Thoth.

Those sacred precincts were probably designated as the god's archives. I wonder what might have been contained in those? After another sip, the Egyptologist continued.

> Register 7: My venerable father Imhotep, instructed me in the ways of the god Heka. She who bore me, Neferka, did likewise, and she entrusted me

> Register 8: with Heka's very words of power. My life was a goodly one: 110 years, 10 months, and 3 days. Under the majesty of the King of Upper and

> Register 9: Lower Egypt, Khufu, Son of Re, Year 14, fifth month of the first season, day 15, I, Djedi, departed from this life. My form was introduced into

Register 10: the Good House (sc. embalming
    chamber), and spent fifty-six days in the
    hands of the priesthood of Anubis, the
    lord of the West. I was conducted in

*Only fifty-six days in the Good House of
purification. The usual for a noble or royal burial was
in excess of seventy. That means his burial was that of a
commoner, at least when it came to his mummy.*

Register 11: peace to my place of beauty (sc.
    tomb) in the West on the first month, of
    the second season, on day 8, to enjoy life
    in the netherworld forever.

Register 12: Violate not this place of beauty
    (sc. tomb)! To do so, the wrath of Wadjet
    will fall upon you! The bites of millions
    of snakes and

Register 13: stings of millions of scorpions
    will find you! Ammit will devour your
    soul! May your nose and mouth fill and
    suffocate in sand!

*And what a curse it must have been given those five
wretches! But then again, Djedi was quite a magician.*

Finished with his labors, Reissen's back cracked
when he finally sat back into his chair. Looking down
at his wrist watch, he had spent over three hours on the
wall's translation. The exercise was well worth it, for
the wall inscription dove-tailed with the account of
Djedi's life as recorded in the *Papyrus Westcar.*

Perhaps more importantly, here was an example of an archaeological discovery corroborating a philological source. He smugly concluded: *Next season will be most intriguing.*

That thought, however, was dashed at the insistent sound of rapid knocking on the opaque glass of his office door.

"Enter."

"Herr Dr. Reissen," a panicked and flush-faced Else Wald said, "we have a problem."

Seeing the extreme alarm in the woman's eyes, the archaeologist bolted out of his office chair, and seated Wald. "Tell me, Else. What's troubling you?"

"These," She passed him four printouts.

Taking the documents, Reissen squinted through his wire-rimmed reading glasses and then frowned. "Else. What am I looking at?"

"The five bodies."

"But, where are they?"

"That's the point, Dr. Reissen. *They* aren't there! In fact, I cannot find any images of the five in the sixty-four digital frames they should be in."

"Camera failure?" the archaeologist hoped.

"Not possible. Look professor," the troubled photographer pointed with a quivering finger. "The meter sticks and signage all appear, but somehow the bodies didn't, including the close-ups of their horrible skin lesions."

*　　*　　*

After Else left, wearing tears of personal frustration, Reissen realized that this Sakkaran site was fast becoming more mystery novel than archaeological site.

I clearly need a second opinion, which prompted him to reach to his right and make an international phone call.

That help arrived two weeks later, or so the Austrian sincerely hoped. A knock at his door precisely at the appointed time buoyed that attitude. Rising to greet his colleague, they carefully embraced so as to not crush her starched white scapular. Reissen guided the tiny befreckled nun to his office's guest chair. Seated, the archaeologist looked into the glowing cherubic face with deep dimples and pleasantly said, "Sister Josephina, a morning coffee perhaps?"

"The gracious offer of a cup of Viennese coffee … now that *would* be sinfully lovely. Thank you, Erik."

The Austrian made a phone call to the departmental secretary. That task completed, "So, how goes the Pontifical College?"

"The same old, same old, Erik. Virtually nothing has changed since your last visit. You know how it is." The nun said with a shrug. "The rector's research policies remain as imaginative as a block of granite."

He chuckled. "How can that fossil hold such an exalted position?"

"Don't ask, Erik. The internal politics of Holy Mother Church are always mysterious, even on the best of days."

"Granted. But what about your new position at the Gregorian Egyptian Museum?" Reissen hopefully asked leaning forward on his elbows.

Sister Josephina Busby, Ph.D. in Egyptology, shifted in her chair and displayed a perky smile. "Yes, Erik, being the head curator does have its perks. Believe it or not, the bureaucratic falderal is far less than at the College." Sister Josephina said with widened eyes. She finished with an exaggerated stage whisper. "Best part: I can assign myself to any research project."

Reissen grunted with approval for his dear colleague from his graduate years. He then shifted the small talk to what no one seemed to want to start. "What did you make of my e-mail, field notes, and images?"

"Curious, and, quite frankly, unsettling. I never thought I would ever see concrete evidence for the efficacy of Egyptian magic." She said shaking her head. "It frankly shook me to the core. Made me reconsider many things. But you want the sober opinion of an expert in ancient Egyptian religion and magic—not that of a frightened school girl. In sum, and especially given the owner of the tomb, I believe that the lack of digital imagery was not due to any mechanical failure. Nor was it because of some dubious electromagnetic energy burst or pulse. Instead, Erik, I believe it to be the signature of dark magic."

"You're kidding." Reissen deadpanned.

"No, Erik. Sadly I am not." She said with a shake of the head. "In fact, I'm quite serious about this. I read that curse very carefully and took note of the surrounding iconography. That curse's content is quite unique and represents something that I would fully expect a master magician would conjure. Those grave robbers succumbed to what the curse proscribed— snake bites and scorpion stings. Your own eyes and field notes recorded that. And, do not forget the dual *Wadjet* images at the base of the ramp's two walls. She, the royal cobra goddess, also had a hand in this. Those poor men didn't have a prayer."

"So what about the imagery or lack thereof?"

"Erik, patience, I'm getting to that." Sister Josephine testily replied. "That tiny grotto you found is the focus of powerful dark magic. As soon as those men defiled that hallowed ground with their chisels, that awful spell was triggered. But what I find so intriguing is that this dummy tomb entrance is so powerfully defended in the first place."

"Dummy!" Reissen blurted out.

Sister Josephina raised an open palm toward her host. "In every respect, Erik, that ramp and its grotto area are nothing more than clever subterfuge and magical kill zone."

"What!" Reissen said almost getting out of his chair.

"Yes, you heard me correctly. The burial shaft of Djedi will not be found before that false door and its offering table. Instead, I predict that you will find it somewhere in the bedrock behind the ramp and grotto."

"Why there?"

"Because, my dear Erik, the location of Djedi's false door does not follow established religious canon. It faces west—the wrong direction. So that means your burial shaft should be located somewhere to the east."

"Huh. You're absolutely right. Now how did I miss that?"

"During the excitement of the discovery, Erik. Remember, you're human. You are the mission's director, you have a lot on your plate. So don't beat yourself up. As for the reason behind the lost imagery, that's where I can only provide an educated guess." The nun declared with her hands neatly folded on her lap. "The curse's phrase, '*Ammit* will devour your soul!' I believe holds the key. Those five unfortunates first gave up their lives in a quite horrible fashion. But that was not deemed sufficient. Upon their death, the five then lost their eternal souls, which were magically destroyed."

Total silence. Reissen sat with his head in his hands, his eyes peeking out between his fingers.

"So, Sister Josephina, you're suggesting that a

corpse without an associated soul cannot be photographed?"

"Yes, Erik." Then the nun's head cocked to one side. "Have you ever heard of Kirilian photography?"

A negative head shake.

"Have you ever heard of auras or halos?"

A positive nod.

"That's good. Some paranormal researchers and religious philosophers believe that there is a correlation between a detectable aura and the soul. That the presence of the former is proof for the existence of the latter."

Reissen wore a glazed look that Sister Josephina immediately caught.

"Erik. Must you always be so unimaginative? Work with me. Kirilian photography purports to detect the electromagnetic halo, or aura, that surrounds all living things. Some believe that the presence of that glow is proof of the soul's existence."

"Okay." Reissen surrendered with a sigh.

"Now consider this. Your Egyptian grave robbers probably believed at some rudimentary level that their soul, the *akh*, was sacred. In their minds, a loss of their soul meant that their opportunity for eternal life, in the afterlife, was forfeit. But the ancient Egyptian soul was made up of many fragile parts. So again consider:" the sister continued now counting with her fingers, "their *ren*, or name, went forever unrecorded as they were most likely illiterate and socially unremarkable. Their *ib*, or heart, which represented the sum total or ledger of their life's worth, was devoured by the female demon *Ammit* before reaching their final judgment. Their *ka*, or vital essence created at birth, was destroyed by the snake bites and scorpion stings. Their *ba*, the unique personality of an individual, came to an abrupt end at their untimely death. But it is my belief that the fate of their *sheut*, their metaphysical shadow or double, is why their bodies could not be photographed. Erik, those poor devils had been rendered soulless.

"But ..."

Sister Josephina again raised her open palm to stop her colleague. "It gets better." The nun said while leaning forward. "Enter the much-feared underworld demon, *Ammit*—a true Egyptian nightmare. This composite demon had the head of a crocodile, the torso of a lion, and the hindquarters of a hippopotamus. This *thing* sat luridly waiting during the last judgment of an individual while his heart, or *ib*, was weighed by Anubis on the scales of Thoth, where the *ib* was measured against *Ma'at*'s feather of truth and righteousness. If the scales did not balance, then the individual's *ib* was devoured by this dark primordial *Ammit* demon. What makes this curse so vile Erik is that it totally short circuits the entire last judgment process."

Mein Gott! Reissen thought with wide eyes.

"Erik, if you can prove that this tomb indeed dates from the Fourth Dynasty, then this is the earliest mention of *Ammit* on record. Usually, we don't hear about this hellish devourer of souls until nearly five hundred years later."

"Yes, you're absolutely right, as a part of the Osirian last judgment."

"Precisely." The nun emphasized with a pointed finger.

"If we find that this tomb is indeed Fourth Dynasty, would you like to write up this observation?"

"I sure would." Sister Josephina said with a firm nod. "It's right up my alley."

"Done. But sister," Reissen softly asked, "If we find the burial shaft, can it be safely excavated?"

"That depends." She said while examining her hands. "Have you ever heard of the Mirgissa Deposit?"

"Why yes, yes I have. That was a ritual human sacrifice found near the Second Cataract."

"Indeed, Erik. So if I were you, I would be on the outlook for broken red pottery covered with enchantments written in red ink, the remains of melted red candles, and of course, any sacrificed and dismembered human remains. If you encounter any evidence of these, I would immediately back off."

With those words still hanging in the air, the departmental secretary arrived with a heavy wicker tray. On it were a carafe of creamy headed coffee, two white mugs, a side of freshly made whipped cream, and two warmed blueberry scones.

*   *   *

Upon returning to Egypt in late January, Reissen had a lot on his mind. On one level, the archaeologist focused his attention on the continued investigations at the Temple of Ptah. The goal there was to trace its foundation and hopefully locate its ceremonial deposits. As with the previous season, Habib, in conjunction with an official from the Egyptian Antiquities Service, oversaw the day-to-day operations at Memphis.

On another level, Reissen, along with a select field team, would return to clear and record the "minor" archaeological site atop the Sakkara plateau. This team included the photographer Wald, the survey team of Peters and Franks, and a late addition, a Bavarian named Sheila Roth. Why? Roth was a credentialed historian and protégé of Sister Josephina on loan from the Pontifical College. Roth was also a student of Robert Gilbert—the leading Cambridge specialist in ancient Egyptian magic. Her dissertation on the magicians of this ancient land was considered authoritative and a must read for those in the field. While she wasn't a trained archaeologist, the risk-adverse Austrian sorely needed Roth's on-site presence and insights. After all, he reasoned, he was trying to find a crafty magician's tomb. Even the tomb of his father Imhotep had yet to be discovered, despite decades of searching for it. Other than Reissen, no one else had been briefed in on Sister Josephine's chilling analysis of the Sakkaran site, not even Roth.

To this team was also assigned an antiquities inspector, a pleasant fellow named Ali Hassan— Inspector Kama's own assistant, who provided governmental oversight during their investigations. A relative from Kama's side of the family, the twenty-two-year-old Hassan presented himself as reasonable, polite, and knowledgeable of his country's history and antiquities. He also had a reputation for getting things done expeditiously and in the most imaginative of ways. If Hassan played his cards right on this assignment, he was guaranteed a long career within the Egyptian Antiquities Service.

Under the gaze of the inspector, Reissen, and his team, Hassan produced a squad of twenty Egyptian laborers, who removed the fill sand and protective tarps from the Sakkaran site. As they chanted to the jaunty rhythm of a common workman's song, the fill rapidly disappeared as plumes of sand were ejected gopher-like from the ramp area. Much to Reissen's relief, the remains had not been tampered with.

After dismissing the men with a full day's pay for a half-day's labor, Reissen turned to his team. "We will sweep this entire area." Reissen said as he handed out short-handled brooms to Roth and the rest. "Uncover any indication of pavement stones or suspicious cracks. Spread out and try to find any hint of an entrance shaft."

Without another word, all got to work, brushing away the remaining sandy grit and fluffy tan powder from the bedrock before the false door and the long ramp that dead-ended against it. The team scoured the area creating neat snake-like piles of fine debris. As Reissen worked alongside them, he occasionally stopped to look around. So far no one had found any evidence of cracks, fissures, or suspicious rectangular cuttings.

Hassan also seemed to be taking in the area, as he blankly looked from side to side, as if his head were a panning motion picture camera. This odd, almost mechanical behavior, the Austrian noted. *What's wrong with Hassan?*

Before noon the team had brushed clean the ramp and flooring. Wald photographed the pristine site and in particular the five chisel marks. Peters and Franks resurveyed it and made several additions. Their upload would provide the team with a state-of-the-art, multicolored, 3D revolving plot of the site.

While all of this was going on, Hassan continued with his robotic behavior as he walked down the sloped ramp toward the inscribed grotto, which he scanned with meticulous care. In the process, he uncharacteristically managed to get into nearly everyone's way. Naturally, they grew frustrated with their inspector's antics.

* * *

That particular day the typically congenial Hassan had not been at all his usual self, which troubled him. The guard felt as if he were sleepwalking, wandering about in a fog, shuffling his feet, staring mindlessly this way and that. He felt that his usual enthusiasm had been sucked out of him. As Hassan stumbled about the archaeological site, he twice almost stumbled over the edge of the excavation onto the ramp below. Only his quick reactions had saved him.

* * *

Meanwhile, a sweaty, dust-coated, and kneeing Roth observed. "Dr. Reissen, I've been thinking. This is supposed to be the tomb of Djedi, the magician. Correct?"

"Yes."

Standing up to dust off her knees, "His father Imhotep was an architect well-known for his innovation, cunning, and subterfuge."

"Yes."

"To date, we do not know where Imhotep's tomb is located. Correct?"

"Yes, that is correct."

With her hands on hips, "Then shouldn't we expect similar innovation, cunning, and subterfuge from his son? Shouldn't we be looking elsewhere for his tomb's burial shaft?"

"Sheila. What an interesting idea. Where do you propose we begin looking?"

At this point the rest of the team stopped what they were doing, ignored their ever blundering antiquities guard, and listened in with considerable interest.

"Have you investigated the exposed bedrock immediately opposite this ramp?"

Roth then turned to the survey team and asked, "What is the orientation of the ramp?"

"270 degrees due West." Peters quickly answered.

"There you have it, Dr. Reissen. Djedi placed his burial shaft 180 degrees from the norm."

This insightful suggestion hit Reissen squarely between the eyes, for that was precisely what his colleague Sister Josephina had told him. Standard Old Kingdom burials of high officials and important personages had burial shafts located before or nearby their false doors. But he reminded himself that Djedi was hardly your run-of-the-mill bureaucrat. He was a magician and high priest of Thoth. He knew of the secret location of that crafty god's most sacred chambers. And after all, he was his father's son. He took all of those facts into consideration.

Wald spoke up, "I like Sheila's idea." Peters and Franks nodded in agreement. Hassan just stood there with a puzzled look on his face.

"Okay then," Reissen said with his hands up in surrender, "let's inspect the opposite side of this outcrop. We have nothing to lose."

Directly opposite the descending ramp, Franks' short-handled sweep brushed away sand, limestone chips, and fine debris. In the process, he dislodged a chunk of weathered plaster, which revealed beneath it a straight two-inch man-made fissure in the bedrock. Following that clue, the surveyor tapped the next several inches of the stony surface with back of his wooden sweep. More shattered plaster camouflage fell away. That tangible result caused Franks to stand up, extend his arms into the air, and let out a victorious shout, "I found it!"

*   *   *

Indeed the ramp and inscribed false door and back wall of the grotto had been a ruse. After an hour's labor by the entire team, a rectangular outline revealed itself to the bright Egyptian sunshine. For over five thousand years, the burial shaft had been cunningly camouflaged with an artful layer of stout plaster, but no more.

Wald photographed the newly found architectural feature and the survey team added to their plot.

Thereafter, Peters announced the obvious, "This rectangle is oriented exactly 180 degrees from the ramp. Congratulations Sheila!"

"What are the shaft's dimensions?" Reissen asked the survey team.

"2.28 by 4.57 meters." Franks responded.

"That's five by ten Egyptian cubits," Reissen observed after making a quick calculation in his head, "Sufficient room for lowering down a burial."

Now the back-breaking excavation began, because everyone knew that burial shafts were just that—rectangular holes cut vertically into the bedrock and then backfilled with rubble. Only Reissen worried that they might encounter more than just rubble.

CHAPTER 4

As the news anchor prepared for the next segment, he muttered to himself, "Must be a slow news day."

"Garbage, garbage, garbage. It's the bane of modern existence, and yet that stinky, rank-smelling, and awful stuff is actually worth something. Don't believe me? Then listen to what our roving international reporter, Jeremy Scott, has to say about the matter."

The broadcast breaks to the image of a young man with his hand up to his right ear, wearing the light and airy clothing of a hot desert climate.

Looking up, "Thank you, Adam. This is Jeremy Scott in Cairo, where I am standing in what could be loosely described as a neighborhood recycling plant."

As the camera view spun around, Jeremy continued to narrate. "All around me is trash, fresh trash, old trash. Be thankful that your device does not have smell-a-vision app."

With the camera back on the reporter, he turns to his right. "The man standing next to me is Ibrahim. Ibrahim's job is to pick up the trash from this high rise building behind us. He literally trudges up and down to each and every back door every day." The camera's lens pans to a poured concrete structure with ten floors, with hanging laundry, and people sticking their heads out the windows. Children grin and wave back.

"But Ibrahim's job is far more than that. Once he collects the daily trash, he delivers it to this reclamation area over here," the image of a chaotic scene, "where he sorts through it. Glass, plastic, paper, and metals go to one side." Then turning, "All edible organics go over here," to a shot of a huge pig sty.

"Yes, ladies and gentlemen, the Egyptians use pigs to recycle their organic waste into … this." He now points to a pig defecating into a splattering wallow over six inches deep.

"That recycled waste is then sold, at a premium," the reporter emphasizes with an upraised finger, "to local farmers, who prefer it to imported chemical fertilizers. As for the non-organic material," the camera now panned to stacks of bound cardboard, clear plastic bags of bottles, and of a boy crushing aluminum cans with a hand-operated contraption, "it is sorted and resold in bulk.

"As for the pigs," a close-up of a filthy example, "they too are a by-product of the system. I'm told that they are highly prized.

"This is Jeremy Scott, on assignment in a Cairo neighborhood, wishing sincerely that he were anywhere else. Back to you, Adam."

*   *   *

The year was 1981, when an infant was born amidst the wretched urban squalor of Cairo. Unwanted by his biological parents, the babe was unceremoniously dumped into a sty at a neighborhood pig farm to be devoured along with the collected urban garbage. Strangely, none of the ravenous swine would touch the babe. Whenever one approached, a near-electric charge would reach out and change its mind with a squeal. For that matter, neither did the endemic black flies light upon it, nor other urban vermin disturb it for the same reason.

Two days later, the newborn's hungry bawling attracted the notice a barren Coptic Christian who was sorting through the recyclable debris, seeking something useful. Taken by its pitiful plight and ice-colored blue eyes, the woman looked down into the little face laying in the rank muck and smiled, "What have we here? It's a precious little one." When the baby grinned back, she snatched it from the fetid enclosure and embraced it as her very own.

When Fatima returned to her tiny but immaculate one room flat, her husband Mohammed al-Razzuli was surprised by what she brought home.

"A baby?"

"Yes, my husband. The Lord has blessed us! Just look at him. He's so handsome."

Looking into her arms, Mohammed saw beyond the grime a smiling, arm waving, and leg kicking little tyke. "Such beautiful eyes! I have never before seen the like." Then, "Fatima, where did you find this child?"

"Orphaned among the pigs."

"What!"

"And what is more, my husband, those hungry beasts did him no harm. He must be blessed in some special way."

That revelation furrowed Mohammed's brow full knowing the nature of those voracious, near-feral pigs.

"I wish us to adopt him, my husband. He deserves a chance."

"Well then, let us begin by washing him." Mohammed said as he reached out to take his son.

As the babe too reached out, no doubt fascinated by his thick moustache, Mohammed wondered, "What name should we give him, my wife?"

"I have been thinking about that ever since I found him. I favor Usire. It is a good and proud name."

A single grunt emanated from her husband. "That's not a popular name."

"Nor is being discovered in a pig's sty. Usire comes to us from divine means. He answers our years of prayer for a child."

"Indeed, my beloved. I agree. So he will be named."

One week later, little Usire was baptized amid

incense and chanting prayer as the newest member of the local Coptic Church. But the attending priest was chagrined at hearing his name, the Coptic form of the ancient pagan god Osiris. In a spirit of compromise, the family agreed to allow the priest to select an appropriate middle or second name. The priest chose Shenouda, the name of several famous Coptic popes. Thereafter, the boy carried the lengthy name of Usire Shenouda ibn Mohammed al-Razzuli.

Within their religious community, Fatima and Mohammed were best known for their care of the neighborhood's many unfortunates. Fatima baked and distributed bread, while Mohammed fixed the unfixable with amazing ingenuity, imagination, and earned with this talent the family's modest income.

But the couple stood apart in yet another way— both were sensitives if not outright adepts who practiced beneficial white magic and folk medicine. With the cost of simple medicines out-of-reach, they considered themselves urban missionaries, bringing comfort within the horrific conditions of a Cairo slum. These charitable acts were recognized by their religious brethren, but while not fully understood, were considered sainted acts nonetheless.

Young Usire observed his caring parents, who despite their modest station, generously gave to those in need. Their charity and care-giving imprinted the babe in the most unexpected ways.

Given that the boy was raised with magic as an everyday fact and tool, early on, he too began to stretch his latent, preternatural muscles—in open imitation of his much loved parents. At the age of three, with a lick of his palm and its application to a forehead, he cured a woman of a migraine. Two years later, young Usire shadowed his father on his rounds while gathering useful bits from the communal dump. During one such foray, Usire encountered a blind boy stumbling about. Witnessing this, Usire cried at the other's difficulty, wiped away his tears, and applied them to the boy's eye lids, curing him on the spot.

By the time Usire turned eight, his name had become a thing of Caireen folk legend. People would travel from throughout the city to seek him out, for his mere touch was considered miraculous. His tears and spit were proven time and again to be curative. Even his feces were highly prized and considered efficacious. His parents, however, thought ill of all this attention, and with the help of their local priest, sent Usire away to be educated at the Coptic monastery of Saint Anthony in the Eastern Desert.

Saint Anthony, the founder of Christian monasticism, had such a profound effect upon his followers that they built a monastery in his name at the beginning of the fourth century. Established at a protected oasis within the parched and pristine Eastern Desert, the monastery was located just over two hundred miles southeast of Cairo and not far from the ascetic's own cave. There, the parents believed, their gifted son would be relieved of the incessant pressures placed upon his narrow shoulders. They also sincerely hoped that their gifted son would find himself and his true purpose.

Life within the walled compound was a big shock for the youngster: eternally cloudless robin's egg blue sky; quiet desert serenity; simple nourishing food; and a rigorous academic regimen. All of these things, including the coarse cotton novice robes, opened Usire's eyes and helped clear his mind.

Structure, scholastic encouragement, discipline, and prayer became the daily rule. Immersion into this highly ritualized, incense-laden, Coptic realm, brought calm and focus. Surrounded by antiquity and continuity, the boy found peace. One of six at his level, life-long bonds quickly formed among his classmates. Best of all, here Usire was not special, just a novice pilgrim in search of inspiration and knowledge— someone who sought his yet unknown and unlimited potential.

Much to his teachers' delight, Usire applied himself with a will and quickly learned this letters. After only two, and rarely three repetitions, the boy mastered his lessons. In the process, the young man developed a deep love for the written word and of books, as the monastery possessed within its walls the largest collection of Coptic manuscripts in Egypt.

The cool confines of the library's white washed walls provided Usire a place where pure thought could take place. Unbridled, his interests grew. With enthusiasm he delved deep into his studies and excelled beyond his teachers wildest expectations. In his tenth year he fully embraced Coptic and Greek. Talk among the monastic faculty dared to breath words like "genius," "prodigy," and "divinely gifted."

In that same year, Usire's eager mind stumbled across an old manuscript in a back cabinet. Far older than it looked, it was a fragile seventh century Coptic version of the ancient Egyptian *Book of the Dead*. The profane vignettes and text, so openly pagan in their content, fascinated the boy, who up until now had been schooled exclusively in Christian verse. Usire realized that he had to learn more about his ancient heritage in order to better understand the many references and the hidden meanings behind the manuscript's iconography. The seed had found fertile soil.

On his twelfth birthday, Usire had a choice to make. The monastery's abbot, Bishop Yustus, approached young Shenouda—for that was how Usire was referred to at the monastery, to pose a question. "Shenouda, your many accomplishments while a pilgrim guest at our monastery are most noteworthy. Your teachers have only high praise for you. Your fellow students find you pleasant. You have labored without complaint in the monastery's bakery, date palm groves, and gardens. Your mastery of languages is superb. But now I must ask you a critical question. Do you wish to remain within these walls as a monk, or to return to your parents and the secular world?"

Before he addressed the abbot, Usire looked directly into the bishop's bespeckled brown eyes, ignoring his large broad nose and full beard lightly flecked with gray. He then knelt, bowed and touched his forehead to the pavement stone, rose, and kissed the man's extended hand. "*Sayenda* (Master), with a most heavy heart, I wish to return to my parents and the secular world."

"Why so, young Shenouda?"

"I wish to study the history of our ancient land."

That brought a grunt of disappoint from the abbot. "Then, my son, may God go with you."

*   *   *

Upon his return to Cairo, Usire's world turned upside down again, but this time by the sheer cacophony of urban civilization, the press of the crowds, its pervasive smog, and ever-present filth. He was repelled by it all. Only in the sanctity of his parent's meager household did he feel he could breathe. He began to question the wisdom of his decision to leave the womblike existence at the monastery—but not quite.

What sustained him was his drive to learn about his land and its antiquities. Like an earth-bound soul he haunted the galleries of the National Museum and committed to memory its public collection. Unknown to his parents, he hitchhiked to the many archaeological sites located outside the city—Giza, Memphis, Sakkara, and even as far as Abu Sir. To sate their son's thirst for knowledge, his parents enrolled him into the preparatory school at the American University in Cairo, where, among other subjects, he learned English. More times than not, once his classes were over, Usire could be found listening in on undergraduate lectures on Egyptology and archaeology.

During his fifteen year, Usire finished his preparatory schooling and took his first undergraduate class in Egyptian hieroglyphs. His professor, Dr. Ahmed ibn El-Mussar, a man with bright eyes and infinite patience, espied the teenager's zeal.

"So, Mr. al-Razzuli," the professor peered over his half-glasses during a student interview, "what do you wish to study?"

"The ancient history of our land."

"Then why are you not enrolled in my colleague's introductory history class?"

"Because I wish to learn hieroglyphs first."

"Ah, I see. You want to be a proper Egyptologist."

A nod of the head.

"Do you have any language training?"

"Yes, professor, I am fluent in Coptic and Greek."

This admission caused El-Mussar to sit back into his chair and take off his reading glasses. For the first time, in a long time, he stopped to consider the possibilities.

"May I ask, Mr. al-Razzuli, how old are you?"

"Fifteen, sir."

"And where did you learn your Coptic and Greek?"

"Saint Anthony's Monastery, professor."

This tidbit again stopped El-Mussar dead in his tracks, for he knew quite well several of the faculty at the monastery, and they were all top-notch—and rigorous. He leaned forward across his office desk.

"Are you prepared, Mr. al-Razzuli, to immerse yourself fully into Middle Egyptian?"

"Yes, professor, in fact, I have already begun. I am on chapter eleven of Gardiner's *Egyptian Grammar*. Frankly, I'm stuck on a construction and was hoping for a hint as to how to proceed."

So began Usire's intellectual adventure into the philological minutiae of his country's ancient language.

* * *

While Usire prospered at the university, his own nation, community, and faith came under attack. Sunni Islamist guerrillas called El Gama'a El Islamiyya made their presence known. These terrorists were dedicated to the overthrow of the Mubarak government and the establishment of an Islamic state within a secular Egypt. To that end, the Coptic Christian community in Cairo suffered greatly along with over seven hundred Egyptian policemen, soldiers, and hundreds of foreign tourists.

During his junior year, one afternoon after classes, Usire discovered his parents' murdered and mangled bodies in the street before their flat. Young, impressionable, highly emotional, and mad with grief, Usire clutched their limp forms in a final embrace and let out a soulful primal scream. Tears flowed as he rocked them back and forth, powerless to bring them back. His hoarse scream again filled the street, but this time in mourning. Images of ancient Egyptian funerary scenes filled his head—processions of mourners, crying, tearing their hair out, throwing ashes, and rending their clothing.

While sitting on the blood-splattered asphalt, Usire then and there vowed a bloody revenge and knew instinctively how to do it—by resorting to old magic, a dark tool of pharaonic state policy. He had been studying a series of execration texts and in the process had understood the key to their primal effectiveness. With such tools at hand, and his powerfully innate will, he knew that he could simultaneously protect himself and exact a deadly toll on those responsible for his parent's death. He knew also that what he planned could not be proven in any modern court of law.

To exact his vengeance, Usire found within a surprising amount rage that had to be appeased, somehow released. So he compiled that night a focused curse text, added the names of the individuals involved, who had claimed responsibility for the act in the newspaper. He painted the curse in red glyphs on a red ceramic bowl, and launched the curse by breaking it.

Instantly, the room of his parent's apartment spun uncontrollably. In his head a great emotional dam of pure energy gushed forth, followed by a pounding, migraine-like headache. His body felt depleted and dehydrated. On his hands and knees in excruciating pain, blood dripped freely from his nose, ears, and eyes. Then, he collapsed unconscious.

*   *   *

Six young men in their twenties sat on a worn carpet below a slowly turning fan. They shared a large ashtray filled with still smoldering butts. In one corner of the room leaned six virgin AK-74s, glinting of gun oil, freshly uncrated, illicitly imported by Iranian friends. In another corner, still crated, sat explosives, also donated by the same friends. Between the six lay a city map of Cairo. On it were four red circles that had been crossed out. What they were so vigorously debating were the locations of their next four targets.

The heated discussion did not last for long, however, for suddenly all of them could not breathe. Something unseen strangled them. Something, no matter how hard they tried to resist, kept up the pressure. After several minutes, all died of asphyxiation. Their blue oxygen-deprived tongues stuck out grotesquely like hard bananas.

Then, a whirl-wind appeared in the room that scattered about the cigarette ash and butts. Once it settled in a fine layer, the tongues, again by an unseen force, were violently ripped out at the root and left beside each of the plotters. This final act ensured that the many falsehoods that they said in this life, would not be repeated in the next.

*   *   *

Usire awoke the next day in a dried pool of blood. Body stiff and with a cotton-filled mouth, he staggered toward a half-filled water bottle and greedily emptied it. That caused his stomach to rumble.

I need food.

Washing from his cheek the cracked pancake of blood, he glanced in the mirror and staggered back. His eyes had changed color. No longer were they ice-blue. Now they were the darkest brown, flecked with gold. This transformation caused Usire to look for other physical changes, but found none. Once again he looked in the mirror and saw the eyes of a face he didn't recognize.

I think I overdid it. I used too much of my will.

Then for some reason he turned on the television and immediate heard of a government crackdown on the El Gama'a El Islamiyya movement. Now headless with their leadership found dead, the announcer narrated, a city-wide search was underway to rid the capital forever of their kind.

All dead? Usire thought. *Was I really responsible for that? Did it actually work?*

Now sitting on the floor next to the dried pool of blood, the Egyptian began to take stock of the situation and shivered in the realization that perhaps, just perhaps, he did indeed have something to do with it. That his plan on revenge had worked. Then, another realization hit. *I have crossed a line. My new eyes prove it.*

The next several days before his parent's funeral, Usire began to take notice of things, odd things. People avoided his gaze, his touch, even his shadow, and moved instinctively to get out of his way—even in crowds. Animals outright ran from him. At the university, others refused to sit next to him in lecture. Flowers wilted at his touch; fruit spoiled in the marketplace. As far as Usire was concerned, he was a changed man. While he couldn't prove it, he knew he was a murderer as well.

Have I become death?

In the following weeks, and finally coming to grips with his new persona, Usire dropped his pious Coptic middle or second name of Shenouda and changed his first to Kek—the Egyptian god of darkness. It felt strangely appropriate.

CHAPTER 5

Right and left
Up and down
Positive and negative
Cold and hot
Good and bad
Darkness and light
They all exist for one reason—balance.

As synagogues, mosques, shrines, and churches throughout the world called their followers to worship and prayer, it's a safe bet that the same occurred for the opposing persuasions' ceremonies and poorly understood practices.

To this alternate persuasion, Kek was drawn, and those of like mind, to him. Parentless, the seventeen-year-old had yet to complete university. Following his parent's funeral, he needed work for the one room flat. While the local Coptic Church would have been a logical place to seek help, Kek wanted to strike out on his own. With this attitude, a well-dressed middle-aged man with dark hair and wearing sunglasses, approached him outside the church after the funeral. Kek did not remember seeing him during the liturgical ceremony.

"Are you Usire, son of Ibrahim and Fatima?"

"Yes, I am."

"I am Mr. Shaheen, and I wish to express my sorrow for your tragic loss. They were such fine people and gave of themselves so generously to the community." He said solicitously. "Sadly, Usire, their passing comes at a time when you are most vulnerable."

"Vulnerable? What do you mean?"

"Are you still at the university?" the man pressed.

"Yes, I am."

"Ah, which year?"

"I am half way through my third."

That caused a grunt and a knowing nod.

"Do you need a job?"

"Yes, I do, very much."

"While I cannot bring back your parents, Usire, I can get you a job. Here is my card." He presented it to Kek with both hands as if it were a precious gift. Taking it, briefly their fingers touched, and a flare of energy passed between them.

Jerking back, Kek said, "What did you just do?"

"I did absolutely nothing, Usire. It was you who reached out to me." He said with a slight bow. "In fact, you are far more powerful and talented than both of your parents combined. Your abilities need harnessing, Usire, refinement, and focus." He paused. "But I suspect that you know that already. Is that not so?" He smiled showing his teeth.

Kek just stood there, mouth open. *How does he know?*

To the teenager's surprise, the stranger answered, "Because Usire, excuse me, *Kek*, it is my job to know." He finished again with that toothy, knowing smile.

"Today, call the number on the card. Then, appear at eight sharp, and your true education will begin."

Intrigued, the young Kek did just that. And as the often-used adage said: down the rabbit hole he went.

*   *   *

Kek wrote down the address to a section of Cairo he had never before visited—never even knew existed. From his parent's flat, and after a brisk thirty-minute walk, he arrived at a manicured neighborhood majestically lined with full, well-tended, and watered trees. The sharp smell of its drying streets and sidewalks betrayed the fact of their pre-dawn hosing. No laundry hung from these neat and freshly painted buildings—their windows intact and backed by expensive curtains.

The college student could find no trash, saw no beggars, didn't smell any street carts. The street did have, however, four foreign flags displayed before embassy compounds. Kek concluded that the block represented the polar opposite of his childhood environment. Standing before the address given to him, he stopped before its pristine glass doors at his unsmudged reflection—a pair of old shoes, faded pants, and a threadbare white dress shirt. Kek lip read from the etched glass at eye level—International Cultural Studies Center in Cairo. He rolled his eyes and knew that he didn't belong, had no business being here, but his growling stomach drove him to reach out and grasp the door's brass handle.

The cool darkness of the narrow lobby's interior caused Kek to stop and blink to get his bearings. Eyes now dilated, he saw that an elevator stood opposite and to his right a reception desk, behind which hung a large, shield-like decoration of beaten bronze. Two other identical bronze shields were arranged on the blank wall to the left.

The receptionist looked up from her computer screen at his approach across the black slate flooring. Perfectly applied makeup couldn't hide her aloof gauntness, nor could her tailored black business suit. This striking impression, plus the haunting hint of jasmine perfume, made Kek self-consciously hide his care-worn cuffs behind his back. Her name tag said, Iskander. Oddly Kek could see his fractured image reflected back in the bronze wall hanging, but not hers.

Her dark eyes languidly appraised him like a piece of lusciously delicious food. Her nostrils flared taking in his scent. Finally, she said in full flush, "How may I be of service?"

"Good morning, Ms. Iskander. I am al-Razzuli. I have an appointment with Mr. Shaheen." Kek nervously stated.

"Ah, I see," she breathed with an all too knowing cocked eyebrow, while efficiently stabbing the sleek phone set's buttons. Iskander's long, red finger nails of one hand darted about spider-like, while smoothly raising the receiver with the other. Kek noted this practiced feat with wide eyes. Never once did the receptionist's predatory gaze leave him.

After a brief, coded conversation, "Mr. al-Razzuli, kindly take the elevator to the third floor. Mr. Shaheen's secretary will receive you." Her vivacious voice said.

The elevator, Kek noted, was lined with brushed aluminum unmarred by fingerprints. On its back wall, centered, was placed another beaten bronze decoration. Most surprising of all, the lift operated smoothly without any jerks or sudden stops. When its doors opened at the third floor, he met another efficient woman dressed in a black suit and matching low heels.

"Please come this way," she curtly directed.

"This way" went across the building's floor plan, which ended at a corner office with double wooden doors. Kek guessed them to be of dark oak or something similar. The secretary knocked once, and opened one. Kek thanked her, and entered.

Mr. Shaheen sat at a broad desk with his hands

folded before him. His face beamed a dazzling smile. "Welcome, Mr. al-Razzuli." It was then Kek got the shock of his life. The color of the man's eyes—a deep dark brown with golden flecks—were just like his *new* ones.

Given that the office did not have a guest chair, Kek had to remain standing.

"Mr. al-Razzuli, I am pleased you chose to visit us. Allow me to be direct. I wish to become your new *Sayenda* (Master). Unlike Bishop Yustus, your former *Sayenda*, you will find me a very generous and influential person. Under my tutelage, you will no longer want for anything." Examining the perfect nails of his left hand he continued, "But like the dear bishop, I too have my standards. They can be quite high." Now looking right through the young man, "I demand excellence, Mr. al-Razzuli. Do you understand?"

"Not completely, sir." Kek blurted out.

"I see. Then allow me to explain … more fully."

For the next several moments, Mr. Shaheen outlined, point-by-point, his expectations. But during this conversation, he didn't utter a thing, but his words nonetheless echoed in Kek's mind with a force that caused the young man to stagger back.

When Shaheen finished, Kek gasped out, "Yes, *Sayenda*, I now better understand … and I will submit." Kek added with a bowed head.

To this clear deference, Shaheen nodded in

approval. "I am pleased that you now appreciate the situation." He then removed from a desk drawer a thick envelope, which he pushed across the desk's blotter.

"Mr. al-Razzuli, take this. Your first steps in creating your new life are to open a bank account, buy suitably professional clothing, and see to your rent. Then, you are to apply yourself to your studies, especially the ones pertaining to ancient Egyptian magic. In return, I expect a progress report every week. See my secretary as to when I am available. As I said before, I demand nothing short of excellence." Then with a dismissive wave of his hand he said, "Now, off with you. I have some things to attend to."

Picking up the heavy envelope, Kek again bowed, left the man's office, and quietly closed the door behind him. Outside, he approached the secretary and explained his need for another appointment. She just handed the young man a black monthly day-planner.

"I have taken the liberty of filling out the next six months' of appointment dates. Be careful, Mr. al-Razzuli. Mr. Shaheen is a very busy man and does not appreciate being stood up," she said with ragged and sharp steel in her voice.

"Mr. al-Razzuli, you have been warned. And, the next time you pay us a visit, wear a proper dress shirt, slacks, coat, and tie. While at the university, dress plainly so as to not draw attention to yourself, but here, you are always to appear professional."

Kek gulped. Ubaid noted this.

"Mr. al-Razzuli. Do you know how to tie a tie?"

"No ma'am."

"Then learn."

Shaken, Kek dashed out of the office in search of a bathroom. Once settled into a stall, only then did he dare open the envelope. Once again shock hit him squarely between the eyes. After counting out the envelope's contents twice, he held fanned out in his hands ten thousand dollars US, the equivalent of nearly eighteen thousand Egyptian pounds. An unimaginable amount, Kek could only lean his head against the cool marble of the stall's wall.

While Kek contemplated his good fortune, Shaheen and his secretary Ubaid discussed his future.

"So, kindly tell me again why are you wasting your time entertaining this street urchin?" she asked.

"Careful, Ubaid, he is immensely powerful, gifted. His mere touch since infancy has been considered curative. When I purposely initiated contact, I actually bit my tongue in a mixture of surprise and pleasure. Yes, he sorely needs our training to develop and focus his abilities. Our arrangement for his parent's removal to isolate him, make him more dependent, and malleable was brilliant. More remarkably, he, in an emotionally charged moment of vengeance, found, and then murdered those terrorist animals with a dark magic of his own design. And that's what I call initiative."

Shaheen said with admiration and punctuated with an upraised finger.

"As for his allegiance, Ubaid, he has few options. Besides, the amount I gave him will seduce him totally." Shaheen concluded with a gesture of open hands.

"Okay. Should I add him to the enclave's roster?"

"No. That would be premature. He has to first prove himself to the rest of the enclave's membership. Then, perhaps."

A nod, and then secretary mentioned, "You may be right about this one. I got a call from Iskander during your interview with him. Iskander said that Al-Razzuli's face fell when he noted her lack of reflection in the lobby's bronze warding devices."

At this tidbit, Shaheen smiled, "Both powerful and observant. Perfect. What else did Iskander say?"

"That old soulless ghoul wanted him for dinner."

Shaking his head, "That will not do."

"That may be so, but Iskander's talents provide us with unmatched security."

"Yes, indeed *it* does." Shaheen pointedly said.

*   *   *

A nervous Kek appeared ten minutes early for his first appointment with Shaheen. At seeing him, Iskander raised an approving eyebrow at his new look. Decked out as he was, *it* wanted him more than ever. At seeing him, Ubaid nodded also with approval, but only after she straightened his tie.

Shaheen sat once again behind his desk, but this time there was a guest chair waiting for him. Kek had the wits to wait until offered it.

Putting down his fountain pen, Shaheen finally looked up, took in his charge, gestured to him to sit, and began. "You look quite smart, Mr. al-Razzuli. However, work on your tie knotting skills. What classes are you taking this semester?"

So the week's review began, with Kek doing most of the talking, stopping only when Shaheen probed here and there.

"Excellent. Now, Mr. al-Razzuli, tell me about your studies into ancient Egyptian magic. What's your overall plan?"

"I posed that very question to Professor Dr. Ahmed ibn El-Mussar." The name Shaheen jotted down. "We outlined a course of study that began with an in depth study of the Big Three, to be followed by lesser, more arcane magical works."

"Big Three?" Shaheen asked quizzically.

"Oh, I apologize, sir; the Big Three are *The Pyramid Texts*, *Coffin Texts*, and *Book of the Dead*. We agreed that once I mastered those, the rest would come. Then, I would push on to the later Greek and Coptic magical corpus."

"Again, excellent, Mr. al-Razzuli." Glancing at his watch, "You are dismissed." Opening a drawer he again removed an envelope and pushed it across his blotter. "And kindly make use of this wisely."

Once Kek had closed his office door behind him, Shaheen muttered to himself, "I really must find some way of rewarding this El-Mussar. He is grooming Kek perfectly."

Then he had a thought and lifted his phone's receiver.

"Ubaid, I need you."

*　　*　　*

Twenty years later, Kek ibn Mohammed al-Razzuli had long established the reputation of someone not to mess with. Dashingly handsome, fit, and gifted, the dark adept showed no compulsion whatsoever to stop once a thing was desired. His own enclave preferred to avoid his presence, claiming a pestilential psychic overpressure that few could bear. Those who could see auras, perceived al-Razzuli's as a black hole—without depth, limit, or shred of humanity.

Now a powerful telepath and telekinetic athlete, the adept had become a practitioner of the magical heritage of his native Egypt. More to the point, he blatantly used that knowledge—its curse texts, figurines, amulets, and other appliances, for his own purpose and advantage. In another time, al-Razzuli would have been an exalted temple high priest and first oracle—literate, influential, and immensely powerful.

This preoccupation explained al-Razzuli's interest in a certain archaeological excavation, which the adept had first learned of during a monthly enclave meeting. That initial information prompted al-Razzuli to contact a well-paid informer. The bureaucrat oversaw Egypt's regional excavations—both legal and otherwise. This particular site al-Razzuli had brought to his attention, full-knowing the man's immense interest in all things monetary.

The adept did not stop there, for he subliminally placed a suggestion, which prompted his inside man to place his relative, Ali Hassan, as the field inspector of the Austrian mission's excavation. Young, impressionable, and above all, easily controlled, the telepath, while sitting from a nearby vehicle, quite literally walked in the young man's shoes as he stumbled about the excavation at Sakkara. Using the inspector's eyes, the adept could not believe what he was seeing—the discovery of a Fourth Dynasty tomb of a legendary magician..

CHAPTER 6

The burial shaft went deep, taking on the look of a mine shaft. To deal with it, Ali Hassan thoughtfully secured for the Austrian archaeological team wooden scaffolding with a pulley, a hemp rope with a lashed loop at its end, and a wicker debris basket on a hook. This act of useful resourcefulness seemed to offset his previous day's blundering in the eyes of the field team. Nevertheless, Hassan continued to study carefully everyone and everything.

Reissen worked alone in the ever-deepening rectangular pit. He took seriously and shouldered the responsibility for his team's safety. How could he in good conscience ask them to dig *and* lookout for any evidence of magical paraphernalia and bobby traps? He jerked twice on the rope and another basket of dusty debris ascended toward the robin's egg blue sky.

The rest of his team took turns at the scaffold's rope, which had been set up to one side of the shaft to make loading and unloading far easier. Each basket of debris from the shaft made its way to the two sifting boxes as each load was examined for cultural remains.

The grad students filled the day with mindless chatter both silly and serious as to which task was worse.

Roth, while standing before one of the sifters in an ever-growing delta of throat-choking fine tan sands and pumice-like powders, lectured Peters, "Every now and then," choke, "I'm finding hellishly sharp microliths. While I'm putting them all aside for later analysis," choke, "I can't decide whether they're natural or manmade. I'm just glad that I have gloves on."

The willowy Wald, while on her stint the scaffold's pulley-rope, "Better watch out Franks," she challenged the Bavarian as she pulled hand over hand, "I'm building my upper body!" While the wooden pulley creaked noisily under the strain of another load of limestone debris, "I'm getting a part-time job when this is over." Grunt. "As a waitress at the Hofbräuhaus. When I'm done here, I'll be able to carry four steins of beer in each hand, easy! I'll be rich on tips alone!"

*   *   *

Al-Razzuli sat patiently in his white Corolla parked along a secondary agricultural road that skirted the base of the plateau. Directly above him, the field team was hard at work. He hated the rented vehicle, its cheapness, its smell, but he knew that its presence would go unseen, while his Mercedes would not.

On his second day monitoring Hassan, he used a defter touch on the young inspector. One that was not so intrusive and heavy-handed. As a result, the rest of the archaeological team had totally ignored him.

Nevertheless, al-Razzuli found several things that he personally found curious. Why, for instance, was the middle-aged team leader Reissen doing the grunt work in the pit? As for the sifting operations, who would willingly submit to such a dirty and choking process all for a handful of trinkets? This entire archaeological process that the adept had once found so fascinating as a youth, had become mind-numbing as a adult. As a result, he left early that day, rationalizing that he had better things to do.

*   *   *

The following day, honest sweat streamed off Reissen's face and dotted his strong forearms, already coated in sweaty limestone clay. His tan shirt and shorts were thoroughly soaked, even to his leather belt. The burial shaft at this point was easily over three meters deep. Still he had yet to encounter any of the items that Sister Josephina had warned him about and the Mirgissa excavation reports had found. He'd checked in the library. While in the shade, the archaeologist did not enjoy one breath of breeze. The atmosphere now taxed his every move, so he sat back on his heels and took a break.

"Water. I need water." He begged to the surface. He looked at his watch after he unsnapped its protective leather cover. "I've got another hour. I can make it." He convinced himself.

Ten minutes later, watered and rested, the Austrian doggedly began again and after placing two handfuls of debris in the basket, stopped dead.

Peeking out from one corner of the shaft lay a broken piece of pottery with a red fabric. Reissen's pulse spiked.

"Would someone drop down a hand brush?" That request caused the rest of the team to stop what they were doing and peer over the edges of the burial shaft.

Roth's curiosity broke the tension, "What did you find Dr. Reissen?"

"Not sure yet, give me a moment." The man said with a tight voice, while he brushed away the dust from the reddish ceramic fragment and its immediate surroundings. Then he saw it—cursive hieratic writing painted in red on the potsherd. His heart fell a mile, while threatening to explode from his chest.

He sat back on his heels and looked up. "Roth, I have something for you. I think it's a fragment from an execration text."

Pause.

"Wald. Send down your camera and a twenty centimeter scale."

"May I come down instead?" Wald wanted to know.

"Absolutely not, Else!" Reissen uncharacteristically snapped.

The find of the curse text fragment brought an end to the day's labors. Washing off the potsherd with her bottled water, Roth turned it this way and that in order to orient herself to the red hieratic writing.

"You're right, Dr. Reissen, this is a part of an execration text." Roth confirmed. Meanwhile Wald, Franks, and Peters didn't have a clue as to what she meant.

"So, Sheila, what's an execration text?" Franks spoke up.

"Basically, an execration or curse text focused harmful magic upon the Egyptian's enemies. Once the naming of its enemies, foreign and domestic, was complete, the curse became effective when the object was ritualistically broken. This was a highly emotional act. In essence, the force of breakage sent forth the curse. Rather quickly, these curses were later adopted for private use. In such cases, instead of listing a series of states with the names of their kings and princes, private individuals were mentioned by name."

"Wow," Franks exclaimed. "Remind me to keep you on my good side!"

Roth playfully wagged her finger at the Bavarian with squinting eyes. "Careful now."

"Okay, Sheila, what kind of execration text is this?" Reissen asked. "A public or private version?"

"It looks private from what I have here, Dr. Reissen. I'll need more of it to make sure, and that means the entire pot."

The archaeologist grunted with a frown.

"But what's fascinating, Dr. Reissen," Roth continued, "is that if this tomb is indeed dated to the Fourth Dynasty, then this execration text is the earliest one known."

"Marvelous," the Austrian sourly replied as he looked at his watch. "Another anomaly. Alright everyone, we will begin again tomorrow, but only after I share something with you."

*   *   *

After a sobering discussion over lunch about Sister Josephina's interpretation on the missing photographic images and why, the group as one voted to continue, but only to recover the rest of pot's fragments. Then, they agreed to stop and reassess the situation.

"Dr. Reissen," Wald confided, "Thank you for sharing with us that explanation about the digital images. When I left your office that day, I thought I was going insane."

"Else, you're a fine photographer in every way. And I sincerely apologize for not sharing that information with you earlier. But I also didn't want to unnecessarily cause worry for either you or the rest of the team. But given what we have now found … " The Austrian concluded with upraised hands.

As the crew broke up, Sheila took Reissen aside.

"Erik, I want you to wear this."

Looking down at her open hand, the Austrian beheld a beautiful, golden image of the eye of Horus on a leather thong.

"Sheila, I cannot accept this gift. I …"

"No buts, professor. Put this on now."

"You're being silly," Reissen began to turn away, but Roth firmly grabbed him by his elbow.

Looking into his eyes Roth said, "You wear boots, don't you? They protect your feet."

A nod came from the archaeologist.

"Then you'll wear this. It will protect your soul. This tomb absolutely gives me the creeps, and it should you as well. Now put this on."

Reluctantly, Reissen did so. Not so much for the supposed protection that it would afford, but because of the wildly intense look in Roth's eyes.

"And you wear that amulet whenever you're on the site. Got that, professor?"

"You're serious about this, aren't you Sheila."

"Deadly serious and you have five grave robbers to prove it."

The next day began with a far greater seriousness. They all realized that the burial shaft and its contents potentially contained far more than just rubble. Peters expressed the situation succinctly, if perhaps a bit too dramatically. "We're potentially sitting on a magical land mine." This comment perked up Hassan's ears as he had not been privy to Reissen's revelation about the photographic imagery of the five.

Magical land mine? Is that some sort of joke?

Meanwhile, Reissen returned to the pit and worked the corner from where the original potsherd emerged. Within an hour he uncovered the rest of the red pot's fragments. Each he photographed and noted in his laptop's field journal. There were twelve in all.

On the surface, Roth washed, and then hovered over the twelve fragments arranging them all just so. Only then did it become clear to her how the ceramic bowl had been ritualistically broken. The uninscribed base had clearly taken the brunt of the blow.

While the rest of the team rested, lounged about, and nervously fidgeted, Roth got down to work. Nearly an hour later, she declared, "Okay, I have a working translation. Here it is."

> All people (sc. Egyptians), all patricians,
> all commoners, all men, all eunuchs, all
> women, and all nobles who plot against

the defilement of my beautiful form (sc. mummy) in this entire land, beware. May every evil word, every evil speech, every evil slander, every evil intent, every evil plot, every evil disturbance, every evil plan, every evil thing, and every evil dream in every evil sleep against my beautiful form be struck down!

Franks said it best. "If you ask me, that curse sounds pretty bland in comparison to the one in the grotto."

Several nodded in agreement.

"So Sheila, if I understand your reading of the text," Reissen opined, "the curse's threat of 'being struck down' is solely based upon the defilement of the coffin and its mummy. Is that correct?"

"Seems so, but I'm not a lawyer." She said with a dead straight face.

"In that case, I vote to continue the clearing of the burial shaft, barring any other developments. How does that decision sit with the rest of the team?" Reissen asked.

In response, four hands were thumbs up.

"Okay then, let's start anew." The Austrian said as he stood up. "Peters, take up the rope while I repel down."

* * *

For al-Razzuli, who sat below the plateau in his rented white Corolla, he had listened in on the proceedings via Hassan. His interest in the fields of Egyptian philology and archaeology had renewed. In fact, the man was absolutely riveted. *The burial shaft actually contained an execration text!*

*   *   *

By the end of the third day, Reissen announced from far below the surface, "I have reached the top edge of a bricked inside passage. Sheila, you'll be happy to know that it's on the eastern side of the shaft. Congratulations! Else, send down your camera and meter stick with the next basket."

Moments later, while awaiting the arrival of Else's camera, Reissen shifted his weight on the shaft's surface, and distinctly heard the sound of breaking ceramic under his left boot, much like a tea cup being crushed underfoot. That sound was accompanied by a hiss that smelled of garlic and something else. Then, the surface collapsed beneath his feet by several inches, startling the archaeologist. Immediately, the skin on his exposed legs began to itch and the Austrian jerked the rope twice with concern, which remained slack as no one was attending it at that moment. The itching, now reached his knees, and the man panicked.

"HELP! Pull me out now!" he called above and jerked again at the rope, which now was firm in his hand. He didn't wait for any assistance and climbed, hand-over-hand, as his legs felt sluggish, his ankles limp.

"Help me, someone!" he called between gasps, and the rope finally began to ascend. Hassan, who appeared next to the shaft, peered in, reached out, grabbed the shaken archaeologist, and pulled him over to one side.

"What's wrong, Dr. Reissen?" Hassan asked with concern.

That question was answered with a mild explosion from deep within the shaft, followed by a belch of gas that ended in a small fireball. Any Las Vegas magician's act could have done better. But in its wake, the anemic explosion blanked the area with the awful smell of garlic and rotting fish. The lower length of the rope that the Austrian had just climbed was charred as was the wicker basket.

Pointing down into the still roiling air within the shaft, Reissen choked out, "That!"

Ten minutes later the Austrian mission's field physician arrived at the scene from Memphis to find his colleague sitting down and greedily drinking water.

"Erik, what happened? Your legs look burned," the former military internist said while opening up his canvas satchel, emblazoned with a white circle and a red cross.

"That's because they are, Lukas. I stepped on some sort of a chemical booby-trap. I got out of the shaft just before things got interesting."

Swabbing down one of his legs with an all-purpose burn ointment that contained a mild analgesic, "Erik, tell me what I am treating."

"I really don't know. I heard a crunch in the soil, felt the soil compact, then a hiss, and my exposed skin began to really itch. Then I climbed out. Maybe twenty seconds later, we all heard an explosion followed by a fireball."

"Well, my friend, you are very lucky. Your legs will mend. They have been mildly burned—second degree at worst. Within a day or two, expect the affected areas to itch and peel.

The medic continued with his smearing of salve, looked directly into the archaeologist's eyes, and said. "I've seen this before, Erik. This is a hydrogen chloride burn. I've treated plenty of them back at the university. Chemistry students can sometimes be very careless. But the gas explosion is far more worrisome. That suggests to me phosphine gas, a secondary reaction. Did you smell anything odd?"

"Yes! Garlic and dead fish."

Nodding at that information, Lukas continued. "It's a good thing you got out when you did. Those smells are indeed signatures of phosphine, a toxic gas that attacks the central nervous system. Did you feel any odd sensations when you were exposed in the pit?"

"Yes! I couldn't stand, so I climbed up the rope hand over hand."

A head shake of disapproval. "That's phosphine. Erik, how do your legs feel now?"

"Like they're asleep, but their feeling is returning."

"Good. Stay put and keep drinking water."

At this point Lukas, a surgical internist who had seen far too much in Syrian medical tents, peeked over the edge into the burial shaft. He could see at its bottom a mild depression at its center. Whatever gas was left he judged dissipated by the explosion in a classic exothermic reaction. What the physician also saw was a distinct orange to brownish tint extending up from the shaft's floor about six feet up its smoothed walls—the harmless residue left behind from a highly ignitable and toxic phosphine gas reaction.

Returning to his colleague once again, the physician squatted down next to his patient. His blue eyes looked straight into his. "Erik, you are one very lucky man. When I was stationed in Aleppo, I had the misfortune of cleaning up an explosion like this. Over twenty men died, horribly, Erik. I'm ordering you to take a break."

"Understood." Reissen replied.

Just to stay on the safe side, the next day all work at the burial shaft took a pause. Dr. Lukas Hampl, with the help of Hassan, acquired a wicker cage with two live pigeons, which they lowered down into the shaft. There, they spent the entire day without suffering any harm. This positive result split the team's decision to continue on, forcing Reissen to cast the deciding vote.

On day five an absolutely driven Reissen—now wearing a gas mask just to be on the safe side—continued on clearing the burial shaft. In the process, he found a broken, internally glazed, and partitioned amphora that once contained the chemicals necessary for the vicious trap. Once he recorded them in his archaeological log, he sent their fragments up for further analysis. As far as he was concerned, this amphora was the first of its kind ever found in Egypt. *Yet another anomaly.*

The Austrian labored for the next two days until there was no more to remove from the shaft. While his team loyally supported him, they naturally began to wonder about his sanity.

Peters said to Franks, "How well do you know Dr. Reissen?"

"Pretty well. Why?"

"Do you think that he is being a daredevil?"

"No. He's doing his job and protecting us."

Wald and Roth overheard the surveyor's hushed conversation.

"What do you think?" Roth wanted to know.

"Dr. Reissen is definitely a driven man. But a daredevil? No." Wald concluded with a shake of her head.

After the last basket load of debris had been raised, the Austrian emerged from the shaft with a victorious smile on his face. "Okay everyone. Else goes down first to photograph the shaft and the blocked up burial entrance. Focus in on the many stamp seals. When Else is finished, the survey team with take their measurements. Inspector Hassan, do you wish to go down as well?"

A vigorous nod.

"Good. Then, after Inspector Hassan returns to the surface, Sheila and I will go down to assess the stamp seals in the plaster."

From the shaft's cleared bottom, the survey team established that the shaft measured fifty Egyptian cubits—22.85 meters or a shade less than seventy-five feet deep. Its smooth sided walls had cut through three different limestone strata. The execration text was placed twenty-two feet down, the booby-trap some eighteen feet beyond that.

What was left unsaid, but was clear to all—the trap had been placed at a sufficient depth that would have prevented anyone from scrambling out without the assistance of a rope.

*   *   *

Al-Razzuli, sitting down slope in his rented car, was beside himself with excitement. He had a front row seat in an exciting drama..

CHAPTER 7

"What do you think, Sheila?" Reissen asked while his flashlight illuminated a particularly complete stamp seal in the ancient plaster. The beam wandered a bit as he bent down and scratched at the itchy and flaking skin of his right knee.

"There is nothing harmful here, Dr. Reissen, at least in a magical sense. In fact, it's very straightforward. This stamp seal says that the tomb was closed by the priesthood of Anubis, in Khufu's fourteenth year, first month of the second season, day eight."

"That squares nicely with the false door's text." The Egyptologist remembered.

But just to make sure, the pair searched the entire plastered over surface of the blocking wall and confirmed that all twenty-four stamps were indeed the same.

"So Sheila, in your opinion, based upon all the magical texts that you know about, should we proceed to break into this tomb?"

"That's hardly my call, Dr. Reissen." The expert in

religion and magic countered. "But yes, from purely a magical standpoint, I would proceed, but very carefully. Frankly, I was initially surprised that we only found one execration text. Usually, tens, if not hundreds, of such smashed pots are found in state-sponsored deposits. But this is a rare instance of a private tomb with only one focused curse to protect its mummy. In many respects, this is all very new to my field."

Another anomaly, Reissen silently grimaced.

"However, for me that chemical booby trap was a real game changer. That represented a last-ditch defensive threshold, but I could be dead wrong. That trap, while not magical in any respect, might be only the first of many. Regardless, its ingenuity reinforced my admiration for Djedi and his tomb builders. So my question for you is: 'are you willing to potentially risk your life on opening this tomb?'"

* * *

Sheila Roth's observations surprised Reissen. He always considered himself a pragmatist. But he found that the uniqueness of this archaeological site had pushed his buttons in ways that he never expected. In the final analysis, the rigidly precise archaeologist discovered that his chosen field of endeavor was actually dangerous as his still itchy legs attested.

But what really challenged Reissen was the sudden

impact of notoriety. He had not considered what his team's discovery of an intact Egyptian tomb would mean. Suddenly, this low-key salvage excavation, budgeted and manned on a shoestring, became the center of the world's attention. To better deal with the situation, Inspector Kama assigned a beefed up security force to keep the curious at bay. Next, the Austrian entertained a stream of bureaucrats from the Egyptian Antiquities Service. Flowing forth like a river, each required a personal tour, which eventually caused the installation of an electrically powered lift system. This contraption the wily Hassan somehow came up with along with the needed generators and fuel to power it.

When the Egyptian Antiquities Service put out a press release on the find, the domestic and foreign media descended upon the site like a cloud of locusts. Reissen's chiseled visage became instantly famous. Pummeled with their endless questions and their daring ploys to gain access to the burial shaft itself, the archaeologist put an end to their circus. Worst of all in the Austrian's eyes, all work had to come to a screeching halt. Then, miraculously, the site no longer was newsworthy, and peace once again reigned supreme.

By this time, the rest of the Austrian archaeological mission at Memphis joined up with the Reissen and his beleaguered band. Having Habib close at hand greatly relieved the Egyptologist. His presence alone would speed the break in and clearing of the tomb. Why? His old friend was a logistical and organizational genius. As it was, Inspector Kama insisted on witnessing the break in. As a consequence, Hassan precariously installed a temporary structure of shaded bench seating that overlooked the burial shaft's opening. Seating tickets were available and appropriately expensive, and a certain *Monsieur* al-Razzuli arranged for a front row position overlooking the shaft itself. Vexed, the Austrian realized that his excavation had become theatre.

*   *   *

Despite all the pumped up media fanfare, the much-ballyhooed grand opening of the magician's tomb turned out to be a disappointment. How some reporters could spin the event as the second coming of Tutankhamen's riches mystified Reissen, but didn't surprise him one bit. A reporter from *Der Spiegel*, best encapsulated the vibe of the moment.

> Overlooking this burial pit, in truth this dark and foreboding entrance to the Egyptian Underworld, I wondered if we would be greeted by the mummy of magician Djedi himself.

With the twenty-four plaster mortuary stamp sealings already removed and sent off to conservation,

Inspector Kama removed several of the blocking wall's central bricks. With the video cameras of two international news agencies rolling, Kama peered into a beckoning black void beyond. Seeing nothing, Hassan handed him a halogen lamp. Kama wore a disappointed look at not seeing the glint of gold that had greeted Howard Carter on that historic day of November 26th, 1923. But what the harsh illumination did reveal was a partial glimpse of a wheat yellow back wall densely covered in painted black hieroglyphs. That was all. With the cameras each taking their turn at the gap, their lenses didn't do much better.

Robbed of his historic moment, Kama dramatically turned to the rolling cameras and intoned, "I will now remove the rest of the blocking wall. Then we can better assess the condition of the tomb." To his credit, the demolition proceeded in an orderly fashion as he lifted out and away each and every plastered in brick. Rather quickly, the cameras stopped recording this humdrum process. Forty minutes later and with all of the debris removed, the tomb's entrance lay open.

With the cameras again rolling and with the halogen lamp in hand, Kama was immediately greeted by five tan ceramic plates of desiccated foodstuffs— beef ribs, pigeon, and quail, three sealed jars of beer, and four blackened flower bouquets placed at the tomb's entrance way. A hint of Lotus fragrance teased his nose, or did he just imagine it?

Carefully stepping beyond these last funerary offerings, a modest, square-shaped tomb opened up to him and the cameras with precious few extravagances. Black hieroglyphs covered the four walls painted in a wheat yellow color. Gold five-pointed stars decorated a cobalt blue ceiling. Occupying its center, a simple rectangular cedar coffin rested upon the traditional four magical mud bricks, one at each corner, oriented to the four cardinal points, which the inspector explained to the cameras, represented the protective four sons of the god Horus.

Glancing about, Kama saw stacked in each corner several walking sticks, some with forked ends. "These forked staves are employed by the tomb's owner to protect him from the demon serpents of the Underworld." To the left of the coffin rested a small cedar chest. "This is the tomb owner's canopic chest. It contains his mummified internal organs in four separate jars—one for the lungs, liver, stomach, and intestines."

"What about the heart?" One cameraman asked.

"The heart," Kama indulged, "the Egyptians believed, is the seat of one's personality and the repository of one's actions. As a consequence, it remained," while gesturing to the left side of his chest, "in the body. Once in the Underworld, the individual's heart, the *ib*, would face judgment."

Moving on, Kama saw to his right, a larger cedar chest with a rounded lid. Again he took the moment to explain to the cameras. "Here, in this chest, is contained the man's favorite personal items. If you look around, you will note that this is a modest deposit of grave goods. This, in itself, is noteworthy for it tells me something about the tomb's owner. He was a man of simple needs."

Finished with his tour, the inspector shooed the cameramen out. "I am very sorry, but these spaces are about to become very cramped."

"Hassan!" Kama ordered. "Fetch the Austrian field photographer. This must be immediately recorded."

With Wald replacing the videographers, Kama finally relaxed, for Habib had accompanied her.

"Madam. Please proceed, but do so with infinite care."

"Absolutely, Inspector Kama."

Wald, while she drank in this historic moment, remembered Reissen's private words. "Step carefully. Touch nothing, especially the coffin, if there is one."

It took Wald almost three hours to shoot the tiny tomb and its contents, while Habib arranged the signage per shot and the measurement scales. While they worked with well-oiled professionalism, Kama and Hassan looked on. The former pleased as could be and impressed at how the photography was proceeding. The latter only half seeing, as his mind had become clouded again.

With the photography complete, Wald and Habib

left. Only then, by prior agreement, did Reissen descend to finally see the fruits of his team's labors.

At the entrance, Inspector Kama greeted him and declared with a hearty handshake, "My congratulations, Dr. Reissen," the inspector magnanimously began. "The discovery of an intact tomb from the Old Kingdom is an extremely rarity. Your team did a fine job. You should be proud of them all. Hassan has told me this, and has reported of your many courtesies toward him. This I will never forget. And as a sign of my country's goodwill, I have secured for your archaeological mission full publication rights."

Reissen, dumbstruck, nodded, "Thank you, sir."

"Now, Dr. Reissen, let us inspect the tomb," as Hassan handed him the halogen lamp. This the Austrian did, taking care to step over the entranceway's offerings while simultaneously ducking down in the cramped confines. For Reissen, this was his moment, his private pay off for his many labors and frightening moments. In some respects, the modest tomb was a disappointment, but the Austrian was quite sure that its inscriptions would prove *interesting*.

"Dr. Reissen, let us discuss the removal and conservation of this tomb's artifacts."

"Respectfully, Inspector Kama, now that this tomb has been thoroughly photographed, we should survey it, immediately reseal it, and fill in its shaft."

"What!"

*   *   *

Meanwhile, some eighty feet above, sat a restive al-Razzuli. While the man continued to use Hassan's eyes and ears as his own personal video link, he could not penetrate Kama's mind and that frustrated the adept.

"Why not just reseal the tomb with a padlocked steel door and its shaft with a secured iron grate?" Kama reasonably asked the Austrian.

"In my opinion, that is not secure enough, inspector."

"I think it is."

"Well, sir, as the inspector of this archaeological district, I will support your decision regarding this matter."

"Thank you, Dr. Reissen. In time, I think that you will come to appreciate this sensible course of action."

*   *   *

The next day, Wald came to Reissen with wide eyes.

"Yes, Else."

"Erik, I found something in several photographs I think you should see," As she handed him two blown up printouts. "The bedrock of the tomb's back wall has settled here, and again here." She indicated with her right pinky finger. "My guess is that these relieving cracks are hiding something. What do you think?"

"I think tomorrow we'll go and take a look." He said with an easy but intrigued look.

With the media long gone, Reissen and Wald returned to the tomb early the following day without the rest of the team and their minder Hassan. Only a half-sleeping security guard was on duty and a sealed hard pack of Dunhill cigarettes kept him happily occupied. Normally, the Austrian would never have dreamed of doing something this covert, but something was driving him. With the workmen due to arrive to install the grate and steel door, now was the time.

Each with a hand lamp, they stepped carefully over and around all the artifacts and quickly reached the subtle ripple and fine cracks in the back wall that the high-definition imagery had revealed. With his fountain pen, an old Monarch, Reissen gently began tapping the wall from right to left.

Tap.

Tap.

Thunk.

Thunk.

Tap.

Tap.

Now sitting back on his heels, the Austrian looked quizzically at Else and then performed the same experiment vertically and earned much the same result. Satisfied, he said, "Else. What you have detected is a plaster plug of some kind. So before I cut into it, I need a favor. I want you to once again photograph this back wall. I know that doing so will be redundant, but I just wish to make sure."

And while Wald redid the wall section by section, Reissen furiously thought about how he should best proceed. Mind made up, he reached for his phone.

"Good morning, Inspector Kama. This is Erik Reissen. I apologize for calling you so early."

"Dr. Reissen. What a surprise. But your apology is unnecessary. How might I be of service?"

"Our photographer has made a discovery, sir. She and I have just confirmed it. May I suggest that you visit the Sakkaran tomb site today?"

"Another discovery? What is it?"

"I do not know at this time, sir. It appears to be a cleverly hidden niche in the back wall. I do not wish to disturb the plaster without you being present."

"I will be there immediately, Dr. Reissen."

True to his word, the pair heard the hum of the electric lift's operation about twenty minutes later.

Huffing and puffing, a red-faced Inspector Kama stood at the tomb's threshold and said, "I am here, Dr. Reissen, as requested."

"Thank you, inspector for your kind indulgence. The anomaly is over here, sir." Reissen pointed at the back wall.

Now with the inspector standing next to Wald, Reissen said, "Kindly listen, inspector," as he again performed the fountain pen test. "What we have here is a plaster plug that is hiding something behind it."

"It surely sounds like it. How do you wish to proceed?"

"Carefully, obviously. I wish to use my pen knife to carefully tease away the plaster."

"Has the area been photographed," the inspector automatically asked.

"Yes, it has, inspector. In fact, *Frau* Wald here redid this wall just this morning."

Grunting with approval at the Austrian's foresight, "Then please proceed, Dr. Reissen," The inspector gestured.

Alternately carving and picking at the highly friable surface rapidly created a pile of dusty chunks at the wall's base. Perspiration dripped from the Egyptologist's nose while he teased the surface. Moments later, he took a break to have Wald photograph the delineated outline in the wall. To the Austrian's relief, only a handful of painted hieroglyphs would be sacrificed in the process of clearing the one foot square.

"I am finished, Dr. Reissen," Wald unnecessarily declared as she stood back.

Glancing back to Inspector Kama, the Austrian said, "Are we committed, sir?"

A simple head nod.

After only several stabs of the pen knife, the plaster

plug failed and fell away in one piece, saving several glyphs intact.

"Very well done, Dr. Reissen," The inspector breathed with admiration at the feat.

Dusty white, the hidden niche in the bedrock revealed an exquisite cedar model of an Egyptian temple—slope-sided with an outturned architrave.

The three gaped with mouths open.

"I have never seen such an artifact before," the inspector squinted in total disbelief.

"Nor I," Reissen confirmed with a furrowed brow. "Else, please capture this moment."

In response, her camera clicked away. Then, remembering, she placed a small scale in the niche, and shot several more.

"Should I remove it, sir?"

"Yes, please," the inspector barely whispered.

"It weighs practically nothing," The archaeologist remarked, while he gently turned the artifact this way and that. "It is a container, a box of some sort. And it contains something, inspector, I felt it move, but I cannot locate a lid or opening."

"Allow me," Kama said with outstretched hands. "Ah, there is an inscription on its bottom, but I too am puzzled as to how to open it," As he handed it back to Reissen, who carefully returned it to the niche.

"Dr. Reissen, we need to clear this tomb's artifacts as soon as possible."

"Yes, sir. I understand."

"You will no doubt be happy to know that I have already made arrangements for them to be sent to the new conservation department at the Grand Egyptian Museum at Giza."

Reissen nodded soberly. "That, sir, would be the best. When will the conservators arrive?"

"Tomorrow morning at the latest."

Then a ruckus was heard from the surface above.

"Ah, the workmen have arrived!" Inspector Kama gleamed. "We will completely lock this site down before sunset!"

*   *   *

While the site would indeed be secured before the sundown that day, one artifact would go mysteriously missing. Unique opportunities in archaeology cause individuals to do things they normally would never consider. Unique artifacts create a lust that only the strong can withstand. The next morning, the acquisitions and conservation team from the Grand Egyptian Museum arrived and cleared the tomb. However, Inspector Kama had recognized his unique opportunity and took it—quite literally..

CHAPTER 8

Stolen petroleum assets are hard to manage, much less cash in on, if you kill off their staffs. The terrorist elements in northern Syria and western Iraq discovered this rather critical blunder only after the fact. Aside from the impossibly insane issue of logistics, which they had also heedlessly destroyed, the breadth of the international oil market, and its arcane bureaucracy, effectively strangled them. Add to that they lacked representation within OPEC and forces were afoot that dried up the black market in crude. Not being able to transform crude into bullets and foodstuffs, they had to find another source of income.

Then one of their group's leadership, an economist, made the observation that scarcity caused the value of something to rise in the marketplace. Looking around in their desolate surroundings, what could possibly be considered valuable *and* readily desirable on the black market? So was established the plan to pillage museums of their artifacts and destroy ancient monuments, all to inflate the black market prices of such antiquities. Sadly, unlike oil crude, there was a healthy black market for such items and those ready and willing to buy them.

Despite their avowed faith-based argument on the Internet and elsewhere, the Sunni Arab Islamic caliphate of Syria and Iraq—variously referred to as IS, ISIL, ISIS, and Daesh, remained a fraud. Their desire for power was economically driven initially by oil money, and when that was denied, the black market sale of antiquities.

In addition, this supposedly religious movement remained exclusively Sunni *and* Arab in character. Therefore, the caliphate possessed little appeal to all Shia'a and non-Arab populations. Further, the leadership of the movement, based out of the Syrian city of Raqqa, was seriously flawed. A legal academic, Abu Bakr al-Baghdadi, was acclaimed as Caliph Ibrahim. The Prince of Believers enlightened domestic policy for all Muslims was defined by frequent beheadings, stonings, crucifixions, slavery, and a return to the *dhimmitude*, or head-tax on all who refuse to convert to Islam. After his fighters invaded the Iraqi city of Mosul, they slew a dozen Islamic *imams*. The caliph then led Friday prayers at the city's main mosque and wore all black—the signature color of the Abbasid caliphs—as if the last eight centuries never happened.

Their eventual fall was imminent. The military powers of the West were closing in. All that was needed was a gentle push and al-Razzuli was more than ready to oblige.

*   *   *

Once again the adept went to the execration ritual of his youth. His sources had provided him with a list of seven names within the ISIS leadership—including the caliph Abu Bakr al-Baghdadi. As before, he gathered his will into a powerful conjuring, and smashed the red ink inscribed red pot upon his outdoor patio's pavement. But unlike his first jejune attempt, al-Razzuli's laser-like focus projected his will ten-fold. He quite literally saw against the night's sky streaming tendrils of his pure, unadulterated hate. They flowed from his fingertips as green ribbons sent to ensnare and strangle seven victims.

The spell completed, he stood breathing heavily, clearly winded, in the cool desert's night air. The papyrus, jasmine, and lotus blossoms of his garden filled his lungs, settling him down after the exertion. His fingertips tingled as if slightly burned. Only then did he smile up at the stars with complete contentment, full in the knowledge of his act.

*   *   *

Three weeks later, proof of his conjuring's effectiveness reached al-Razzuli's ears from a flat-screen television. The accomplishment caused him to tighten his fists in moaning pleasure.

ISIS Defeated in Raqqa as 'Major Military Operations' Declared Over

US-backed forces fighting ISIS in Raqqa say "major military operations" in the city have ended and that the jihadists have lost control of their self-declared capital.

The development marks a decisive victory in the fight against ISIS, though US officials said there were still pockets of resistance in the city.

"Major military operations in Raqqa are finished but they are now clearing the city of sleeper cells—if they exist—and mines," Talal Salo, spokesman for the US-backed Syrian Democratic Forces, told CNN. The SDF is a coalition of Arab and Kurdish fighters.

"The situation in Raqqa is under control and soon there will be an official statement declaring the liberation of the city."

By Hilary Clarke, Nick Paton Walsh, Eliza Mackintosh and Ghazi Balkiz, CNN. Drone video sourced by Waffe Munayyer, CNN. Wednesday, October 18, 2017.

CHAPTER 9

The door chimed within the darkened cave of the antiquities shop. A heavy-set man hurriedly entered with a wrapped object under one arm. As he did, he passed through the mixed aromas of fresh tea and stale cigarettes.

"Welcome, my friend." The shopkeeper greeted. "It has been some time since we last met. The shopkeeper offered with open hands and a slight bow of the head. "How might I be of service? Perhaps some tea?"

"Indeed, it has been some time," the visitor said, "but I do not have time for polite pleasantries. I have a unique artifact I wish to sell," the man said as he unwrapped and displayed on the counter a delicately carved cedar object.

The shopkeeper's eyes widened with wonder and no small amount of sheer avarice. "My friend, where did you get this? From where did it come? A tomb? An excavation perhaps?" He said with an upraised eyebrow.

"That is not your concern. Both you and I know

such an artifact is extremely rare, if not unique." After a quick glance at his wrist watch, "is your shop interested in acquiring this?"

The shopkeeper stroked his smoothly shaven chin, stalling for time to think. "May I pick it up?"

"Most certainly."

It weighed almost nothing, but while handling it, the shopkeeper sensed that it contained something. "How do you open this?"

"I have no idea. Are you interested in buying it?" the visitor pressed. A rivulet of nervous sweat ran down the side of his face.

Putting the object down and then pinching his lower lip, the shopkeeper made a low-ball offer. The visitor, without quibbling, accepted it, which the shopkeeper thought was telling in a most troubling way.

Retreating to his safe, the shopkeeper returned with the amount agreed upon. The visitor took the bank notes and stuffed them in several pockets. Padding himself down, he nodded to the shopkeeper, and left.

The shopkeeper stood stunned at the proceedings. Looking over at the wall clock, the entire transaction took a mere six minutes and that too worried the man.

*   *   *

A bald man sat before the flat television screen, his lips murmured at the horrible things portrayed. Every now and then, the seventy-something would point and shake a spotted and arthritic finger at the images, cursing in a tongue long dead, full in the knowledge that no one could possibly understand his ravings. *These days,* he reasoned, *one could not be too careful. Walls have ears.*

"May you drown in the urine of Set!

"May Amit devour your soul!

"May Apophis' venom blind you forever!" He raged in ancient Egyptian.

First came Iraq and the senseless destruction waged against the ancient Assyrian capital cities of Ninevah and Khorsabad and the appalling damage to Roman Hatra. Next, they blew up the Fourth century Christian monastery of Mar Behnam, the Islamic Imam Dur Mausoleum, and Mosque of the Prophet Yunus. The Mosul Museum and its libraries they looted, burned. His mouth hung agape.

The insane treatment of antiquities only continued in Syria with the city of Roman Palmyra—an architectural jewel, not to mention the ravaging of the Roman cities of Dura-Europos and Apamea. Both Christian and Islamic shrines felt their mindless scourge. The systematic looting of the Bronze Age city of Mari brought tears to the man's eyes.

Such a waste.

But it didn't end there. Extremists now ransacked the antiquities storage magazines of his own beloved country—Egypt. Looters, without conscience, openly dug in the desert fringes. The antiquities guards, well bribed, turned their heads unseeing. The devils even dared to desecrate the Cairo National Museum. *Where will it end?* He asked himself during a coughing fit. He spat the bloody phlegm into a handy napkin which he discarded into a waste basket.

To say Professor Dr. Ahmed Ibn El-Mussar was sickened with the troubles of the modern world would be an understatement. Agitated, the Egyptologist could not believe what his eyes told him—the systematic ideological rejection of history and its legacy. *This is utter madness.*

His phone rang, jarring his attention from the late afternoon news. Almost dropping the heavy receiver, El-Mussar listened.

After several intent nods El-Mussar replied in fluent German, "I understand." Glancing at his watch, "I can be there in one hour." Pause. "Yes, that would be grand."

Hanging up he thought, *perhaps, just perhaps, I can save this one.*

The cab ride to Khan el-Kalili that early evening took the rail thin philologist only thirty minutes. El-Mussar knew that bustling area quite well, because he had grown up within the bazaar's narrow and uneven streets. As a boy he had favored the many antiquities shops, making it a game to guess the authentic reproductions–the many scarabs, figurines, and coins which had been fed to a goose to produce the desired patina, from the originals. And in so doing, El-Mussar learned many clues and even more about his ancient heritage, ultimately driving him to pursue it with a single-minded passion.

He passed by The Old Papyrus House on the corner of Sekat al Badstan and Rbaa al Selhdar. Glancing through the windows at its wares, he smirked at the gaudily painted papyri designed to attract a tourist's eye. At the corner, he turned right and made for a narrow maroon awning, dusty and faded with age. Even its once golden fringe drooped in sad submission. Squeezed in between two jewelry shops, the narrow store front seemed to disappear in a surround of glitter, silver, and gold. The old man ducked into its cramped entrance, also feeling dusty and faded with age, but excited with anticipation.

The poorly lit place smelled vaguely of a hay barn, but for El-Mussar that was a good sign. It brought back memories of being in the field, excavating at Memphis. *Ah, the smell of antiquity.*

The long and narrow confines of this shop placed an emphasis on an efficient layout. Lined along each wall stood simple floor-to-ceiling wooden shelving, upon which hundreds of shoeboxes waited, each carefully identified with a label. Getting to the uppermost reaches was made possible with two slim-tracked library ladders on wheels. Down the shop's lone aisle lay a worn and threadbare maroon carpet—the only attempt to muffle squeaky wooden floorboards. Two shiny iron tracks of the ladders bordered it.

This was not a shoe store, but rather the most reputable antiquities shop in the entire Cairo bazaar. First opened by a defrocked ex-patriot German archaeologist at the turn of the nineteenth century, the shop managed over the years to "acquire" interesting items museum curators and private collectors hungered for, all the while avoiding the wrath of the Supreme Council of Antiquities. The rumor was this shop had exported to Berlin the famous painted plaster bust of Queen Nefertiti within a bale of raw Egyptian cotton. At the same time, the shop provided a vital back-channel of gossip for the Egyptian authorities that had proved most valuable—all too often. Hence, an uneasy truce was established between the illicit sale of ancient culture and the very custodians of it.

The shop's current owner, Manfred Schmidt, was El-Mussar's boyhood friend. While just as bald as the Egyptian philologist, Schmidt was physically his polar opposite. Heavy, if not obese from too many honeyed sweet cakes, the man suffered from gout. Decades before these two street urchins had learned at Herr Gerhard Schmidt's knee, the shop's founder and Manfred's father, every trick to ascertain an artifact's genuineness, and many lessons in art history and ancient technology as well. For the boys, it was a grand game. But now it was serious business, which for the most part, ranged far outside the law.

Near the glass-topped wooden counter with its brass antique register Manfred held court next to tiny round wicker table. A stool made of the same construction awaited his guest, along with a well-used and piping hot silver tea service. An exotic aroma wafted from it that filled the space.

"Manny, it is always wonderful to see you." El-Mussar greeted him in German, throwing in a deferential bow to his seated host for good measure.

Now standing with a grunt, Schmidt chuckled at the theatrical antics, took both of El-Mussar's hands in his, and kissed them. "And you as well, old friend. Come, sit. I have even brewed a pot of your favorite licorice tea."

After the traditional first sip was savored, Schmidt began. "My brother, do you remember how we used to compete with each other in dating my father's pottery?"

"Indeed, I do," El-Mussar said with upraised eyebrows, "And I recall with pleasure how your father always treated the winner with one of your mother's powdered almond cookies."

That memory generated another chuckle from Schmidt, causing his jowls to bounce like Jell-O. "Yes, indeed, but times have changed, have they not?"

El-Mussar could only muster a sad nod.

"Ahmed. I called you because an artifact has come

into my possession that needs a safe place."

"Oh? And why is that, Manny? Just look at these shelves." El-Mussar gestured, "How could anyone find something here?"

Another merry chuckle, but one far briefer. "No, my friend, I need to pass this artifact on to someone I trust."

"Then, why not the Supreme Council of Antiquities? Do you not trust them?" El-Mussar asked.

"Frankly, no, I do not," Schmidt said with a flat and unreadable look. "This artifact I suspect is far too...controversial. I do not wish it to fall into the wrong hands."

"Manny, why such melodrama," El-Mussar asked with spreading hands "What do you mean?"

"One moment," the shopkeeper said. He reached down behind his stool and produced a shoebox. "I am entrusting you with this, because I believe you to be of sound mind and good character." Only then did he hand over the shoebox to his friend.

The solemn words caused El-Mussar to stare back at his old friend, a hard business man, who dealt with a shadowy clientele within a dark realm on a daily basis. "Your words trouble me, Manny. Just what have you given me, old friend?"

"Something unique to the modern world that should not be on the black market. Suffice it to say, I found it, at least potentially, to be very troubling."

Schmidt raised his finger in dark emphasis. "And, Ahmed, do not open the shoebox here. Instead, open it within the secure sanctity of your office, and study it there. Only then, will you understand."

*   *   *

Having finished his tea and bade farewell to his old friend Manny, El-Mussar took an agonizing forty minutes to return to his flat. True to his friend's request, he did not open the two pound shoebox. Now within the "secure sanctity" of his office, surrounded by overstuffed shelves of academic books and file cabinets piled high, the Egyptian turned on his desk lamp and carefully lifted the shoebox's lid and peered inside.

The faint smell of cedar hit him first from the rectangle that lay within. Its ruddy color guaranteed great age. Donning a pair of cotton conservator's gloves, El-Mussar gently lifted it out and immediately saw that he held a craftsman's masterpiece. *It's a tiny temple, carved from a single block of cedar! Complete with sloped sides, entrance gates, and a papyrus architrave along its roofline. How delicate.*

As he turned the artifact this way and that in the lamp light, the philologist noted the delicate low relief hieroglyphic inscription covering the temple's underside. *What have we here?*

Scanning the glyphs with curiosity, El-Mussar

could not believe what he read, or perhaps better, what he thought he read. *That just can't be.*

Gently leaning the wooden model on one side, he reached for a legal pad, a yellow Number Two pencil, and transliterated the text that was arranged in six vertical registers. That task complete, the retired Egyptian philologist translated the stock phrases with ease.

> *O noble one, you hold the power of the universe. Respect me in accordance with what you know. I am he whom the Unique Lord made before anything had yet come into being.*
>
> *I am the son of Him, who gave birth to the universe, who was born before his mother yet existed. I protect that which the Unique Lord has created. I am he who caused the Ennead to live.*
>
> *You hold my words of power. Only a clever one will find them. I stand before you to receive my dignity, for to me belongs the universe before the gods had yet come into being. I am Heka.*

Heka! This artifact purports to be the property of the primordial Egyptian god of magic! And it challenges me to find his words of power.

In response, El-Mussar dared something that he normally wouldn't do—he gingerly shook the object like a wrapped gift pilfered from beneath a Christmas tree. This action rewarded El-Mussar with a subtle movement from within. *Ah, so it does contain something.*

Under normal conditions, when he had access to the conservation laboratory at the university, the Egyptian's first step would have been to measure, weigh, photograph, and then x-ray the object—standard conservation procedures all. But to even gain access to the lab, much less its x-ray equipment, required logging in the artifact, the establishment of a paper trail, and the inevitable answering of many questions that the retired philologist could not begin to answer. Without question, this object had no archaeological provenience, was probably illegally excavated without a permit, and had found its way onto the black market.

With a heavy sigh El-Mussar sat and stared at the exquisite cedar box, while he considered his options. *Manny gave me this artifact to safe-guard. I now know why. Should I store it away? Or, investigate further?*

With his mind made up, he turned the beautifully carved object in his hands, taking in its perfect proportions, its sheer artistry and craftsmanship. While doing so, he looked for what "only a clever one will find." For all practical purposes, the tiny temple appeared to be a solid block of wood, but the inscription and his tactile senses told the philologist quite another story.

El-Mussar examined the base once more and then

saw it—the two outer register margins of the inscription were ever so slightly more distinct. Now holding the artifact along its two longer sides, he gently pressed and pushed the base with his thumbs, and was rewarded with a subtle hiss of air. Lo' and behold, the base moved several inches revealing an access panel, which after some gentle coaxing, he removed.

Within lay two papyrus rolls, one bound with three red strands of yarn, the other with blue. Also within, was wedged a rectangular golden amulet hung from a string of lapis lazuli beads. Upon it stared back at him a magnificent image of the Eye of Horus.

El-Mussar knew that the ancient Egyptians chose their magical colors purposefully—red for that which was harmful or aggressive, blue for beneficial spells or curative magic.

The smell of fresh hay wafted forth. The tawny-green color of the rolls looked in surprisingly good condition. El-Mussar lifted out each little bundle and placed them on the leather pad of his desk.

With purpose, the Egyptologist first selected the papyrus roll with the red yarn, teased them away with a tweezers, and placed each loop back in the open recess for safekeeping. Now unrestrained, the document unrolled itself, almost as if commanded to do so.

Fully relaxed, the papyrus sheet lay open before El-Mussar, as if to dare, "Here I am. Read me." And the philologist did just that.

The sky trembles, the earth quakes before [NN].

The magician is [NN]. [NN] now possesses my power.

[NN] is the god/goddess to perform your bidding.

The god/goddess under your yoke is [NN].

[NN] (god/goddess) can be told of its dominion as [XX]. [XX] is the extent of [NN]'s power.

[NN] are the enemy, the prey. The enemy and prey are [NN].

The magician [NN] who wears the Eye of Horus commands [NN] (god/goddess) to do its bidding.

[NN] (god/goddess) is yoked by the magician [NN] to follow his commands.

The philologist immediately recognized the formulaic nature of the papyrus and the purposeful gaps provided for the names (NN) and parameters (XX) of a frighteningly powerful magical spell. *By Allah's beard, to conjure and command the Egyptian gods to do one's bidding. What a horrific power this papyrus represents!*

With care, a tremorous hand placed the first papyrus aside while he attended to the second, the one bound with three blue yarn loops. Once freed, it too opened itself and El-Mussar read the following:

> *The sky trembles, the earth quakes, before [NN].*
>
> *The magician is [NN]. [NN] now possesses the power of Heka.*
>
> *The god/goddess [NN] is commanded to return and slumber in the Underworld.*
>
> *The magician [NN] who wears the Eye of Horus commands the god/goddess [NN] to do his bidding.*
>
> *The god/goddess [NN] is yoked by the magician [NN] to follow his commands.*

One to summon. One to place into slumber. Magical "on" and "off" switches! And the Eye of Horus will provide the magician the needed protection.

For several moments, El-Mussar just stared into space, thinking. *Manny, Manny. What a burden you have placed upon my shoulders! What a gift of pure poison,* unconsciously punning on the German word for poison—*Gift. Only a temple high priest would have access to such a spell, such potential power. Not even a pharaoh would dare,* but then his facile mind easily saw several possibilities, where warrior pharaohs had made remarkable conquests.

He shivered at the vast array of implications.

With a sigh and a decision made, with utmost care, El-Mussar rebound, returned the two papyrus rolls, and resealed the artifact. While the tiny temple sat before him, his mind tried to place it within an historical context. Given the architectural style of the tiny temple and its extraordinary craftsmanship, the Egyptologist judged it to be anywhere from Old, Middle, or New Kingdom in date—a vast swath of time of over one thousand years. He considered, and re-examined the inscription itself, specifically its style of carving— delicate low relief. Again, the same temporal assessment came to mind. Finally, El-Mussar focused on the orthography of the inscription itself and it was there he found the clues he was looking for. The inscription had been composed using the vocabulary, glyphs, and mannerisms of the early Old Kingdom, a time over four thousand years ago.

As to what this artifact's provenience was, he had not a clue, and his friend Manny had not offered any hints. But given the vast funerary fields and complexes of nearby Giza, Sakkara, Heliopolis, and Memphis, any of those could have easily provided this looted cultural treasure.

Without another thought, he secured the artifact and its contents in his personal floor safe, beneath his study's desk. Then he burned his roughed out translations in the kitchen sink.

* * *

That night, while El-Mussar returned to his flat, four men entered the antiquities shop on Rbaa al Selhdar.

Schmidt, who was putting away his tea service, said in Arabic, "I am very sorry, gentlemen, but my shop is closed for the day. It is late."

The shortest one of the four, perhaps thirty years old, spat, "Indeed you are closed. But not for us." As he signaled the other three, who spread out, and secured the shop door's lock with a loud snick.

Coolly, Schmidt replied, "My shop has nothing of interest to you." Gesturing toward his antique register, "Here, take whatever you can find, and leave."

Now sneering into Schmidt's face, "I don't want your money, fat man, I want the artifact!"

At this supposed challenge, the shopkeeper's face split into a wide grin as he toed an emergency security button next to his counter.

"Artifact? Which one, sir? Can you not see that you are surrounded by them?" as he waved to the shelved walls. "No, wait. Let me guess. You're looking for the big gold one, right?"

The short thug slapped him. "No, you stinking pile of camel dung! I'm here for the cedar box!"

"What cedar box?" Schmidt asked, stalling for the authorities to arrive. That earned another vicious slap.

Schmidt, for his part, was hardly defenseless. On his person were secreted no less than four knives and one loaded 9mm, but still he waited.

"Who sent you? The Supreme Council of Antiquities?"

The question caused the short thug's eyes to bulge in disbelief. "Where's the artifact!"

"Ah, now I understand." Schmidt continued, "Your handler is not the Council. Is that correct?"

Another slap across the face.

At this point, Schmidt began to wonder what was taking the bazaar's police force so long to arrive. Usually, they were quite prompt to a call for help. Then he considered the distinct possibility they had been bribed to stay away. The German theatrically sighed in resignation, looked down at his shoes, crossed his hands before him in feigned submission, and with blinding quickness drew from his coat sleeve a knife that slashed deeply across the short thug's neck. Thick gouts of blood flooded out splattering the shop's threadbare carpeting, staining it deeply. While the victim choked and gripped his throat, the other three turned, and pulled their knives. Schmidt escalated the threat by brandishing his 9mm. In moments, the other three were dead.

Wiping his brow on his sleeve, "So it begins."

CHAPTER 10

Reissen returned to the Imperial City as a local media celebrity. With his heavily bronzed skin on full display, the glaring video camera lights greeted him at the airport's baggage claim as a conquering hero. Overly attentive interviewers with intrusive microphones fawned over his every word. Effectively corralled between no less than three network cameras, with their incessant questions, he sincerely wished that had only carryon. Finally, his two bags arrived, and he gratefully escaped.

The archaeologist saw this notoriety as a personal invasion and hindrance to his work—that is until his departmental chairman paid a visit to his office.

"Erik, you look wonderfully fit and well-tanned. Egypt clearly agrees with you. Welcome home!" Professor Dr. Gustav Höhenfelder cheerfully declared with a hearty handshake. Taking a seat in one of the office's visitors' chairs, the chairman continued, while leaning forward with his hands on knees to better deliver his pitch. The stance also allowed for his substantial paunch.

"Your discovery and excavation of the Djedi tomb truly reaches far beyond the walls of this department. I know that your personality does not suffer well in the spotlight. Granted. But please, Erik, consider the following. With the proceeds from one public lecture alone you could fund several more seasons. With one appearance on 3Sat, you could reach all of Austria, Switzerland, and Germany. Think also of the prestige that our department would enjoy. And Erik, finally consider how such exposure would establish *you* as the Indiana Jones of Vienna."

Reissen, wide-eyed, "Gustav, are you serious?"

"Completely. Think about it, Erik. Imagine the students who would eagerly flock to you and our department. Think about your career, man. That tomb has put you on the map. The public's memory is short, just look at how they forget about our politician's blunders and missteps. The time to strike is now!" He concluded with a buried fist in a palm.

"3Sat you say."

"Their representatives have already contacted me. They want to interview you for their program *Kulturzeit* in two days time at their station's headquarters in Mainz. Will you do it?"

Reissen stared back at his pleading chairman, a man, who to date, had treated him honestly and fairly. "I'll do it, Gustav. But," Reissen smirked, "I won't wear a brown fedora."

Clapping his hands together, Gustav gushed, "Excellent!"

*　*　*

The television interview went well as far as Reissen was concerned. Else Wald had provided him with a thumb drive filled with images that the station shared with the public. For the scoop, he and his department received a hefty honorarium from an ecstatic station director. Reissen had driven a hard bargain, while the station landed an historic coup ahead of several international television networks.

As for the on-air archaeological funding appeal, funds had begun to trickle in. But these would swell considerably after his public lecture at the university. Never before had he made a presentation to a packed lecture hall that was standing room only. Looking up from the podium, he saw a field of eight hundred plus eager and expectant faces on all three of its levels. He whimsically thought, *so this is what it's like to be a soccer star.*

*　*　*

Following that whirl-wind two weeks, Reissen, with both his department's and his excavation's war chests now flush with donations, finally settled down to work. First on his agenda was a translation of Djedi's tomb.

Designating the tomb walls A through D, he then assigned numbers to each wall's vertical registers. With that task behind him, the philologist could now create references and cross-references easily.

After only a cursory examination of Else's imagery on his flat screen, Reissen stared back in absolute shock to discover that he recognized the content of the tomb's text.

Mein Gott! His silently exclaimed. *These are The Pyramid Texts! These are Fifth and Sixth Dynasty creations, not Fourth!*

Sitting back in his office chair while his mind scrambled to grasp the possibilities, all he could do was shake his head.

Yet another anomaly.

Pause. *No. What this means is that either Djedi blatantly borrowed a pre-existing collection, or perhaps better, collated himself that most ancient collection of magical spells!*

Still not quite believing what his eyes were seeing, the Austrian went back to the flat screen and began to scan through the many funerary spells, hymns, and incantations. He recognized them all and was uniquely able to do so, because *The Pyramid Texts* had been the subject of his *Diplomstudium* or master's degree.

But the entire focus of this collection of magical spells was markedly different in one key respect. *The Pyramid Texts* of the Fifth and Sixth Dynasty adorned the entire interior of their pharaohs' pyramid burials. Those spells specifically mentioned by name only those kings and their concerns for the afterlife.

But not here. Here, the benefactors of these supposedly royal spells are mentioned in the plural nominative and without specific attribution. The only hint of their identity, mentioned countless times, is to "those most beloved." Erik, this is another anomaly.

*   *   *

Simultaneously, as Reissen pored over the translation of Djedi's tomb inscriptions, other scholars and members of his team were busy as well. Franks and Peters had perhaps the least to prepare for publication. Their marvelous 3D representation of the Djedi tomb site, in multiple colors, was a work of art. Their biggest challenge, however, was an editorial issue. Would their survey plot fit on a separate folded sheet designed for a book pocket or instead would they insert a bound, fold-out. Other than that, they're work was done.

By prior agreement with the Egyptian Antiquities Organization, all images of the five tomb robbers were embargoed and specifically excluded from any future publications for cultural reasons. The dirty little secret that none of the grave robbers appeared in the Austrian mission's sixty-four images was not shared with the EAO. Consequently, that restrictive requirement suited

Reissen just fine as none could be produced. However, that minor fact had not been shared with the medical forensics team at the Grand Egyptian Museum, who per their usual intake procedures, photographed them again, and again, and yet again. Only then did the lead forensics physician step in to clear up the issue, and discovered that he couldn't. The five tomb robbers remained shyly non-photogenic. This then led to a full scientific investigation of why this was so. Numerous detection devices and techniques, both nuclear and non-nuclear, were employed, all with no positive result.

What the medical forensics team did confirm was that the five tomb robbers had died from massive infusions of multiple poisons. Their saturated remains, in all five cases, remained dangerously poisonous if hydrated. After some expert sleuthing, the laboratory technicians managed to trace the toxins to two vectors: the Egyptian cobra (*Naja haje*) and the Egyptian fat-tailed black scorpion (*Androctonus crassicauda*)—the "fat-tailed man killer."

Djedi's coffin and grave goods were left to another team within the acquisitions and conservation department of the Grand Egyptian Museum. Initially, all were catalogued in the museum's database and had unique acquisitions numbers assigned. That list was then attached to an e-mail sent to Reissen, who passed it on to Wald so that she could label her many images for the Austrian mission's upcoming publication.

The physical analysis of the amphora booby trap came next. The forensics team demonstrated how the unique multi-chambered vessel had been constructed to collapse under the pressure of a man's weight. Their subsequent chemical analysis of the amphora's remaining residues confirmed what Dr. Lukas Hampl had feared: an energetic hydrochloric and calcium phosphate reaction.

More surprises were in store for the acquisitions and conservation team at the Grand Egyptian Museum. The coffin of Djedi, by strict departmental procedure, could not be opened until it was x-rayed. That directive saved the entire team, and perhaps even most of the personnel at the museum, because the x-ray revealed that Djedi's coffin did not contain his mummy. Rather, the coffin did contain what appeared to be a crude chemical bomb.

What the x-ray revealed were eight sealed beer jars, all connected by copper rods to delicate ceramic nipples at mid-girth. These eight jars were in turn surrounded in a yellowish-white powder up to mid-jar. The copper rods were attached to the lid of the coffin in such a cunning way that if someone either jarred or opened the coffin, the rods would break the ceramic nipples.

At this point, the coffin was eagerly transferred to a bomb laboratory at a nearby Egyptian army base, where they managed to defeat it. Upon investigation, the heavily glazed interiors of the eight beer jars remarkably still held their sloshing contents of hydrochloric acid. As for the powder packed around them, the army technicians confirmed that it was pure calcium phosphate. In short, the coffin had been transformed into a massive nerve gas bomb.

With so much industry occurring in Egypt, Sister Josephina Busby was hard at work on her contribution on an early attribution for the demon god *Ammit*. At the same time, her protégé Dr. Sheila Roth of the Pontifical College worked up her piece on the execration text that had been found in the burial shaft.

*   *   *

While Else Wald could not produce images of the five tomb robbers, she did encounter serious trouble while trying to match up her images with the artifacts' list from the conservation department at the Grand Egyptian Museum. In short, their acquisition numbers did not match up with her imagery. What should have been a tedious exercise, turned out to be a real head scratcher of a mystery. An artifact she had photographed multiple times was not on the acquisition's list from the conservation department. Apparently, it had never reached that repository.

Thinking that she was being resourceful, Wald e-mailed an inquiry back to the Egyptian acquisitions and conservation official, copied Reissen, and thoughtfully attached the missing artifact's image.

On that same day, Reissen learned from Wald, by way of the Grand Egyptian Museum, that Djedi's mummy had turned up missing as well.

Then all hell broke loose.

CHAPTER 11

When al-Razzuli found out about the failed attempt at procuring the artifact, he went into a silent rage, not so much at his dull henchmen, but with himself.

Sayenda Shaheen always counseled me to take on and see through that which is important—myself. I have been lazy. The failure of my four men was my fault.

* * *

Schmidt opened his antiquities shop at ten sharp. It smelled from the chemicals of the carpet cleaner, who had labored nearly the entire previous day to clean up the bloody mess. Then the German had to deal with the authorities, who wanted to know in no uncertain terms what had occurred. Fortunately for the shopkeeper, all four of his victims were known criminals. But still, considerable *Baksheesh* had to be forked over to ensure his innocence.

He made some tea, an important custom in the successful landing of any transaction. That chore complete, Schmidt stood behind his counter's register sipping at his first morning tea and humming, while he wondered what the day would bring.

Schmidt's firm and Lutheran upbringing did not include the paranormal in any respect. He did, however, believe that such things might exist, especially with unusually successful archaeologists. But for some reason, just before eleven, he glanced at his silver pocket watch and frowned. Something bothered him—a sort of mental itch he just could not place. He shook his head and returned to his ledger.

The door chime announced his first customer of the day—a tallish Egyptian strolled in wearing a finely tailored suit, dark, pin-striped, and well-pressed. Middle-aged with expressive dark brown eyes and a thick moustache, Schmidt judged him to be a wealthy banker or businessman.

"Are you Dr. Schmidt?" the finely turned out man said in literate Arabic.

"I am, sir. How might I be of service?" Schmidt said with a slight bow.

"I am searching for a specific kind of artifact. A cedar box carved in the shape of an ancient Egyptian shrine. Do you know of it?"

The German blanched at the mention of the box and the well-dressed man easily read it.

Now shaking his head, Schmidt said, "No, sir. I do not stock such an object."

Then a curious buzzing began in his head. Building

in intensity, the overweight German had to sit down while he held his head in his hands. He murmured in his Bavarian dialect, "Such pain…"

After several more moments, the buzzing suddenly went away, leaving the shopkeeper gasping with relief.

"Dr. Schmidt, where is the artifact?" the well-dressed man asked again.

"I don't…" and once again the buzzing, like an angry hive of bees, returned, but this time, far more intensely.

"Please, please, make it stop," the German begged.

And it did.

"Dr. Schmidt. I am a busy man who does not possess an infinite amount of patience. For the final time, where is the artifact?"

Standing up, the shopkeeper reached for a small pad of paper and quickly jotted down a nearby Caireen address. "Here, sir. He has what you seek."

Now reading the address, Razzuli smiled. "That was easy." The buzzing returned, intensified, and spiked with deadly effect. The German, now on his knees, reached out in agonized submission, sighed his last, and collapsed on the newly cleaned, threadbare carpet that still smelled of cleaning fluids.

Razzuli viciously kicked the corpse just to make sure of his handiwork. Satisfied, he murmured to it, "I despise those who traffic in my country's cultural heritage, be they Egyptian or otherwise."

*   *   *

That early evening, El-Mussar, while watching the latest cultural carnage on the evening news, heard a knock at his flat's door. Peeking through his door's security port, he spied a well-dressed man.

Curious, something prompted him, "May I help you?" He said through the door's cracked opening.

"Are you Professor Dr. Ahmed ibn El-Mussar?"

"I am." Now standing marginally taller.

"Wonderful. While you might not remember me, you taught me hieroglyphs at the university."

"I did?" El-Mussar answered with a furrowed brow, struggling to make a connection between this finely dressed man with any of his former students.

"It was a long time ago, professor. But the reason that I am here, is that an associate of yours, Dr. Schmidt, recommended that I make a visit."

At hearing his friend's name, El-Mussar bowed his head and said, "My apologies, sir, please come in. I am not accustomed to receiving visitors, Mr..."

"Kek ibn Mohammed al-Razzuli."

"Please come in," as El-Mussar guided the well-dressed Razzuli to an ancient but comfortable chair. Then his mind screamed at him.

Kek! You imbecile! That's the ancient Egyptian god of darkness! What have you let into your apartment!

Turning off the blaring television with its images of senseless cultural destruction, El-Mussar muttered about the atrocity of it all, turned, and offered to make his visitor some tea, while a fine layer of perspiration began to form on his smoothly shaven upper lip.

"No, Professor El-Mussar that will not be necessary. Please sit. I suspect that we have much to talk about."

Once El-Mussar seated himself, the visitor began.

"Professor El-Mussar, I must be candid with you. Not only did you teach me hieroglyphs, you also introduced me to the world of ancient Egyptian magic, and for that, I am most grateful."

El-Mussar stared at his visitor and felt raw fear as he began to piece together his visitor's face. But something was just not right.

"I also note that you do not approve of what is happening throughout our region, specifically what is happening to our cultural heritage." He gestured toward the television's images of a newly destroyed ancient monument. "Trust me, when I say, I am in complete agreement with you."

El-Mussar forced a weak smile at the sentiment and said, "The execration texts. You were the student who liked to read them so … But you look so very different …"

Genuinely smiling, "That is correct, professor. You provided me with a truly in depth introduction into the darker side of our ancient heritage. However, Professor El-Mussar," al-Razulli continued, "I also know, because Dr. Schmidt told me, that you have in your possession a fascinating artifact, a model of an Egyptian temple, carved in cedar wood. Is that not so?"

The panicked astonishment on the old philologist's face did not require al-Razulli's telepathic skills to divine. He had it. The only question was, where?

"Sir, I don't know…" El-Mussar whispered, but his words suddenly failed him when the well-dressed man raised his left index finger.

"Professor El-Mussar, I respect you as my former teacher. My fond memories of your patience with me and my studies I cherish to this very day. Now sir, take me to the artifact."

At that point, El-Mussar lost thirty minutes of his life. Thereafter, and none for wear except for the time lapse, the Egyptian philologist returned to watching his noisy television, occasionally cursing its content in fluent Middle Egyptian. If he had bothered to visit his office, El-Mussar would have found his floor safe open and empty.

* * *

Now with the artifact and its precious contents in his possession, al-Razzuli quaked with anticipation. The secret panel quickly revealed itself as he had read of its workings from his old teacher's mind. Long a master of the ancient Egyptian language, both in its hieroglyphic and more fluid shorthand style of hieratic, the adept sight read the content of the two secreted papyri. Upon doing so, he smiled with immense satisfaction as he raised the golden amulet and placed it around his neck.

This is true power. The power of the god Heka himself!

* * *

A magician practitioner with a decidedly scientific bent, al-Razzuli decided to test Heka's spells on a small and insignificant target. First, he chose someone he found particularly hateful—a man who purportedly defended his land's ancient monuments, but who had profanely profited from their sale. Next, he searched his soul for an appropriate demon or divinity to exact his vengeance. After some consideration, al-Razzuli decided, and whispered. "How appropriate to be ripped limb from limb by a goddess of Re's own creation— Sekhmet."

If that first experiment proved successful, he would surely increase his influence within the enclave, perhaps even to ascend to its leadership. Like all power-hungry megalomaniacs, al-Razzuli believed in the arachnidan manipulation of his environment and did not think small.

CHAPTER 12

Sister Josephina Busby stood straight and tall behind her podium. Her seminar notes lay neatly before her. A fresh bottle of water waited on the shelf beneath. A total of nine graduate students sat attentively before her, by anyone's standards that constituted a packed house. Of them, four were pursuing degrees in Egyptology. As for the rest, four were social anthropologists, and one an historian. She had checked. It was always wise to know your audience.

"Today, ladies and gentlemen, I would like to share with you a bloody tale."

The mention of "bloody tale" predictably perked up their attention that early morning.

"The title of this magical tale is *The Book of the Heavenly Cow*."

The good sister waited for the snickers to fade, but she couldn't resist adding, "That's *'Heavenly Cow'*, not Holy Cow." Now she firmly had their attention.

"As is usually the case with such ancient Egyptian tales, it is filled with illusions and references that we moderns struggle to understand, but we will dissect. As for its composition, let us provisionally assign it a New Kingdom date—making it a relatively late mythological document. What is so odd about that fact is that this tale references events that took place during Egypt's most primordial times. In short, and as usual, we have ourselves a real head scratcher. So sit back, take notes, and listen very carefully."

> *It came to pass, that the Majesty of Re, who came into being by himself, having been king of mankind and the gods, discovered that mankind plotted against him. They believed that his Majesty had grown old, his bones becoming silver, his flesh gold, and his hair of lapis lazuli.*

Sister Josephina paused, and remarked to her class, "Note here what the Egyptians believe to be the indications of old age—bones of silver, golden flesh, and hair of lapis lazuli. The parallels to mummification are clear." Then she continued.

> *His majesty learned about the plot against him devised by mankind and said to his retinue, "Summon to me my Eye, the gods Shu, Tefnut, Geb, and Nut, and also the ancient god Nun, bringing his courtiers along with him. But do so secretly, lest mankind sees and their hearts flee. All should come to the Great Palace, so that they may give me their council."*

So these gods stepped forth, and lined up on his two sides, bowing their heads toward the ground before his Majesty, in order that he might speak his words in front of the father of the eldest gods, the Maker of Mankind.

Sister Josephina again paused in her narration. "This mention of 'the father of the eldest gods' refers to Nun or Atum. This primordial is rarely depicted in their art, and when he is, it is usually as the primeval mound of creation." And on she went.

They said to his Majesty, "Speak to us, so that we may hear it!"

Then Re said to Nun, "O eldest god in whom I came into being, and You ancestral gods! Behold, mankind is plotting against me. Tell me what you would do about this. I seek not to slay them before having heard what you might have to say."

The Majesty of Nun replied, "O my son Re! God greater than his maker, be seated on your throne! Great is fear of you when your Eye is on those who conspire against you!"

A student raided their hand.

"Yes, Mr. Grant." Sister Josephina acknowledged.

"This Eye of Re, is it the same or like the Eye of Horus?"

"Excellent question. The Eye of Re, on the one hand, is the right eye of the god Horus. But on the other, it is a feminine entity of brutish power that Re can unleash at will. Again, good question, as it will make clear this next passage."

> *Re said to his father, "See, they have fled into the desert, their hearts being afraid that I might speak to them."*
>
> *The retinue of Re said to his Majesty, "Send out your Eye that it may smite them for you, those conspirers of evil! No Eye is more fit to smite them for you. May it come down upon them like a lioness in the desert, as Sekhmet!"*
>
> *And so the Powerful One, the lioness Sekhmet, came into being.*
>
> *The Majesty of Re was not finished, for he created another Eye. This one was to be his guardian son, Horus, the Protector of Mankind.*

Sister Josephina paused yet again. "Note the balancing act mentioned here between the Eye of Re and the Eye of Horus—the former the tool of Re and the latter that which protects mankind from harm. The Egyptian culture strived for balance in all things. This is why the goddess *Ma'at*, the very personification of balance, was so important to them. *Ma'at* quite literally was the divine check against a predatory pharaoh."

And so the Powerful One, the falcon Horus, came into being.

The Powerful One Sekhmet said after slaying mankind in the desert, and the Majesty of Re said, "Welcome in peace, Sekhmet, Eye who did what I wished!"

Said the Powerful One Sekhmet, "You gave me life, I vanquished mankind, and it gladdened like a balm my heart."

At the end of her reading, Sister Josephina noted that all had remained riveted to her words. A hand rose, one of the anthropologists.

"Yes, Mr. Bradley."

"With all due respect, sister, that was one bloody tale. I always thought ancient Egyptian mythology was more elevated than that—more intellectual and philosophical in nature."

"Well, Mr. Bradley, allow me to disabuse you of any such notions. At their core, the ancient Egyptians possessed a brutish, cruel, and ruthless side that we moderns have chosen to blithely overlook. The evidence is everywhere *if* one chooses to take note of it. The inscriptional material alone is replete with examples—the smiting of heads, decapitations, trampling, the removal of hands and penises. And guess what, Mr. Bradley, the Egyptian magical world was a far more gruesome copy of what we call reality. Welcome to the magical worldview of ancient Egypt."

*   *   *

Drunk to the point of collapse, the lioness Sekhmet's heavily lidded eyes wandered about without focus. Her limbs refused to respond. Her stomach filled with reddened beer almost dragged upon the ground. Then, several men gripped her flaccid legs, lifting them, dragging her limp form like an antelope kill. Sekhmet didn't know where these energetic ones were taking her, but the mud changed into warm sand. Soon they approached a dark opening and entered into its coolness. The besotted lion-goddess purred with pleasure as her sweat cooled her face. Held to stand upright, she swayed like a wind-blown reed. But not for long as the lioness felt the others wrapping her in fine linens, which quickly bound the goddess tightly in their embrace. Panicking, she could not move, or fight them, much less run away. Layer upon layer they applied in the flickering lamp light. All they left was a narrow gap across a set of bewildered eyes.

Then Sekhmet heard a single, authoritative voice through the bindings, who chanted the following words:

> The sky trembles, the earth quakes,
> before Ankh-Ptah.
>
> The magician is Ankh-Ptah. Ankh-Ptah
> now possesses the power of Heka.
>
> The lion goddess Sekhmet is commanded
> to slumber and return to the Underworld.

> The magician Ankh-Ptah who wears the Eye of Horus amulet commands the lion goddess Sekhmet to do his bidding.

> The lion goddess Sekhmet is yoked by the magician Ankh-Ptah to follow his commands.

Sekhmet felt her eyes tire, relax. Just before the fog of slumber overtook her consciousness, the lioness sensed being placed upon a smooth surface. Sekhmet lay at perfect rest. Then all was darkness, silence.

The spell complete, the entrance to the narrow niche in which the lion-goddess lay was sealed in with rude rubble and common plaster. The seal of the oracle and high priest Ankh-Ptah stamped into the drying plaster warned of dire consequences for anyone who might disturb the portal. Once dried, a final plaster layer was trowelled into place and artfully smoothed to appear as the native bedrock.

*   *   *

Al-Razzuli realized that before he could summon the lion-goddess to do his bidding, he must first be able to approximately locate her resting place. While a challenge certain, he had resources and a magical acumen.

He began by laying out a series of detailed topographical maps of the Nile Valley and its surrounding desert fringes. In all, four colorful 1:500,000 scale maps decorated the tiled flooring of his four acre villa outside of Cairo. These British military maps he had procured just for the purpose and for a tidy sum.

Next, he erected a tripod above the northern-most sheet from which hung a swinging plumb bob on a length of enchanted waxed yarn the color of wheat.

As the plummet settled and yarn finished its twisting first this direction and that, Razzuli rested both of the Djedi papyri on the map. It was a gamble, but the adept figured that the papyri's innate magical properties could assist him.

Sitting on the floor next to the sheet, he relaxed, focused on the plumb bob, and slowly intoned a common locator spell—a *locus devotio magica*. The plummet twitched, but failed to point out a location on the sheet.

Not to be deterred, Razzuli shifted gears and employed an ancient Egyptian spell that was used for divining water sources. While the plumb bob moved, it jerked randomly between a number of water sources.

My problem is specificity.

An hour later, the adept crafted a female wax figurine with the name Sekhmet affixed in red hieroglyphs. This time the *locus devotio magica* worked! The plummet pointed rigidly toward South Sakkara at a point just below the 250 foot contour!

Somehow, I am not surprised in the least.

Quickly sliding the wax figurine off the map, the plumb bob returned to its neutral, vertical position. Razzuli placed a second map sheet over the first—this one with a 1:50,000 scale resolution. Again he placed the figurine in contact with it, repeated the *locus devotio magica,* and received another steady reading that indicated a barren location almost due west of the Step Pyramid of Djoser.

Now I have you! Tomorrow, I will summon you.

* * *

As Sekhmet struggled to dig out, her sweat slicked legs and body quickly became coated with sand. The goddess ignored the many abrasions to her tawny hide as she struggled to work herself free. The urge to shake her coat, to groom herself was great, but she had no room. Sand even threatened to choke her muzzle. But after a final supreme exertion, she emerged from her tomb. Finally free, she lifted her face to her beloved father Re, whose warmth she hadn't enjoyed in millennia.

Her chest heaved in the desert's dryness mixed with a verdant air that tasted of freshly cut hay, cooking fires, and something different, unrecognized. Stretching like a house cat in the warming rays, the last remains of her wrappings—long deteriorated by ages of decay, fell away. Then, unbidden, a primal hunger made itself known, followed by a single thought, *who called me from my slumber? Who now beckons me?*

Sekhmet's golden eyes scanned her surroundings seeking threats. Seeing none, she stood atop the ridge of a desert plateau overlooking a vast green river valley bathed in the shadow of early evening—full of life and many other things. Sekhmet yawned wide and again stretched her forepaws—*my beloved Kemet*, as once again that hunger voiced its displeasure. *I must feed.*

*   *   *

Al-Razzuli while wearing the gold amulet chanted the summoning spell at dawn while cradled in the rich leather of his white Mercedes 450 CSL. He parked the vehicle in the bus parking lot next to the Step Pyramid, figuring that would be a perfect observation point for anyone emerging from the Western Desert. There, he waited, and as the hours past, began to second-guess everything. Had he recited the spell correctly? Could the goddess hear his repeated psychic calls?

Dusk arrived at the Sakkara Plateau and an almost dozing adept took a swig from a warm plastic water bottle. He started as he saw a silhouette, low and slinking, on the ridge in the fading sunlight. Part of him could not believe it. The other half shuddered in horror as a larger-than-life lioness homed in on his vehicle.

Gliding and sliding down the sandy slope on massive paws, Sekhmet psychically reached out to him in a hungry wail, *"Who beckons me?"*

Getting out and leaving open the rear passenger door, al-Razzuli returned quickly to his place behind the wheel. Frightened out of his wits, he waited for the big cat to approach. Not peeking into either his side or rearview mirrors, he again called out to his quarry, *Come to me, Sekhmet!*

Suddenly, the suspension of his vehicle sagged under a great weight as the lioness had literally bounded into his back seat.

I am here, sorcerer, she purred out, *and I must feed.*

Daring to look over his shoulder, an extremely exotic and sultry woman now stretched out across the tan leather of his back seat. Her shoulder-length, straight jet black hair had sand mingled within it. Her golden almond-shaped eyes speared his heart with their intensity and his groin moaned. With golden-colored skin, only the brown of her nipples provided any contrast.

I must feed. The goddess Sekhmet repeated.

"Yes, goddess. Immediately!" al-Razzuli said as his foot hit the gas with the passenger-side rear door slamming closed at the sudden acceleration. Gravel flying, the adept drove like a man possessed to the government office of the Egyptian Antiquities Service in Memphis. While en route, he reverently addressed his passenger, more to keep her distracted than anything else. "Beloved goddess Sekhmet, Inspector Kama is who you seek. He is like a fatted calf. You will feed well."

Pulling to a stop at the curb before the administration building, al-Razzuli saw that the interior lights were on inspector's office. He knew that the man was there as he tended to work late, and besides, was expecting an appointment to arrive. He opened the passenger side rear door and pointed towards the light. Sekhmet understood as she slithered out of the vehicle and with a single mind made her way in that direction. Never before had al-Razzuli been so aroused by a naked female—never before more frightened.

"I will await you, goddess," he said to her back.

She acknowledged his words with a flick of her hand.

The goddess's divine visitation had not taken long, perhaps ten minutes. She reappeared while wiping off her chin, her tongue still licking her sensuously engorged lips. Her quick strides on long toned legs, however, could not betray the swelling of her gut. She had indeed feasted. Al-Razzuli, taking this in, inwardly shuddered while he held open the passenger side rear door.

As he drove back to the bus lot of the Stepped Pyramid, his thoughts were locked returning the goddess from whence she came. She heard his words.

"Sorcerer. Your words were most truthful. That fatted calf sated me. I am grateful, but I sense your passion. Your desire for me. You smell like an Apis bull preparing for rut. Is this not true?"

Al-Razzuli, despite the golden amulet around his neck, almost panicked as he pulled to a stop in the parking lot. Instead, he reached into his console, retrieved an item, and got out of the Mercedes. While opening the passenger rear door with one hand, he read from a piece of paper several passages in Middle Egyptian,

> The sky trembles, the earth quakes, before Al-Razzuli.
>
> The magician is al-Razzuli. Al-Razzuli now possesses the power of Heka.
>
> The lion goddess Sekhmet is commanded to return and slumber in the Underworld.
>
> The magician al-Razzuli who wears the Eye of Horus commands the lion goddess Sekhmet to do his bidding.
>
> The lion goddess Sekhmet is yoked by the magician al-Razzuli to follow his commands.

The goddess stood dutifully before al-Razzuli pouting, while he recited the slumbering spell. She reached out and gently stroked his chin in a parting caress, turned, and transformed back into a mighty lioness that ran off into the Western Desert.

The adept just stood there legs astride, panting, his member fully engorged, and regretting that he should probably should have taken her up on that generous offer. *Perhaps next time.*

CHAPTER 13

Rarely do e-mails to a conservation department cause a stir. But Wald's did. For within a world dominated by careful procedure, acquisition numbers, and lot locations, error was an abhorrent thing not to be tolerated. Even worse, Wald claimed a highly distinctive artifact was missing altogether from their acquisition register. This claim, at first, was taken as quite an affront by the lead conservator assigned to the Djedi archaeological site, Dr. Aziza Hassan—Ali Hassan's older sister. She and her team had accounted for, packed, loaded, and unloaded all the Djedi artifacts. Add to that, she had absolutely no recollection whatsoever of such an exquisite cedar box. Her memory was quite good.

That said, the lead conservator immediately attempted to resolve the matter by contacting Inspector Kama and his assistant, her younger brother, Ali Hassan. While Inspector Kama could not be reached, she did reach her brother, who tellingly arrived within the hour at her office next to the conservation laboratory.

"Beloved sister, what is troubling you so?" a concerned Ali Hassan asked.

Looking up at her brother from her laptop, she made a few keystrokes and spun it around to face Ali. "Read." Was all Aziza said with crossed arms.

Moments later, "I know this Else Wald. She is the photographer with the Austrian archaeological mission." Then looking at his older sister. "You mean to tell me you have never before seen this artifact?"

"No! Have you?"

"No, never, and I did not see it during the tomb's opening either."

A cloud of frustrated silence hung in the air between them.

Aziza broke it. "Ali, did anyone have private access to the tomb after it was opened?"

"Not to my knowledge. No, wait. That's not correct. Inspector Kama made a visit the next day after the grand opening, while the workmen were installing the security door and grating. That was the day before your team arrived."

"I called his office. He didn't answer." Aziza sourly said.

"That's odd," Ali commented, "he's usually good about such things. Do you want me to visit his office?"

"Would you, dear brother? I really do not wish this to get beyond this office."

"Understood. I'll go right now."

*   *   *

Ali Hassan knew his boss well. He considered him reasonable and fair, if a bit of a worry wart and stickler for detail. As he approached his office door, Hassan could tell that something wasn't right. Inspector Kama's door was ever so slightly ajar and his lights were on—two things that didn't add up given that the man liked his privacy and it was early afternoon.

Respectfully knocking on the jam, the Egyptian heard nothing, but most definitely got a nose full of something that smelled dreadful. Pushing open the door, Hassan's eyes bugged out at the shocking scene and then promptly threw up in the hallway when the putrid stench hit him.

Having emptied his stomach of his lunch, the inspector's assistant wiped at his chin and stumbled away. Leaning against a wall, he reached into his pocket and called security, full in the knowledge that his life was about to change.

*   *   *

It was three in the morning and Ali Hassan was now on his fifth interrogation. Thirsty, hungry, and emotionally drained, the first five hours he spent with three unreadable men from security who didn't believe a word he said. They then turned him over to the Egyptian Antiquities Service. After endless waiting and eventually a grilling before four high-ranking bureaucrats, Hassan figured out with considerable relief that he was no longer a murder suspect—just a person of interest in an antiquities scandal.

His mind confused and blurred, the man just wanted to go to sleep. Sitting on an uncomfortable wooden chair with no arms, in an empty and unpainted office in the Grand Egyptian Museum, Hassan had indeed managed to just fall asleep, but then was jolted awake by someone shaking his shoulders.

"Wake up Assistant Inspector Hassan!" he groggily heard. "Your superiors have more questions for you!" the armed security guard said as Hassan, somehow, got on his feet.

The walk was painful as his stiff legs did not want to respond. Regardless, four security guards marched Hassan, one of their own, through a dizzying maze of corridors and hallways. Finally, bleary-eyed, he was shepherded into a nicely furnished office. The first security guard sat him down in comfortable leather chair before a desk. On it sat a steaming hot plate of food and three bottles of water.

"Eat and drink, my friend," the first security guard said. "You've earned it."

Ali Hassan didn't need to be told twice as he downed first a bottle of water and then attacked the plate of roasted chicken, rice, vegetables, and bread. When he was finished, one of the four men who had questioned him earlier from the Egyptian Antiquities Service, Dr. Hamid Gohar, arrived.

"Mr. Hassan. On behalf of our organization, we wish to apologize for any distress that you may have suffered. Given the circumstances of Inspector Kama's death, we had to make sure. And, given the strong possibility of a lost artifact, we have to be doubly sure. You are free to go to your home, and get some sleep. And while you are doing so, I have some pleasant news for you. The council has decided that you, Mr. Hassan, will temporarily act as the inspector of the Memphite archaeological district. Several members of the council were impressed with your demeanor during this unfortunate time. Further, your reputation for resourcefulness and consistently high marks among the many foreign archaeological missions has put you in good stead. Until further notice, you are now the acting-Inspector of the Memphis District. Congratulations, Mr. Hassan." Gohar concluded with a hearty handshake.

As Hassan stood there, he sincerely thought he was dreaming.

*   *   *

Reissen was about to go to bed when he received an unexpected telephone call.

"Good evening. Is this Dr. Erik Reissen?" a voice asked in passable, but halting German.

"I am Reissen. Do you know what time it is?" he answered with annoyance.

"Dr. Reissen, I truly apologize for disturbing you. My name is Dr. Hamid Gohar, I am a member of the Egyptian Antiquities Council. I wish to ask you some questions regarding the recent murder of Inspector Hussain Kama."

That slapped Reissen into another reality altogether.

"What! Inspector Kama is dead?"

"Yes, Dr. Reissen, sadly Inspector Kama was murdered yesterday evening. While I can assure you that you, sir, are not a suspect, there remains the issue of a missing artifact. One of your archaeological staff, *Frau* Else Wald, brought this to the attention of Dr. Aziza Hassan, of the acquisitions department here at the Grand Egyptian Museum. Are you aware of this?"

"Yes, I am, Dr. Gohar. Else Wald, my field photographer, informed me of the situation."

"I see. When did you last see this artifact?"

"In the tomb of Djedi. *Frau* Wald and I discovered it in a hidden niche. I had informed Inspector Kama of our suspicions prior to its discovery. In fact, he was there to witness its discovery. That is when *Frau* Wald photographed it."

"Did you, Dr. Reissen, remove this object from the tomb?"

"No, sir. In fact, Inspector Kama, *Frau* Wald, and

myself left the artifact in the tomb along with the rest of the grave goods. When we left the tomb, it was because of the arrival of workmen, who were there to install the tomb's security door and grate."

"I see."

"In fact, Dr. Gohar, the acquisition and conservation people from your museum arrived early the very next morning and cleared the tomb. That process involved no members of my mission nor myself, just Inspector Kama."

"Thank you, Dr. Reissen. What you have just told me has been very helpful. Good evening, sir, and once again please accept my apologies for disturbing you. Good bye."

As Gohar put down the receiver, he still had one missing artifact. He did, however, have a suspect. He concluded, but could not prove, that Kama must have removed the artifact sometime after the securing of the tomb and prior to the arrival of the GEM conservation staff. What Kama did with the artifact was a matter of pure speculation, but his money was on its sale on the black market. But who bought it? Only time would tell.

Reissen, on the other hand, just stared numbly at his receiver. He mumbled, "A missing artifact and now a dead inspector. What are the odds the two are connected?" He just shook his head.

*   *   *

Criminal acts, and especially murder, are generally handled the same way throughout the world—inspect the crime scene for clues; question those close to the murdered party; and above all, establish a motive.

The murder of a government official, such as a district inspector of archaeological monuments and excavations, perforce received close scrutiny. While the capture of finger prints held importance, few, other than the victim's, appeared and those few were inconclusive. What truly intrigued the forensics team were three lion footprints and two of a barefoot human. Unfortunately, the dermal ridges of the latter could not be lifted.

The medical coroner and his team, however, had their collective hands full. Their photographer, a grizzled veteran of several regional conflicts, captured the dismembered corpse with a clinical detachment. The victim's head, gutted torso, and right arm rested in the office chair, with the limp and nearly decapitated head lolling on the desk's top. The tongue was missing, no, bitten off. The beckoning look from the victim's still open eyes was particularly chilling. A partially gnawed left arm lay separated from the torso against the wall. In its grasp was a fur tuft, which was collected by the coroner and passed on to forensics team. Also removed and mostly eaten were the legs and genitalia. The clothing throughout had been shredded into tatters. The throat was bitten through as if by a large animal. Most, if not all, of the internal organs were missing, leaving behind a vacant and open torso that had been violently wrenched apart. The lungs and heart could not be found.

In general, Inspector Kama's office had the look of a blood-splattered butchery. Blood covered everything, pooled here and there, and formed stringy veined patterns on many surfaces. Bits of gore, sinew, and yellowed fat lay all about. The coppery smell of the place was heavily masked by the rank, sweet odor of the corpse's overall decomposition.

Based upon the preliminary on-scene investigation, the coroner concluded Inspector Kama had been mauled by a lion. The facts, as he saw them, led him nowhere else.

Those colleagues in the inspector's neighboring offices, when questioned, had not seen or heard anything. All had gone home long before the early evening murder, judged by the coroner to have occurred between 1800 and 2000 hours. And besides, given the immense cat paw tracks and the condition of the corpse, the murderer's motive was clear—hunger.

*   *   *

Inspector Kama's murder, while a personal tragedy and regrettable loss for his family, was also one of great interest red flagged by Dr. Gohar and the International Cultural Studies Society of Cairo. So much so, that after the Egyptian forensics team had left the man's office, another team of forensics experts followed in their wake in the middle of the night. Four in number, each brought an expertise that at best could be considered arcane: a vampire, Gohar himself—an extreme sensitive, an empath, and a spell whisperer.

As they stood outside the office door festooned with bright yellow crime tape, Gohar addressed them. "Dear colleagues. What we are about to see will be shocking at several levels. But gird your loins, as we have to know who did this to the inspector. Let us begin, right here, in the hallway, before we stick our heads into that fetid butchery."

Dr. David ibn Ibrahim Fakry was the first to pick something up. A vampire and spawn of an impregnated sixteenth century victim from Istanbul, his nose was sensitive. He opened his mouth as well to taste the air.

"I have something. There's a tell-tale scent amid all the humankind tracks that is very rare, very old." Now on his hands and knees sniffing at the floor like a blood hound, he circled about and stated while doing so. "It came in through that doorway from outside and left by the same route. Very feline. Very old. Very powerful."

Gohar was next as he carefully reached out to touch a wooden panel of Kama's office door. His reaction was classic—like an electric shock. "I concur. It touched his door. I would only add extreme darkness to my impression."

Haley Johnson, an expatriate from Malta, a powerful witch and empath stood with her arms tightly wrapped around her. "Such unbridled hunger. Bestial rage. And an almost toying playfulness. Whatever murdered Kama was one real sicko."

The spell whisperer just stood there with his hands in his pockets. Richardo Gambini, born during the High Renaissance in de Medici Venice, knew to make his determination, he had to get his hands dirty. In many respects, Gambini would have made a fine county coroner. "Okay. Enough with all the touchy, feely stuff. Open that God damn door and let's get this over with."

* * *

Thirty minutes later the four sat in Gohar's vehicle. He sipped a bottle of water in a vain attempt to forestall his queasiness. Fakry yearned for an extremely rare steak. Johnson cried her eyes out. As for Gambini, he knew who'd done it, but not who conjured the murderer.

"This is really some deep, dark, shit. The goddess Sekhmet did the deed. Of that there's no question. Her saliva is all over the body. She feasted on that poor sucker. Took her time too.

"But who sicked her on Kama? That's what I can't figure. The magic is so old, so primordial, that it verges on mythic. I'm sorry, Hamid, but that's the best I can do."

CHAPTER 14

The next archaeological season for the Austrian mission would be a juggling act for Reissen. Fortunately, a departmental colleague responded to his pleas for help. Gretchen Gunner, Norwegian by birth, managed the continued effort in Memphis at the Temple of Ptah. From under her enormous sun hat, one third of the temple's outer circuit, known as the Great White Wall, was scheduled to be investigated. To date, its magical foundation deposits had eluded discovery. Good old Gretch wanted to find them. Meanwhile, Reissen and the Sakkaran team of Habib, Wald, Roth, Peters, and Franks, revisited Djedi's tomb up on the Sakkara Plateau. They had a simple goal before them—find where the crafty magician Djedi had secreted his mummy.

When they arrived at the tomb's site, the newly-minted Inspector Ali Hassan was waiting there for them. While getting out of the truck, Hassan greeted Reissen and each of his crew with an infectious smile and wide open arms of welcome. Seeming more like an old home week celebration, this gathering surprised several of the nearby security guards with its boisterous enthusiasm.

"Ali, my good friend," Reissen said with an embrace, "I am so happy for your promotion!"

"Thank you, Dr. Reissen!"

"No, Ali," the Austrian said as he gripped the Egyptian's shoulders, "my name is Erik." He mouthed very clearly. "Please use it from now on."

"Thank you, Dr. Reis ... Erik."

At Hassan's stumbling reply, the entire team burst out laughing. At that, the new inspector waved goodbye as he had many visits to make throughout his district.

The Austrian, glancing around and noting that the burial shaft's grate had already been opened for their arrival, then rubbed his hands together. "Okay, everyone. Let's get to work!"

*   *   *

Never before had Habib, Reissen, and the rest, been crammed together into Djedi's tomb. Now cleared of its coffin and grave goods, they just fit. Once everyone settled down and stopped shuffling their feet, the Austrian addressed them. "You already know that Djedi's coffin was found empty. Our task is to figure out where he is. Spread out and look around you. Each of you has a hand-broom, use it."

While everyone began meticulously cleaning a

portion of the tomb's flooring, Reissen turned and went directly to the niche in the back wall. For some reason, it seemed to practically beckon to him. Squatting down, he peered in and felt around. Feeling nothing, he took out his fountain pen and began his tapping test. Still nothing. The stubborn archaeologist continued to stare at the niche and then noted its precisely centered location in the back wall—both vertically and horizontally.

Now that surely cannot be a coincidence.

Reissen now took out his faithful pen knife, a battered Swiss Army knife that his father had given him as a boy. To the Austrian's surprise, the material at the center of the niche easily fell away to the blade. Rolling a fragment in his fingers, it easily broke apart. Reissen realized that it was plaster and not limestone.

Huh.

The archaeologist continued to pick at the center and was rewarded with an exposed straight edge carved into the limestone. So he persisted, and soon a small pile of plaster debris began to form at his feet.

"Habib," he called. "Please come and take a look at this."

Habib did, first turning his head this way and that. "Erik, it almost looks like a square socket. How odd ... How deep does it go?"

After everyone else took a look at Reissen's discovery, Reissen got back to work expanding the suspected socket. When he was finished, it appeared to be a perfect cube.

Seeing this Peters asked, "Erik, is there a plaster layer around that socket?"

"Why, Jürgen?"

"Because if Ali is correct, and that's a socket, then it is meant to *turn*."

"Ah, now I understand you."

The picking with the Swiss Army knife's blade began anew and Reissen indeed did find a thin plaster layer that ran across the back of the entire niche. As the fragments flew, the archaeologist uncovered first a gentle curve, then a half moon, and finally a complete circle carved into the limestone. And true to Peters' observation, the socket occupied the circle's precise center.

"Jürgen?" Reissen called. "Is this what you meant?" the archaeologist pointed.

A broad grin. "Yes, professor. Yes, indeed. That's a socket for sure. That means the circle is probably the end of an axle. Professor, we are looking at some sort of mechanism."

"Else. We need shots of this feature."

"I'm on it."

Once Wald finished with her photography, everyone took a peek at Reissen's handiwork, ooing and ahhing.

Then, Habib looked around and spoke up. "At long

last it seems I now have something useful to do," as he handed over his hand sweep to Reissen. "Will someone please precisely measure the interior of that socket? Then I'll build a spanner to match it."

*   *   *

The next morning, the Austrian team arrived at Djedi's tomb carrying short-handled sweeps. Only Wald was without one, burdened as she was with her camera gear and signage. As for their Egyptian foreman, he had with him a short wooden post, an odd metal fixture, and four sawed off shovel handles—each about three feet long.

"What's that?" Reissen reasonably asked.

"My spanner."

"Oh."

Down within the tomb, only then did Habib reveal his cunning ingenuity.

"I once read that Archimedes said, 'Give me a place to stand, and a lever long enough, and I will move the world.'" The Egyptian said. "With these items I believe that we can work wonders."

Habib began by inserting the short post into the wall's square socket. It fit perfectly. He slipped over the wooden post the metal fixture formed in a square with four pipes welded to its sides. It fit snuggly. Finally, he firmly inserted the shortened shovel handles into each of the pipes.

Standing back to admire his make-shift four-handled creation, Habib just smiled and said to the Austrian, "I need three strong backs."

With each sawed off shovel handle a meter long, Habib figured that sufficient torque could be brought to bear. So with Wald photographing the entire scene and Roth taking the field notes, Habib, Reissen, Peters, and Franks put their collective grunt into it. Unconsciously following the rule of "righty tighty" and "lefty loosy," on their first left-handed attempt, the four stout handles bent under the groaning men, snapping one with a gunshot-like report. Fortunately, no one was injured, but there was considerable grumbling as the socket hadn't budged a millimeter.

"Wait one moment," Roth exclaimed, "The Egyptians do everything backwards: their north is our south; they write from right to left. God only knows how they did a lot of things. Why don't you just replace the handle and try again in the other direction."

Now with the spanner repaired, the four-some tried again, but this time turning to the right. Their straining muscles were rewarded with odd sights and sounds—a gathering dust cloud, the grinding of stone, and the fracturing of plaster.

"Stop!" Reissen fearfully yelled. "Everybody get out!"

With the team standing in the open air of the burial shaft, wisps of plaster and limestone dust leaked out.

Fortunately, nothing structurally collapsed or chemically exploded.

"That was quite a start," Roth whispered loudly.

Once the dust cleared, Reissen reentered. "Else. Come in here. Everyone else stay back."

What the photographer recorded with her lenses were long horizontal and vertical cracks on the right side of the tomb's back wall and that a portion of that wall had actually, somehow, moved to the right leaving an inch wide vertical gap just right of the niche.

"Else," Reissen observed, "get some close-ups of this gap. It looks like this dummy wall section is actually a wooden frame of some kind."

To successfully capture the moment, the Austrian archaeologist held a flashlight to illuminate the narrow groove while Else clicked away.

Satisfied, Reissen called the rest of the crew to come in and see what they had wrought.

"This is incredible!" Habib whispered.

"Yes, it is. Team. Should we continue?" Reissen asked.

"Perhaps we should first test the rest of the tomb to see if there are any other false walls." Habib reasonably suggested.

"Absolutely. A fine suggestion. Everyone. Listen while I tap out the difference between the solid wall here," Reissen placed his hand above the niche and its socket, "versus the dummy over there." Methodically, the Austrian began with his black Monarch fountain pen moving from left to right.

Clink.

Clink.

Clink.

Thud.

Thud.

Thud.

The archaeologist stopped about a third of the way across the dummy wall section. "There you go. Now spread out and gently tap with the backs of your sweeps the rest of this tomb's walls."

Chapter 15

Within the sometimes quaint but always filthy chaos of the old train station, an American couple alighted from a first class train car. It had just arrived from Alexandria. A continuously rocking and lurching trip, the couple was pooped. After an insane and anxiety-filled ten minutes, they finally located their luggage, and paid the obligatory *Baksheesh*. Per the usual, the porter claimed it wasn't enough, but the husband ignored him and the baggage man's all too quick hand gesture that flicked a cigarette ash in his direction. Weaving their way out of the Ramses Train Station, they hailed an all too willing cabbie.

For the Porter family, this trip to Egypt was a dream come true. For Jim, a structural engineer, he couldn't wait to see the Pyramids of Giza, the vaults and huge bull sarcophagi within the Serapeum at Sakkara, and the monumental statue of Ramses the Great at Memphis. For Nikki, she saw Egypt as the ultimate source of her Afro-American roots and a spiritual homecoming of sorts.

Their grinning cabbie loaded up the couple's two

wheelies into the dented trunk of his mostly black and white vehicle. Sitting in the back seat, sans seat belts, Jim's former basketball knees seemed to almost touch the headliner. Then he noted with some alarm that both side view mirrors had been decapitated at their door mounts.

Once the engineer told the driver "Nile Hilton," off they went at a breakneck rate that made Jim smile and Nikki cringe. About to merge onto the 6th of October Bridge Boulevard, the driver saw the densely packed traffic, and without a thought opted to take the wide open opposing lanes on the other side of the median. Now flying along past a flood of stalled traffic, against non-existent traffic, Jim laughed aloud, which encouraged their driver to even more NASCAR-like antics.

Within view of their stately hotel, at a crosswalk, a pedestrian stepped out. The unthinkable happened. The cabbie blind-sided the pedestrian as he careened down the wrong side of the boulevard. While such commonplace things never make the Caireen news, two American tourists, much to their horror, watched in slow motion as the vehicle went into a four wheel skid, crumpling the figure.

*   *   *

Tarek el-Masry lay within the crosswalk coughing up

gouts of blood. Looking down he clinically assessed the ruined mess that once had been his torso and abdomen. Immediately, the man's thoughts were filled with sardonic mirth. Here, the great and famous Tarek el-Masry, "the Egyptian", who just the day before had celebrated his two thousand and forty-seventh birthday, had been mortally sundered by of all things—a black and white cab.

*　　*　　*

Jim bounded out of the cab and rushed to the fallen man, a very old one, dressed now in a very bloody Savile Row business suit and silk tie. Unthinkingly, he removed his sport coat, rolled it up into a pillow, and gently slipped it under the old man's head. At his contact their eyes locked. The old man looked up at him and crinkled and blinked his thanks at the comforting gesture. The squatting American then felt a warm tickling sensation pass through his hand that rested on the Egyptian's bloody forehead. For whatever reason, he began to sob uncontrollably crocodile tears that ran down his lean athletic face. Wiping them away, Jim, for again whatever reason, then dampened the injured man's forehead with them and followed up that gesture by whispering into his ruined upturned ear, "Safe journey venerable old one. May your *ka* find a worthy host."

With those kind words, the old man's eyes again blinked a silent thanksgiving to his comforter, and breathed his last. With his life force, quite literally his *ka*, so suddenly extinguished, his long overdue and magically extended physical form wanted to collapse in upon itself, but not quite yet. With a final excursion, el-Masry psychically reached out.

Jim felt it—the shock of its pulse. The *ka*'s transfer caused him to abruptly sit back on his heels, knocking him squarely onto his backside. He instantly sensed two things: one a warm feeling of brotherly sharing; the other, of a spiteful hatred.

Nikki, now at his side, said, "Are you alright, honey?"

Jim wore a blank look, robotically looked up at her and said, "Yes, I am perfectly fine."

Looking back between his splayed knees at the fallen man, Jim watched as his jaw relaxed open, his tan color faded, and form sagged into the pavement.

Standing up, he scanned about as if looking for something or someone. Jim saw nothing, but did find their cabbie hysterically babbling into his radio's microphone.

"Call an ambulance!" Jim commanded in Egyptian Arabic.

"I am," the cabbie snapped back.

"No you're not," Jim sneered, "you're blubbering to your wife! You haven't a fucking clue! Now call for an ambulance you disgusting pile of donkey shit!"

Thoroughly shocked, the cabbie cut off his wife in mid-transmission, and did just that.

Jim, steaming and feeling the blood rush to his face, turned to his equally shocked wife. She didn't know her husband could speak Arabic.

"Honey." Jim said in English, "We got to get out of here." Now pointing. "See that building over there about two blocks away? That's the Nile Hilton. We're hoofing it from here."

Turning back to the still seated cabbie, Jim stuck out his hand and ordered in Arabic, "Keys." After he retrieved their wheelies from the trunk, he dropped them into the dumbfounded cabbie's lap.

Before the ambulance arrived, el-Masry's body had deteriorated into a pile of grayish ash. A passing breeze scattered all evidence of his passing, leaving behind only a bloody business suit and tie.

*   *   *

"Jimmy, I didn't know you spoke Arabic," Nikki lightly bantered as they walked passed by the many parked taxis that lined the hotel's U-shaped driveway. It had been her first words since they abandoned the taxi.

"Yeah, I thought it would come in handy for the trip." This was news to his wife of fourteen years, who knew how hectic his professional life was first hand.

At reception they checked in only to discover they had been upgraded to a full suite. What the Porter's found amounted to a small, multi-room apartment, a king-sized bed, with marble amenities everywhere. An electronic greeting on the large flat-screen proudly displayed, "Welcome Dr. James E. Porter and Spouse."

"See honey, I told you that it pays to be an MIT-graduate." Nikki bubbled.

That evening, after a quaint and tasty alfresco Italian dinner, the king bed experienced considerable commotion. While this activity was unexpected from Nikki's point of view, she relished her husband's new-found energy, twice. But just before she drifted off to sleep, she paid a visit to the bathroom because one thought kept nagging at her. *Now how can a man with advanced prostate cancer do what he just did?*

*   *   *

Al-Razzuli, who watched the accident scene from across the median, observed the couple leaving the taxi and walking toward their hotel. Biting his lower lip, he worried whether that old jackal el-Masry had transferred his *ka* to the tall black man, because his quick scan of the area had passed dangerously close to his Mercedes. He shook his head. *That damn cabbie just hit his brakes too soon. My control must be slipping.* He berated himself.

CHAPTER 16

The sudden demise of Tarek el-Masry triggered an extraordinary meeting of the International Cultural Studies Center in Cairo. For the membership, it was an unsettling event, as el-Masry had occupied the enclave's Senior Chair for as long as anyone could remember. The old one—an avowed Neo-Platonist, had enthusiastically embodied the spirit of the enclave itself. He was the one who had argued that the enclave's meetings take place within the palatial setting of the Egyptian Museum. In defense of his wish, el-Masry claimed the museum's monumental exhibits were warmly familiar and felt like home. Who could argue against such a sentiment, even though many found the venue cramped and poorly lit?

That night, four days after the accident, the membership met in the museum's northern hall. An open chair at one end of the rectangle remained temporarily unoccupied out of respect. Shaheen, the First Chair, took his seat opposite and all looked to him to initiate the proceedings.

After the usual preliminaries, Shaheen spoke with a

shaky voice. "It is with profound sadness that one of our own has passed on—all the more so as it was our Senior Chair. As a consequence, a realignment of status will commence forthwith. Second Chair, please proceed."

With her laptop opened, Fazilah Rahman pretended to search for the next oldest member, but everyone already knew who that would be. "First Chair," she finally said, "Iskander is the next in line for the Senior Chair."

"Thank you, Second Chair, for that confirmation." Shaheen smoothly said.

Among the twenty-five there was a stirring—a sense of change about to occur, much like a fast approaching storm front. Iskander, always an odd creation of nature that was barely tolerated, nonetheless held high value as a powerful ally. Shaheen, the appointed First Chair, found himself clearly at an impasse as he had to work seamlessly with it. Worse, everyone knew it. As did al-Razzuli, who had precipitated the entire situation with his subtle manipulation of a cabbie's reflexes.

"By long and time-honored precedence, the oldest member enjoys the privilege of occupying the Senior Chair. By our enclave's chronographer's reckoning, that honor now falls to Iskander..."

No one actually saw the ghoul take the seat opposite Shaheen, but some did sense the breeze of its passing. Within Shaheen's stomach a slow twisting began as he now had to face the gaunt and preening monster in its full glory. The broad and gloating smile, filled with fangs, sufficiently managed to repulse him.

Swallowing his disgust, Shaheen bowed his head toward the other end of the table, and intoned, "Welcome, most honored one to our table. May your words forever provide us with wisdom and guidance."

To Shaheen's surprise, as well as and the rest of the membership, Iskander spoke. "I do have a request."

"And that is?" Shaheen prompted.

"Our next gathering should be at the Serapeum."

This caused immediate shock, as that manmade funerary grotto, buried in the sands of North Sakkara and dedicated to the burial of Apis bulls, was hardly a convenient location for an organization with the locative "of Cairo" in its name.

Instead, Shaheen smiled solicitously and asked, "Pray tell, why there, Senior Chair?"

"Because there, I was made."

That simple statement brought stunned silence as no one had ever before heard of this tidbit of detail, especially from the tight-lipped Iskander.

After a long pause Shaheen said, "I see." Then turning, he addressed Dr. Hamid Gohar. "Sir, is this request possible?"

The dark-haired and mustached Egyptian opened his hands, shrugged, and demurred. "First Chair, anything is possible. The vault can be, however, cool and very dusty." What the politic board member of the Egyptian Antiquities Department did not say, was the venue appropriate.

Again, Shaheen said, "I see." Then daring a glance toward Iskander, "I will personally look into the matter."

This answer seemed to mollify the new Senior Chair.

At this point, al-Razzuli, the youngest member of the enclave, indicated that he wished to speak. *In fact*, Shaheen thought, *this was his first time to do so after nearly twenty years of membership.*

"Mr. al-Razzuli wishes to be recognized. Sir." The First Chair said with an opened hand gesture of invitation.

"Thank you, First Chair." Al-Razzuli said with proper deference for the man who made him.

"I wish to ask the membership why we cleave to a tradition that allows our enclave to be now directed by a barely coherent monster, tolerated only for its sheer viciousness."

The bald statement caused a sharp intake of breath from twenty-three of the members, while Iskander narrowed its eyes into slits. A drooling hiss slithered from deep within its throat.

Ignoring the obvious threat, al-Razzuli continued. "Why not instead consider, besides the wisdom of age, one's genealogy? Heaven forbid perhaps even one's sheer ability?"

Iskander, Shaheen saw, was clearly being baited. Both of its hands were poised atop the table, elbows akimbo, as if ready to launch a pounce. Meanwhile, within the shadow cast by a statue of the goddess Sekhmet, a large, low slung figure patiently waited for her moment.

To everyone's surprise, the youngster blithely continued on with his needling.

"Can anyone here present actually imagine what the leadership of our community would be like under the current Senior Chair? Fellow colleagues, think for a moment. Consider what sort of utter madness…"

Al-Razzuli did not complete that inflammatory thought, because Iskander attacked. Its two hands squeezed his throat. Kneeling upon the table before its soon-to-be-victim, the ghoul grotesquely displayed its fangs. Its mouth unhinged in the process. Strings of drool dripped across al-Razzuli's face. Its breath reeked of rotten flesh.

A tawny blur flashed across the table and Iskander was gone. But in the darkness of the next aisle of the museum, a furious fight was underway. Clear roaring of a lion was heard, joined by inhuman screams of effort mixed with utter fear. Gruesome sounds of liquid splatter, tearing, growling, gurgling, and pitiful begging ensued.

In an instant, the quartet of Fakry, Gohar, Johnson, and Gambini immediately looked at one another with wide and knowing eyes of positive recognition. Fakry's nose flared in confirmation of the scent. Gohar's mind went through a kind of whiplash. Tears flowed down Johnson's cheeks. Gambini needed more data. Gohar sharply broadcasted to them, *Hide your thoughts*.

Then all was silence as a beautiful woman, naked, and with a supremely regal bearing, appeared from behind an exhibit case. Bloodied, and with several scratches, she serenely walked over to stand behind al-Razzuli, where she protectively placed her red stained hands on his shoulders. A golden amulet with the image of the Eye of Horus now hung around his neck. Her presence engorged the loins of men too old to remember. Her confident presence and unabashed nudity caused the women to swell with pride and with more than a bit of jealously. Gambini now had his absolute proof.

After a theatrical cough and rub of his bruised neck, al-Razzuli continued. "Are there any questions?"

After two minutes of discussion, Sekhmet walked off into the shadows of the museum's Ground Floor and al-Razzuli occupied the formerly designated Senior Chair.

The quartet remained stone-faced with rigid jaws, minds closed tight, and not daring to glance at one another. Never before in the history of the enclave had such a bold coup occurred. The four-some realized as one that Tarek el-Masry's death had not been an accident, but rather only the first move in a grab for power and prestige. Also decided on the spot, the quartet would not let this stand.

CHAPTER 17

Like donkeys tied to a mill wheel, the Austrian team once again put their backs into Habib's ingenious contraption. Revolution after revolution they torqued it, until it would turn no more. Amid clouds of dust, failing plaster, and ragged-sounding scraping, the gap now measured precisely three Egyptian cubits, 1.42 meters, or a bit over four and a half feet. Reissen checked just to make sure. Far more alluring was the dark, descending passage behind the dummy wall, which yawned open with darkness behind it.

Reissen looked at Roth, "Good call, on the direction that is."

"Thank you," the blushing historian said.

"But a tight fit," Reissen remarked.

"What's a tight fit?" Habib queried.

"If this is a burial passage, it would be a 'tight fit' for a coffin."

The Egyptian nodded now understanding.

"I want this fallen debris swept up and removed for Else's images." Reissen directed. "Then, we proceed." Roth, Peters, and Franks made light work of that.

*   *   *

The Austrian archaeologist sat cross-legged in deep thought, his chin in palm, before the dark passage. He listlessly flicked his flashlight this way and that across its maddeningly smoothed surfaces looking for something, anything. Then, he saw it.

"Team," The Austrian said, "Am I just seeing things or does the wall and ceiling color of this passage's entrance look odd?"

Wald was the first to make the connection. "Erik, that color looks just like what the chemical explosion made on the walls of the burial shaft!"

With that observation, the rest grimly nodded.

"Looks like the result of a construction accident to me." Peters concluded.

"My thoughts entirely." Reissen said. "Which means this passage is booby trapped as well."

Groans erupted behind him as he now swept the descending passage's floor with the light, looking for a clue. And there is was, a brief scrap made by the passage of the dummy wall across its entrance. Picking up a sweep while the others looked on, he carefully fussed about the threshold between the tomb's floor and the passage. In short order he detected a straight line. With a victorious grunt, he followed it across a good portion of the entrance's width to confirm his suspicions. He also uncovered two suspicious notches at the edge of the plaster that had been camouflaged with packed plaster dust. Then, once again with his fountain pen, he tapped his way from the tomb's flooring to about a foot into the passage.

Clink.

Clink.

Clink.

Thud.

Thud.

Thud.

Sitting back, the Austrian declared. "This section of the passage's flooring is a trap. It's made of plaster. Plaster flooring typically hides man traps."

"Else, please record this feature."

Standing up, Reissen turned to face Habib, "Somehow, we need to carefully remove this flooring. But before we do, we will need wooden planking to bridge the man trap."

Wide-eyed at the prospect, Habib said, "That I can find."

"Good. Go now while I organize my thoughts as to how to defeat this obstacle." Reissen paused, and added, "And Habib, find an empty fifty-five gallon oil drum as well—without a lid."

While Habib ascended the shaft with his curious laundry list, Reissen turned to the rest of his team. "We need to talk. This tomb is fast becoming more a hazardous chemical waste dump than an archaeological relic. So far we can count on *at least* one man trap."

"What's a man trap?" Roth asked.

"Sheila, Imagine a four to five meter shaft with smoothed walls. That's just deep enough to break your legs, *if* you're lucky. But if Else is correct about the discoloration in the passageway, and I believe she is, the bottom of this man trap will have one of those toxic, exploding booby-traps."

Reissen let his words hang in the air while his charges digested their weight. Looking around, all were wide-eyed, swallowing, and pale.

"That said, *if* we are to proceed, we need to carefully lift away at least one plaster flooring section. That's why we need the wooden planks, both to place them under the sections in order to slide them away in one piece, and secondarily to act as bridging. Any questions?"

Peters spoke up, "Why the oil drum?"

With a sly smile, "You'll see."

"Alright then. Let's call it a day. Without the planks we cannot go on. Besides, I need to think about how we *might* accomplish this without needing to call in a chemical weapons disposal team." The Austrian said with a wicked smile.

"In the meantime, grab those four shovel handles. We're going to make them into levers."

*   *   *

That evening, the Sakkaran team got together after dinner to discuss the situation over several ice-cold Egyptian Stella beers. Reissen noted that the mood was somber, which he well understood. So he decided to break the ice.

"Alright everyone, who is in for removing the fake plaster flooring?"

Four tentative hands rose, which hearted the archaeologist.

"But what about the booby-trap!" Franks wanted to know.

"Good question, Willi." Reissen acknowledged. "We will have to isolate it in such a way that when we're finished, a professional bomb disposal team can remove it from the site."

That answer seemed to calm the team, but then Peters piped up. "That's all well and good, Erik, but frankly I will not work around them, while they're still in the tomb. You'll have to find yourself another surveyor."

That ultimatum found receptive ears among the team, the archaeologist noted.

"Frankly, Jürgen, I don't blame you. I feel much the same. So how about this. Habib and I will remove the fake plaster flooring. We will locate the booby-trapped amphora—if any, *and* for those we do find, we'll secure them by covering them over with a fifty-five gallon oil drum. Then, once the entire passage has been cleared, we call in the pros to remove the booby traps. How's that?"

"That sounds good, Erik. I can find no fault in your plan."

"Oh, my friend," Reissen said, "There's plenty of fault in it to go around. And here's why." The Austrian emphasized with an upraised finger. "*If* Habib and I fail to remove any of the fake plaster sections intact, they will fall. If they do, we die."

After that terse statement, both Franks and Peters voted no to continue as the hazards were too great. Roth, with a deeply furrowed brow, remained undecided. Wald voted to continue, on the stipulation that Erik and Habib wear full clothing and gas masks, and that Dr. Hampl would be at the ready onsite.

*   *   *

Hampl took Wald's suggestions one step further as they both wore bright yellow HAZMAT suits with shielded hoods and respirators. He stood there with his medical gear in the tomb; she with her cameras. Both had thoroughly hydrated before donning their gear, full knowing how hot they would be getting.

As for Habib and Reissen, they wore full clothing. Their pant legs were duck taped to the tops of their boots. Both wore gas masks only. Peters and Franks, who made themselves available on the surface in the event of dire emergency, thought that the Austrian and the Egyptian were bat-shit-crazy.

Under Hampl's intense gaze and Wald's clicking camera, Reissen and Habib carefully levered up the fake plaster section taking advantage of the two notches the archaeologist previously had found. Using the whittled down ends of two shovel handles, the plaster section rose with surprising ease. While so elevated, Habib slid under the plaster plate a wooden plank along each of its outer edges. He did so to take advantage of the nearly five-inch-wide edge in the limestone bedrock that the faux flooring had been fitted into. Seemingly moments later, the two men extracted the roughly foot square plaster slab in one piece, much to everyone's relief. Meanwhile, Wald had captured the entire nerve-wracking drama.

Now with the man trap exposed, Habib and Reissen got down on their hands and knees and peeked in.

"Mein Gott!" the Austrian declared, "This must be over five meters deep."

"Easily," his colleague replied. "And look at how smooth its walls are. This is truly disturbing, Erik."

"Agreed. Let's take a water break. I can tell that we all need one. Then, we will get the scaffolding and tackle into position."

*   *   *

After a half-hour of hydration and rest, everyone got back to work. Using the five-inch wide border cuttings, Habib and Reissen erected the wooden scaffolding. They fed through its pulley a fresh length of hemp rope that ended in a lashed loop. It was agreed that Reissen would descend to locate the booby trap, while Habib would use a wooden bar across the passage's entrance to belay and tie off the rope.

With a halogen lamp in position, its glare within the limestone pit created stark shadows as Reissen slowly descended.

"Damnation! If I am going to die, I want to do it 'under the lights.'" He darkly joked. Then in a moment of reflection, Reissen looked up from the pit's bottom and said, "Thank you, my friend. I knew that I could depend upon you."

While he couldn't see Habib's face, he did hear his reply, "Always, my friend, always."

Stopping six inches above the fine gravel surface and breathing heavily, the archaeologist brushed away at the pit's center with his sweep. Images of the *Mission Impossible*'s secret agent Tom Cruise, similarly suspended, played in Reissen's mind. Moments later, he uncovered a delicate looking, flat, drumhead-like ceramic top about fifteen inches wide.

"Erik. How is it going?" Habib called down.

"I have located it," Came his muffled reply.

Satisfied, he brushed elsewhere around the pit's

flooring, and finding nothing else, called for his retrieval.

Reissen emerged from the pit like a white ghost. His sweaty clothing had been thoroughly coated in limestone dust.

After another pause for water, it was time to lower down and position the fifty-five gallon oil drum into position. This would be a tricky feat to pull off as the drum had to be carefully lowered down over the booby trap. While Reissen manned the rope, which he had wound twice around the bar, Habib guided the open drum from overhead, and gently eased it into position. With that task complete, the Egyptian slid down the rope, he had insisted, untied the drum, and squared it over the booby trap with several twists of its bottom flange. Then Reissen pulled him up.

During their water break, the pair discussed their strategy, as Peters and Franks lifted out the first fake plaster section. Then they began speculating.

"How long do you think the descending passage is?" Habib asked his stress-exhausted Austrian friend, whose eyes were red from the limestone dust.

"Good question. So far all of the tomb's dimensions are in whole cubit measures. By the look of the passage, maybe forty, fifty cubits. There's no telling as we cannot see its end. The grade is too steep."

Habib closed his eyes and made the calculation. "Anywhere between eighteen to twenty-three meters."

"Yes, but maybe longer."

Now looking the Austrian in the face. "So what is the chance that there is another concealed man pit?"

The weary response, "Possible to very possible."

"Somehow, I knew you would say that." The Egyptian said bumping his head against the wall.

*　　*　　*

The next day, the team discovered that the descending passageway, which measured just shy of seventy-five feet, ended at a bricked up doorway. Along the way, the intrepid duo of Reissen and Habib did not detect any more booby-trapped man pits.

While sitting on the surface, drinking water, and luxuriating in a breeze that chilled them to the bone, a nerve-frayed Habib remarked, "Erik, this is absolutely crazy. This man was not a magician. He was insane and paranoid."

Reissen just weakly smiled. "Perhaps, my friend. What we can say is that he took the security of his tomb quite seriously. But I ask you, what haven't we found?"

Habib shrugged.

"We have found absolutely no evidence of an intrusion. In fact, the obstacles are proof positive that behind that blocked entrance there is an intact tomb. I, for one, cannot wait to make that break-through tomorrow. And my friend, I have just learned from our dear inspector that he has notified the Egyptian military to remove the booby trap. This, they will do, within the next several days. Then, joy of joys, the media will descend upon us like locusts to record the historic opening."

At this news, Habib just shook his head in submission. "When, Erik, will all this end?"

CHAPTER 18

An aroma of fresh coffee filled the air as Nikki rose the next morning refreshed. Caught up on her jet lag, and feeling like a contented cat, she stretched her fists to the ceiling. The previous night's adventures had brought her back to a more youthful time and a hope for more of the same.

As for Jim, he sat with his bare back to her, typing on his laptop. Next to him on the desk lay two crumbled up two coffee packets.

"How long have you been up?" She called from the warmth of the sheets.

"Oh, a couple of hours."

Peeking around him, Nikki could see that the laptop's screen was filled with a language that she didn't recognize.

"Honey, what's that?"

"Huh?"

"On your screen."

"Oh, that's Hellenistic Greek." He murmured.

"What's that?"

"A kind of ancient Greek, something called *koiné*,

which means 'common'. It was popular for centuries."

Now it was her turned to say, "Huh."

Jim turned around to face her. "Honey, something's different with me."

"What do you mean?"

"Since the cab accident yesterday."

"I'll say! First you speak Arabic, and then love me up like you're eighteen again."

"Yeah, but it goes a whole bunch beyond that."

"Like how?"

"I suddenly can read ancient Egyptian hieroglyphs, Egyptian hieratic, and Hellenistic Greek for starters."

"What's hieratic?"

"A cursive form of hieroglyphs, kinda like the Palmer Method to us."

"What caused all of this?"

"Honey, when that old man died, he changed me."

"What!"

"Yeah, I know it sounds crazy, but just before he died, he transferred all of his memories to me."

Nikki's mouth formed a perfect "O" at that admission.

"And honey, there's more. That old man was really old, like thousands of years old."

"How do you know?"

"He told me, in his own way." Jim said. "In fact his birth name was Wennofre. He was once a high priest of Isis in Alexandria."

"Honey, you're scaring me with all of this foolishness."

Grinning, "Not to worry, babe. When we go to the Egyptian Museum today, I'll prove it to you."

*   *   *

"Okay, Nikki, we're going to play a game called 'Try to Stump Jim.' It's really easy. Here we are in this big old museum." The structural engineer said expansively while waving his hands about. "All you have to do is pick any statue, any monument, any artifact with an inscription, and I'll try to read it. And, just to make sure that I'm not cheating, you have to cover up the label. Are you game?"

"I suppose." Nikki said with a frown.

The couple wandered amid the Ground Floor's countless statues and display cases. Then Nikki stopped at a tiny black granite pyramid inscribed with outstretched wings, a pair of eyes, and lots of hieroglyphs on its triangular surfaces. Placing her hand over its explanatory signage, she smugly said, "Okay, champ, tell me all about this."

Without skipping a beat, Jim said, "That's the top of a pyramid, honey. It's called a pyramidion."

"But what is this all about?" Nikki pointed.

"Oh, these are two royal cartouches that contain the names of a king named Nimaatre here and Amenemhat there. It's the same guy, just two different names for him. However it is by this name, 'Amenemhat' that we refer to him today."

"Okay," she said peeking at the label for confirmation, "but what about all of this down here?"

Scanning lower on the shiny black surface, Jim focused in on two dense rows of hieroglyphs. "There are some gaps here, but I'll try to do my best." He then began to sight read the inscription,

> May the face of the king be opened so that he may see the Lord of the Horizon, when he crosses the sky. May he cause the king to rise as a god, lord of eternity and indestructible…Horakhti has said I have given to the king of Upper and Lower Egypt the beautiful horizon who takes the inheritance of the two lands…so that you may unit with the horizon…the horizon has said that you rest upon it, which pleases me.

Finished with his demonstration, Jim turned to Nikki grinning like a school boy. "How'd I do?"

Nikki, bending over to check the old and yellowed cardboard label said, "Not bad. When was it carved?"

"No clue, but by the style of the inscription alone, it's definitely pharaonic in date, and not Hellenistic."

"Okay, smarty pants, let's find you another."

While tapping her front teeth in thought with a fingernail, Nikki slowly spun in place looking for the next challenge among the skyline of artifacts. Stopping, she briskly walked over and pointed. "Translate that."

It was a small display case filled with what looked like brown sheets of paper, squeezed between two panes of glass. Each example was covered with a black writing that looked to her like spaghetti splatters. Again, she purposely positioned herself so the signage was covered.

"Okay, honey, which one?"

"The one in the center." She pointed.

"Okay, first off, this is a letter written in cursive Hellenistic Greek on a sheet of papyrus. That makes it late, like Ptolemaic in date. This is what it says,"

> We have granted to Publius Canidius and his heirs the annual exportation of 10,000 measures of wheat and the annual importation of 5,000 Coan jugs of wine without anyone exacting anything in taxes from him or any other expense whatsoever. We have also granted tax exemption on all the land he owns in Egypt on the understanding that he shall not pay any taxes, either to the state account or to the account of me and my children, in any way in perpetuity. We have also granted that all his tenants are exempt from personal liabilities and from taxes without anyone exacting anything from them, not even contributing to the occasional assessments in the districts or paying for expenses for soldiers or

officers. We have also granted that the animals used for plowing and sowing as well as the beasts of burden and the ships used for the transportation of the wheat are likewise exempt from 'personal' liabilities and from taxes and cannot be commandeered. Let it be written to those to whom it may concern, so that knowing it they can act accordingly.

Make it so!

Nikki was flabbergasted, as were several other tourists standing about during Jim's translation. In fact, they clapped at the end of the performance.

Jim blushed at the attention, but then said, "You know, honey, this is quite a tax exemption. I doubt Congress could come up with something better. But this sign off of, 'Make it so!' could only mean one thing."

"What's that?"

"Either a king or queen dictated this."

Nikki then revealed the label. "Will Cleopatra VII do? You're two for two, sport. Want to go for the whole enchilada?"

"Sure, why not?"

Again Nikki wandered about, this time settling on a huge black granite monument the size of a VW bus.

"Read this one," she pointed.

Jim's eyes squinted, "This is late Egyptian, honey. By the way, this is a coffin for an Apis bull."

"A bull!" Nikki blurted out.

"Yeah, a full, mummified bull. Here goes,"

> The Majesty of this god departed for heaven in Year 23, 3rd month of Peret, day 6. He was born in Year 5, 1st month of Akhet, day 7. He was taken to the domain of Ptah in the 2nd month of Shemu, day 18. The duration of this god's perfect life: 18 years, 1 month, and 6 days. Made for him by King Amasis, given life and authority, eternally.

"Do you want me to continue? There's more."

"No. I've heard enough smarty pants. I'm thirsty. Let's find something to drink."

On their way out of the museum, Jim stopped dead before at a partially preserved column and craned his neck to read its long vertical inscription. Finished, he rested his forehead against it. Heavy tears flowed down his face.

"What's wrong Jim?" Nikki said while clutching his elbow.

"This was his, honey, Wennofre's. This column is from the Isis temple in Alexandria. The temple that he used to serve as high priest for."

"But the label says here that it's from someplace called Coptos."

"That's bull, honey. Someone misidentified it. Trust me, I … he was there for its dedication."

Now sitting outside the museum on one of its many

low walls for the purpose, Nikki asked, "What else did that old man give you?"

Looking down into his hands, Jim quietly said, "Well honey, a whole lifetime of memories. For instance, he was born on the day Cleopatra committed suicide. That makes him over two thousand years old when that cabbie ran him down—two thousand and forty-seven years old to be precise."

Silence while she sipped on her barely chilled Coke. Then, "Can you separate out your memories from his?"

"Oh, yeah. That's simple enough. It's like shifting gears of a transmission. The challenge is that his long life was such an interesting one, and by the way, Wennofre was a master physician and magician as well as a high priest of Isis."

"Oh?"

"Yeah. Old Wennofre managed to extend his life by following a common sense diet mixed with some healthy magic."

At the mention of magic, Nikki's eyebrows threatened to disappear into her hairline.

"And," Jim emphasized with an upraised finger, "The temple of Isis was renowned for their ritualistic orgies." Jim said with fluttering eyelashes.

But he continued on with a far darker demeanor. "Honey, I also know who really killed the man."

"Wasn't it the cabbie?"

"No." Jim said with a shake of his head. "The cabbie had been manipulated. Someone was screwing around with his reflexes. That's why he didn't see Tarek el-Masry in time, much less apply the brakes soon enough. He was flat out murdered."

"Who is Tarek el-Masry?"

Smiling, "That's old man's modern day name— Tarek 'the Egyptian'. See the pun? El-Masry means 'the Egyptian' in Arabic."

CHAPTER 19

After that performance in the museum, nothing short of a staged ambush, Shaheen knew a reckoning was in the stars. His protégé had timed his choreography quite well. He had even managed to cow the membership in one swift act of defiance and political maneuver. He now possessed the Senior Chair.

*   *   *

As he had done so many times in his youth, al-Razzuli sat before Shaheen in his office. *The student adept and his master.* He wondered. *Now who was whom?*

Shaheen sat with his hands folded on the desk before him. "Careful Kek. I heard that comment. You are either getting lazy or extremely sloppy with your thoughts. Do not forget your blocking. Always employ it. Do not give your rivals undo advantage." He lectured.

Al-Razzuli blushed in embarrassment. He had indeed been sloppy. "I wish to discuss our relationship, *Sayenda*."

While Shaheen inwardly appreciated the mention

of that revered title, he didn't believe it one iota. He saw it for what it was—a verbal bluff, a diversion. "Speak your mind, Kek," Shaheen said while leaning forward on his elbows.

"I wish us to act as one, in harmony, for the good of our enclave."

The two stared at each other in a frosty silence for the next several minutes, while each calculated the true meaning behind those words. What added another layer of chill to the room was both had closed off all access to their minds. It was a standoff.

Finally, against his better judgment, Shaheen broke the stalemate. "Kek. You have been a member of this enclave for only twenty-one years. For many of us, that represents only a tick of a clock. And now you think you can barge in, and take your place at the rudder of this society? You're delusional."

To Shaheen's surprise, al-Razzuli countered, "Yes, I would be delusional to do so. So, guide me. There is absolutely no reason why we, together, could not guide this enclave. I am reasonable, far more so than that abomination I removed."

But to al-Razzuli's amazement, his former teacher responded. "This entire conversation would not be happening if Tarek el-Masry had not been killed in that accident. While the timing is odd, its result remains the same—a change of status regarding the Senior Chair. You are playing a very dangerous game, Kek."

"Are you accusing me of murdering el-Masry!"

"Absolutely! Your shielded mind only confirms it. Tarek was a good man, who possessed a brilliant aura of bright teal. He deftly, time after time, shepherded our enclave through God knows how many crisis. You, on the other hand, are a blood-thirsty young pup with an aura that looks like a black hole."

Al-Razzuli sat in his chair glowering at his former master. While not powerless, Shaheen had seen through his plan of attaining the Senior Chair through the murder of two members of the enclave. So he calmed himself down, and stayed the course.

"I wish to work with you, not against you. Is this possible?"

"Only *if* the murdering stops now." Shaheen said with an authority that al-Razzuli felt vibrating in his chest.

After a pause of several seconds while the pair locked eyes, al-Razzuli visibly relaxed, and opened his mind to allow his master in. Like a viper waiting in the dark folds of a carpet, al-Razzuli quickly searched the other's unguarded mind. And there it was—all the evidence he needed.

Suddenly, Shaheen's eyes bulged like hard boiled eggs, blood exploded from his eyes, nose, and ears. The former apprentice adept stood over his flailing teacher and benefactor. A pool of rich red blood formed on the desk blotter beneath his still twitching form.

"Die! You miserable worm! Murderer of my parents! Never again will you be master over me. Now I am the *Sayenda*!"

CHAPTER 20

If Reissen and his Austrian archaeological mission thought that they had already experienced the full brunt of the international media, they were sorely mistaken. Six days later, after the Egyptian military had grunted out the booby trap from the man pit, seven camera crews, complete with talking heads, vied for their place in the media sun. Recognizing the insanity for what it was, Inspector Hassan did his best with the local security force to hold them at bay. In the meantime, the Egyptian Antiquities Council conducted an auction for access. The North Sakkaran archaeological site had become the much-coveted object of a bidding war.

As for the Austrian team itself, Reissen held a meeting and strictly outlined which topics were open for discussion and which were not. Specifically, the missing images of the grave robbers, Egyptian dark magic, and the four booby traps were made totally off limits. All agreed and signed confidentially paperwork to enforce the information embargo. Otherwise, anything else could be discussed.

Acting as the gatekeeper for himself and his staff,

Reissen granted interviews first with the 3Sat reporters, per their previous understanding. Thereafter, it became a feeding frenzy. After only three hours into the first day's ordeal of incessant and repetitive questions— some absurd, and others openly offensive, the entire team removed itself from the scene.

All had gone according to plan until someone in the media had ferreted out the fact that an Egyptian bomb squad had paid a visit to the archaeological site just days before. At that point, Reissen and Hassan put their heads together and decided "to defuse" the matter.

One individual from the conservation department of the Grand Egyptian Museum conducted a bone dry presentation on the chemical traces found on the triggered booby trap remains, but did not linger on their significance. Another, a ceramic specialist, discussed the amphora trap's construction and its many compartments, but again, failed to logically follow through on those revelations. These were followed by a brief report made by a representative of the Egyptian bomb disposal team, who made his delivery in French, and not English—by design. While Sherlock Holmes or Hercule Poirot would have had no problem piecing together the importance of what was being reported, the dullards of the media, as one, became restless and bored.

Reissen actually heard one news network commentator say to another, "What a pile of crap. And here I thought that some terrorist group had tried to bomb an Egyptian monument!"

*   *   *

Two days later, and after the lottery, only four networks remained on the scene. Each had one hour to deploy, shoot, and remove themselves from the cramped confines of the tomb. Of those four, only one had earned the right to film the tomb's opening and that was 3Sat. Naturally, the others cried foul, but they had no avenue of recourse. The Egyptian Antiquities Service had made their decision.

While two video cameras rolled, Inspector Hassan began digging away at a central brick of the blocked entrance with a hand pick. Reissen, who was down in a squat beneath him with a hand sweep, tried to keep things neat as the plaster fell upon the wooden bridging above the third man pit. It did not take long to remove the first brick in a shower of grit, only to find a second behind it.

Slightly embarrassed, Hassan turned to the cameras and said, "Sorry gentlemen, but we have at least two layers of bricks to remove." And with that he returned to his demolition.

"Strip away the outer layer first," the Austrian archaeologist suggested. And this Hassan did, and quite rapidly now that he knew how deep he had to go.

Fully twenty minutes later, Reissen had both piled up against the descending passage's wall the first layer of bricks, some forty-three in all, and had swept up a considerable pile of plaster. Seeing this, Hassan called for a halt in order to remove all the debris. The cameramen, obvious pros, silently shut down their rigs and backed out of the passage.

Habib and four workmen hustled in to remove the debris.

During this interlude, Hassan whispered to Reissen, "We are very close, my friend."

"How do you know?"

"The second layer is teetering. I will have to remove a top brick. Otherwise the entire plug will cave in."

"Good strategy. Use it." The Egyptologist nodded with encouragement. "If you feel it giving way, just tell me when to duck!"

*　　*　　*

The 3Sat videographers stood breathlessly as the Egyptian inspector removed an upper level brick, and when he did so, only a black void could be seen.

"Erik!" the Egyptian said, "We're finally through!" The audio clearly caught the moment's excitement and emotion.

"Careful now, Ali. Work slowly, and remember to

pull away each brick. Do not let anything fall inward."
The archaeologist coached.

With fully four courses removed, the inspector
dramatically turned to the cameras and said words that
would become instantly famous, "Gentlemen. It's high
time you took a look."

With both cameras and their lights shooting side-
by-side in the slit-like opening, their lenses initially
flared with reflected light. Quickly dialing down their
lens apertures, their eyes dilated at what they were
taping—golden walls covered with hieroglyphic writing
and shadowed forms beneath their view.

One Brit cameraman said as he backed away, "Guys,
use your torches! You've just got to see this!"

CHAPTER 21

Death, and so many so soon, did not sit well with the enclave's membership. An aging society content to remain static and unchanged, regarded al-Razzuli as a dangerous upstart and outright threat to their anonymous tranquility. Lacking the cohesive will of a leader, they were powerless in the face of this young adept, who was strong, aggressive like a cobra. Worst of all, he had been nurtured by one of their own—Shaheen. To put a sharp point on the situation, after Iskander, Shaheen had been the strongest among them. This band of Hidden Folk, adepts, magicians, and paranormals had to unite in order to rid themselves of a pestilence.

Several among their number, besides the quartet, grasped the gravity of the situation. Cornelius Rhodes, a British expatriate and entrepreneur who made his fortune during the Roaring Twenties, saw this coming. Like a withered stick leaning on a far healthier-looking cane, Rhodes' powers of precognition had actually made the man contact el-Masry before his fatal stroll. He had openly begged "the Egyptian" not to leave his flat. Since "the Egyptian's" passing, Rhodes saw the falling dominoes and he didn't like it one bit.

Marsha Ledbetter, an occasional companion of Rhodes, was an attractive sixty-something witch with a hot temper and nerves of forged steel—all contained within a ninety-eight pound frame. She had vehemently voted not to have the young upstart initially join their group. Why? Because he was far too pretty a package. Besides, she sensed his darkness, peered into his vacant black aura without depth, all the while recalling his childhood antecedents as the next miraculous wonder child. Anyone who could undergo a geologic shift that drastic meant that al-Razzuli had to be unstable.

Mohammed Ghazi was a wizened snake-charmer with a hefty bank account. His casual understanding of Cairo's street life could fill the *Britannica*. He knew the pulse of the pavement and could anticipate events with startling accuracy. His investments soared. His snakes were not overfed and lethargic like his competitors', because they spoke to him, told him things that *they* saw, showed him respect in exchange for his attentive care. He had seen al-Razzuli as a child, raised as the son of a modest Coptic family. But he also knew that he had been adopted, an abandoned child found in a city pig sty. That fact chilled the superstitious man to the bone. To him, al-Razzuli was a thing of beasts, and perhaps, was the Beast himself.

The last of this four-some was the vampire, Dr.

David ibn Ibrahim Fakry, born to impregnated victim. How he managed to survive his infancy haunted the man. As a consequence, and perhaps conveniently, the good doctor currently busied himself with medical research, specializing in, what else, rare blood disorders. He too could view an individual's aura, and in his experience, Fakry had seen few like al-Razzuli's. And of those, none deserved the breath of life.

Three days after the passing of their First Chair, Shaheen, the seven met for dinner at the 139 Terrace Restaurant of the Mina House Hotel, a famous institution that was nestled at the base of the Pyramids of Giza. The 139 is one of those marvelous old school experiences with fresh linens, sparkling settings, and waiters in starched white uniforms from a different age. Lotus and jasmine scents flooded every terrace table colored by a waning sunset that backlit the Great Pyramid.

"My dear colleagues," Fakry began, "I chose this location," while raising his glass of white wine in tribute to the recent sun set, "because of the magnificent gardens and the imposing presence of antiquity."

He sipped as did the others. "Also, we are here to discuss a problem, a serious cancer that cannot be allowed to take hold."

Solemn nods agreed with his words.

"I want that brat dead," Ledbetter casually said just before the waiter arrived.

After making their choices, the waiter left, and Ledbetter continued without blinking an eye.

"He's a menace. He's claimed both our First Chair and Iskander. And that woman who accompanied him … she is pure evil."

"I've been thinking," Rhodes said while playing with the stem of his wine glass, "About the passing of our dear friend Tarek. I see a falling row of dominoes. None of this would have happened without Tarek's passing. I think al-Razzuli had his hand in murdering the man, thereby precipitating a chain of events."

Gohar caught the eyes of the rest of the quartet, and drily stated, "Actually, you're quite right, Cornelius. Al-Razzuli indeed claimed not only our Senior Chair," which caused three pairs of eyes to widen, "but also the former archaeological inspector of Sakkara. All in all, he has been very busy."

"That would explain a lot," Fakry said.

"Indeed," Ghazi nodded, "The word on the street was the cabbie had been impaired in some way. Hadn't seen Tarek until the last minute."

"Did your snakes tell you that?" Ledbetter cracked.

"No, Marsha, the police report." Ghazi politely said.

"So, dear colleagues," Fakry reeled them back in, "What are we to do about him?"

"He's intelligent and plans ahead." Ledbetter pointed out the obvious. "So we kill him."

"How?" Ghazi asked.

"I've been thinking about this quite a bit," Rhodes offered, "Tarek was a good friend. So here's what I have in mind."

CHAPTER 22

With the last of the blocking material removed to the surface, the first videographers from 3Sat created a dazzling effect when they turned on their camera lights. Beyond stunning, their combined illumination revealed a smallish square tomb, cramped with three coffins, grave goods, and walls covered in gold.

As before with the first or outer tomb, flower bouquets lay across the floor of the entrance, effectively blocking all progress. These Wald recorded with scales and identification number signage. Only then did the conservation staff on hand from the GEM remove them.

The entrance clear, the cameramen filmed for the next hour. Given the size of the tomb, care had to be taken so the glare from one camera would not step on the filming of the other. These consummate professionals, one Brit and one Dutchman, wove back and forth, all the while touching absolutely nothing. Reissen was amazed at their choreography. Their hour up, they exited and returned to the surface soaked to the skin and grinning like boys who had stolen the whole cookie jar. And in many respects, they had.

To better appreciate their skilled choreography, the two videographers worked around three cedar coffins that had been placed lengthwise near three walls. Next to the coffins of Imhotep and Neferka lay beautifully inscribed square cedar chests along with their associated boxed canopic jars. Djedi's was missing as it had been used in the first tomb as a ruse. Most unusual, a scribal desk and chair took pride of place in the tomb's center, facing the entrance as if in greeting.

This same procedure was repeated three more times, once each for the other three network crews, each monitored carefully by Inspector Hassan and Reissen. By one in the afternoon all four crews had completed their video. Now, Hassan, Reissen, Wald, and Habib made their tour. Rather quickly, Reissen realized an unavoidable reality.

"Inspector Hassan, this tomb is quite cramped. I propose that we leave the professionals to officially record it. What do you say?"

"I agree totally. Besides, we need to talk."

Once back to relative fresh air of the burial shaft, Reissen asked, "What's on your mind, inspector?"

"What arrangement did you and my predecessor make regarding publication rights?"

"Inspector Kama granted the Austrian mission full publication rights."

"I see." Hassan said while chewing on his lip.

"What's the issue?" Reissen pressed.

"There is no paperwork to that effect."

"Well," The Austrian said with a furrowed brow. "Mr. Inspector, is there any reason why the Austrian mission would not have such rights?"

"Frankly, no I don't. But given the recent involvement of the Supreme Council of Antiquities regarding this archaeological find, I cannot guarantee your mission anything."

Reissen could feel the heat rise on his face, but remained cool in spite of it. "If that is the case, Mr. Inspector, then who would better know each and every inch of this site?"

"No one, Dr. Reissen."

I am no longer, Erik, the archaeologist realized.

"Given what you have just said, Mr. Inspector, are you telling the Austrian archaeological mission to walk away from this find, after all of our work?"

"No, in fact, quite the opposite. I wish your mission to proceed. I also want you to carefully secure all your imagery and notes. A goodly part of my argument on your mission's behalf will depend upon what you uniquely possess. Do you understand?"

"Sadly, Mr. Inspector, I do."

* * *

The following day, the staff from the conservation department arrived to begin the task of emptying the tomb. Given what he could see, Reissen figured that it would take a good two weeks to finish that process, more than sufficient time for the Egyptologist to rerecord this or that as need be. That was why Wald and her cameras joined him.

Of paramount interest early on was an inch by inch examination of the three coffins, all which were pedestaled on magical bricks. All were simple rectangular boxes constructed of imported cedar. When close to them, the resin still provided its distinctive scent despite the millennia. As Reissen hovered over each, reading their inscriptions, he quickly realized that before him was a family. *Mein Gott!* The coffin along the left wall contained the magician and architect Imhotep, the one along the right wall the sorceress Neferka, and the third their magician son, Djedi. The significance of this family grouping was staggering.

"Just to make sure, Else, please rerecord these inscriptions up close and with scale."

"Not a problem."

Then the Egyptologist thought to add, "What are the odds Else that any of these coffins contain chemical booby traps, just like Djedi's first coffin?" He darkly hypothesized. "I frankly would not be surprised one bit, after all we have gone through just to get this far."

Else's response was an ashen face and wide eyes. "Do you think, Erik?"

"I'm going to specifically warn the

conservationists about the possibility, and Inspector Hassan as well. When these are removed, I absolutely prohibit anyone from our mission to be on site."

That said the pair moved on to inspect the rest of the grave goods. The dome-lidded cedar trunks were found to be filled with rolls of bound papyri. By the inscriptions on their tops, they represented the personal archives or *per-medjat* of Imhotep, Neferka, and Djedi. Neferka's chest alone was filled to the brim with papyri bound in red and blue yarns, causing Reissen to remark, "Else, these are the spells of an Egyptian witch. Can you imagine what they might contain?"

The photographer responded with multiple clicks from her camera, just as she had done with the other trunk's contents, all stuffed with papyrus rolls.

Looking down on them, Reissen remarked, "Else, these scrolls represent treasure beyond measure. Even though they are so well preserved, it will take a small army of philologists to make heads or tails of them."

The Egyptologist walked around to stand behind a scribal table and chair that had been placed like an island in the center of the tomb. On it, laid a papyrus held in place by four smoothed river stones; next to it a scribal palette with a dried black ink reservoir and quill. On the papyrus in florid glyphs Reissen read aloud,

> He who opens my most beautiful place
> must now be responsible for its contents.
> This will require wisdom, for such

> knowledge in the hands of an evil one
> can be as dangerous as a hippopotamus
> or crocodile.

"Mein Gott!" Reissen breathed. Then looking at Wald, "This is extraordinary, Else. This tomb is so full of warnings and anomalies."

"But where are the grave goods?" Wald wanted to know.

"You have already seen them." The Austrian expansively gestured. "All of these papyri in these chests are the family's treasure, their personal archives, their *per medjat,* or 'house of books.' At their core, Else, this family collected knowledge."

"But what kind of knowledge?" Wald wanted to know.

"There is only one way to find out. And that is to read this entire collection."

The last three items to examine were open cedar boxes that contained four alabaster vessels each, each jar with the beautifully carved but unpainted head of a baboon, hawk, human, and jackal. Inspecting their inscriptions, Reissen announced, "These are the canopic jars of Imhotep, Neferka, and Djedi. They contain the mummified remains of their lungs, stomach, intestines, and liver. Pointing to each, the archaeologist explained, "These are the four sons of Horus. *Hapi*, the baboon, contains the lungs. *Duamutef*, the jackal, protects the stomach. *Imsety*, the human-headed one, holds the liver.

And *Qebehsenuef*, the falcon guards over the intestines."

Glancing around, Reissen made another observation. "You know, Else, when you think about it, there is really nothing in this chamber that could be considered a personal item, like clothing, toiletries, and the like. My guess is, that at least for Imhotep and Neferka, this was a secondary burial."

"What do you mean by 'secondary'?"

"I think Djedi removed his parents from their original tomb and buried them here. I also think that process must have been a very quick and secretive affair. Hence the total lack of the mundane.

"By the way, Else, have you bothered to look up?"

The ceiling was painted in a cobalt blue decorated with bright yellow, five-pointed stars.

"Oh my!" And her camera started clicking anew. While the photographer began a section by section bracketing of the ceiling, Reissen leaned in for a close inspection of the three golden walls of the tomb. Gently tapping with his finger, his suspicions soon were expressed.

"Once this chamber is cleared, I want you to record these three walls fully. This is beaten gold foil embossed with hieroglyphs. To my best knowledge, such a decoration has *never* been found before. You, Else, will be the first. You will be making history."

"What do the hieroglyphs say?"

"They are a version of *The Pyramid Texts*, Else. Instead of a king's name being mentioned throughout the text, the names of Imhotep, Neferka, and Djedi have been inserted. You will need Habib's help here, because to capture all of this, you will need some careful lighting."

Leaning in close and at an angle, "You're absolutely right, Erik. Shooting these highly reflective walls will be a pain."

* * *

Later that day, Reissen called up Inspector Hassan, and as luck would have it, caught the man just before he left his office.

"Inspector Hassan, this is Dr. Erik Reissen. May I speak with you a moment?"

"Dr. Reissen, I was just leaving for the day, but yes, of course, what can I do for you?"

"The conservation team is arriving tomorrow from the GEM. Is that correct?"

"Yes, it is."

"Wonderful, then may I suggest they remove the golden walls of the tomb as well."

"What! The walls too?"

"Yes, Inspector Hassan, you heard me correctly. The golden walls are a thin veneer. They can be removed. I have found the joints between their sheets."

"I see, I do not know …"

"And there is one other matter that you should tell your colleagues at the GEM about."

"What is that?"

"That extreme care should be exercised with the removal of the three coffins."

"Dr. Reissen." Hassan said with exasperation, "The conservation staff at the GEM are professionals who know what they are doing, furthermore, …"

"Excuse me, Inspector Hassan, but I suspect that at least one of the coffins might be another chemical booby trap."

"Oh. I hadn't considered that, Dr. Reissen." Pause. "Tomorrow, when they arrive, I will inform them myself about the possibility. But as for the gold walls …"

"Inspector Hassan, please excuse me, but you are a good man. What do you think will happen once the tomb is aired on the television? Do you want to be the one responsible for not preventing the theft of those walls, while you're the Inspector of Sakkara?"

A heavy sigh. "Erik, you're absolutely right … once again. Thank you." And a now very worried inspector hung up the phone.

Meanwhile, the Austrian had one week left to wrap up what turned out to be an historic archaeological season.

CHAPTER 23

By late June, all the smothering fanfare, interviews, and well-wishers had died down. That allowed Reissen some quiet time to review the season's imagery on his office's large flat-screen. He saw that Wald had again been brilliant. Next, he had two reports to write—one for the Egyptian Antiquities Organization and another for his departmental chair. Fortunately, the former with only minor edits, would satisfy the latter.

Slowly panning through Wald's imagery helped him to remember, to organize his thoughts. A peaceful two hours into this, the Austrian finished a rough draft. Pleased, he stretched to the ceiling and heard more pops and cracks than he wished. *I must be getting old*, the forty-seven-year-old chided himself.

Then his computer chimed that another e-mail had arrived. Glancing over to that part of the screen, he saw that this one was important. The addressee was none other than Ali Hassan's older sister, Dr. Aziza Hassan, who worked within the GEM's conservation department.

The Magician's Tomb

Dear Professor Dr. Reissen:

I trust that his e-mail finds you in good health! I am writing to you and copying your field photographer to inform you that the Djedi artifacts have been received and catalogued by my department. Ms. Wald's kind list of images, sent separately, match perfectly with what we now have in inventory.

Attached are their acquisition numbers.

After x-ray, the second Djedi coffin was not another chemical booby trap. Instead, it contains the remains of an elderly man. As for the other two coffins, they were unremarkable as well, containing the remains of an elderly man and woman.

The multiple papyri caches provided considerable joy. In all, the Neferka cache contained forty-three scrolls; the Imhotep cache twenty-seven; and the Djedi collection nearly one hundred.

The golden foil that covered the tomb's walls presented us with many challenges, but in the end, we successfully removed them and have built frames upon which to display them. They are truly breathtaking artifacts. In all, there are eighteen sections and they also appear in the attached acquisition's list.

My brother and I have discussed at length the outstanding issue of publication rights. I can assure you and

your staff that I have lobbied heavily on
your behalf.

Yours sincerely,

Dr. A. Hassan

After Reissen immediately responded with
gratitude for the frank and forthcoming support, he
nonetheless came away from the communication with
mixed emotions. He had colleagues who were
chomping on the bit to study those papyri scrolls.
Careers could be made or dashed based on a
bureaucrat's decision as to who was granted the
publication rights. The value of the imagery alone to his
department's finances was considerable. The
departmental funding for the tomb's publication had
been earmarked, but could not be held on the books
indefinitely. On and on it went as the ramifications ever
spooled through the Egyptologist's mind. *Let's get on
with this!*

* * *

Three days later, Reissen, finished with the edits of his
last season's field reports, sent them off with a sigh of
considerable relief. That task finished meant that he
could dive into what he called, *The Golden Pyramid
Texts*. Because of his intimate knowledge of entire
corpus of *The Pyramid Texts*—in all over six hundred

spells, incantations, and hymns, he progressed quite rapidly. In the process, he realized that what he was working through represented a pared down version of what later appeared in the pyramids of the Fifth and Sixth Dynasties. In retrospect, that made a lot of sense, since the second Djedi tomb chamber lacked the sheer square footage of the later pyramid chambers.

Then, like a bolt out of the blue, the next morning his good friend and colleague, Sister Josephina Busby, paid his office a surprise visit.

"Sister Josephina! What a grand surprise." Reissen genuinely gushed. "Please, take a chair. Coffee perhaps?"

"Yes, please, that would be wonderful, Erik." She beamed.

Sitting down, the Austrian reached for his phone, dialed his departmental secretary, and made a request, finishing with, "Yes, *Frau* Miller, that too would be grand."

Grinning ear-to-ear, Reissen asked with a serious tone in his voice, "Why Josephina, other than a coffee, are you here?"

Reaching over from her seat, Sister Josephina placed a thumb drive before the archaeologist.

"What's this?"

"The drive contains Sheila Roth's and my contribution to your excavation's publication. I think that you will find both to be quite interesting, if not ground-breaking in ancient Egyptian religious theology."

Wide-eyed, the Austrian said, "Thank you, Sister Josephina. I will indeed read both with interest, but ..."

"You're still not sure you have the publication rights in hand." She interrupted.

Surprised, "How did you know?"

"Erik, Erik, I have my sources, and they're not Sheila Roth by the way. I hear rumblings, let's just say."

Still holding the thumb drive in his palm, Reissen said, "Yet, you could have easily sent these documents to me via e-mail." Now leaning forward, "So what's the real reason for your visit?"

"Erik, there are times when you can be marvelously perceptive." Looking down at her folded hands as if they could provide the good sister with inspiration, she began.

"Erik, I am here unofficially on official business— Vatican business."

"Oh, how so?"

Looking deeply into his eyes, Sister Josephina held his rapt attention. "Erik, as a graduate student you've spent time at the Pontifical College. You and I know that the Vatican community is a very tightly knit bunch. It's a family, that at times can be quite dysfunctional, but in the end, it's still a family that closes ranks around its own. Vatican departments gathers information. The

Pontifical College shares information. The Vatican Library stores information. The Holy See, as an umbrella organization, oversees all that information *and* all things diplomatic. Erik, I work for a little known Vatican organization called Pro Deo—literally 'for God.' The outside world believes that it disbanded after the Second World War, but in reality, it went deep underground. It's amazing how something publically disbanded can be completely ignored."

"Who does this Pro Deo organization work for?

"The Holy See."

"Ah."

"Within Pro Deo, Erik, I am assigned to its paranormal section. It's my job to take note of that which is curious, odd, and dangerous. And that is where your research into the tomb of Djedi comes in. It seems that your recent find has caused, how shall I say, a ripple in the paranormal world."

"What! How?"

"Do you remember that flap about a missing artifact?"

Reissen, at its mention, turned pale. "How did ..."

With a raised open palm in his direction, "Erik, it is my job to know such things."

At that moment came a rap on his office door.

"Herein bitte," Reissen absentmindedly answered.

The secretary entered with a groaning wicker tray loaded with a large carafe of creamy coffee, china, and a generous mound of scones. Rising and taking the burden from the struggling woman, Reissen said, "*Danke*, Marta."

Alone again, and after everyone had their coffee and *Kuchen*, Reissen continued without skipping a beat, "Sister, you were saying."

"That missing artifact was sold to an antiquities' dealer, who the next day killed four thieves in his shop. He then turned up dead the following day. Egyptian forensics recorded that the man died of a massive cerebral hemorrhage. However," Sister Josephina said with an index finger in the air, "magic, any kind of magic, once used, leaves behind its signature. In this instance, the antiquities' dealer died of lethal magic."

Reissen sat riveted while his coffee cooled, his scone untouched.

"Three days later, a man who you knew, Inspector Hussain Kama, died horribly in his office. Egyptian forensics said that he had been mauled by a lion. However," again with that index finger, "the truth is Kama was mauled by extremely ancient dark magic. In fact, our in-house spell whisperer, who investigated the case, had never before encountered such a case."

Reissen now held his head in his hands. "Josephina. What's a spell whisperer?"

"Think of it as magical forensics."

She took a sip of her coffee and continued. "And the word on the street is that missing artifact is believed to be the cause of many other murders. More significantly, however, it must have been acquired by someone who knows how to use such dark magic."

Sister Josephina again paused to take a sip of her coffee and followed it with a dainty nip of her scone.

Reissen just watched her and wondered how she could do so given the subject matter.

She said, "Erik, I am sorry to burden you so, but I am afraid there's more. The individual who killed Inspector Kama and the others is not finished. Once he learns of the Imhotep, Neferka, and Djedi archives, they will act again to acquire their magical scrolls."

Reissen cringed at that news. "What can I do to stop them?"

"Well, Erik, the obvious. Don't find any more magicians' tombs. That aside, I have been authorized to make you an offer."

"What kind of offer?"

"To join the faculty at the Pontifical College in Rome, and become a quiet member of Pro Deo."

"Sister Josephina, why would I want to do that? Especially given what I know about the Pontifical College's petty politics? My God, even you, the most patient person I know on the planet, took another job outside of their walls."

"Well, Erik, you have several advantages. Number one, you already know that the college is a snake-pit filled with overblown academic egos. Second, they already know you because of your graduate work within their walls. That automatically makes you one of them. And by the way, your current notoriety carries serious clout. Third, you're a member of the laity and not the clergy. That means considerable freedom. But best of all, you would have a ready source of funding for your research. Those are the advantages of the Pontifical College."

She stopped to take another sip of that divine coffee, timed perfectly to give Reissen the opportunity to mull over what she said.

"As for Pro Deo, Erik, there are things, secrets, and paranormal insights that would be a great aid to your understanding of *The Pyramid Texts*. And they have independent resources as well."

Another sip, and finally the Austrian did as well, but then grimaced at its fallen temperature.

"Finally, Erik, someone has to study all of those scrolls. I believe that scholar is you, Erik. Right now, right this moment, the Vatican, via the Holy See and Pro Deo, are making every effort to gain possession of them."

"Why?

"Because Erik, they are potentially very dangerous. Consider this: six people died over the illegal acquisition of just one Djedi artifact. How many more will do so over the scrolls of two ancient Egyptian magicians and a witch?"

CHAPTER 24

"My plan," Rhodes outlined, "is simple. We provide sufficient honey, the bee flies to us, and we squash it."

"So what is this exquisite nectar that will cause al-Razzuli to cast all common sense to the wind?" Ledbetter fluttered her hands and wanted to know.

"I have recently heard from Gohar of the acquisition of over one hundred and fifty tantalizing scrolls by the GEM's conservation department. These scrolls come from a certain Sakkaran tomb that has enjoyed of late considerable publicity."

"The Djedi tomb." Ghazi stated as a fact.

"Yes. That one." Rhodes confirmed.

"All of this is well and good, but how do we 'squash' this pestilential bug?" Fakry asked.

"One of us, and I volunteer," Rhodes offered, "tells the man about the scrolls. Explains that the scrolls are for sale, and asks if al-Razzuli is interested. If so, the same individual, me, would meet the man at a place of his choice to consummate the deal."

"Again, all well and good, but how do we squash him?" Fakry pressed.

"Surprise, my good vampire. Before he pays up, I will offer him the chance to inspect the goods. While he's so engrossed, then all of us pounce upon him."

Skeptical looks surrounded him.

"Oh, come on! Look at what we have at our disposal. David here represents speed and strength. I suspect that you can remove a man's head in the blink of an eye."

Fakry nodded in agreement. "It's true."

"Meanwhile, my powers of mental prediction can also block my thoughts. If I appear befuddled and simple-minded, I won't give anything away."

"Marsha, do you have any *perturbare* spells handy? If you can cast one to dull his wits, that would be most helpful."

"That I can certainly do." Ledbetter assured.

"Finally, we need some backup. Mohammed: can you come up with something that might distract him?"

A knowing smile, "Yes, my friend, I indeed have an idea for one."

"This honey," Ledbetter asked, "is it the real thing, or just something ginned up to appear authentic?"

"No, Marsha, just several blank rolls of papyrus. Think of them as props on a stage."

*　*　*

Plans within plans within plans. This is why the military train so much and so often. Individuals are assigned tasks, which are to be efficiently completed at or near a specific time. Such tasking orders are layered one upon another, all in the hope that a mission's critical operation will succeed. As one might expect, preparation is foremost, task proficiency ingrained, and the sharpening of an individual's situational awareness and creative inventiveness tantamount.

These four lacked most of those qualities. Above all, they were of a solitary mindset, individuals, and not an experienced and trained team. Only Fakry was an accomplished killer. The others rarely touched a stranger. They did, however, rehearse their assigned parts several times, in their heads, and privately. What could possibly go wrong?

*　*　*

Rhodes successfully contacted al-Razzuli with the news of a new-found cache of magical papyri. He enticed the adept with the claim he had several in his possession. Would he be interested in buying any of these scraps? While the doddering old man's pitch didn't convince the adept of his claim's validity, his own inside contacts within the Egyptian Antiquities Organization had. Indeed they had recently inventoried over one hundred and fifty scrolls, purportedly once owned by an ancient Egyptian family made up of a witch and two magicians.

To further reel in their quarry, Rhodes left the venue of the meet up to al-Razzuli's discretion, but had insisted upon a public place. Perhaps out of pure whimsy, the newly appointed Senior and First Chair of the enclave chose to meet within the Khan el-Kalili bazaar of Cairo. The date was set at eleven, at the El Fishawy Café, located on the alley of the same name, for mint tea.

To visit the roofed over alley is to experience the stuff of *A Thousand and One Nights*. The eye is caught by intricately carved cedar panels, fans, tiny round granite-topped tables, and wicker chairs. The nose is assaulted with hookah pipes and the aromas of rich coffees and delicious teas. Everywhere one is the eye-dilating wash of sumptuous and gaudy color, and above all, the ever present bee-like thrum of conversation.

Al-Razzuli took a table in the cramped and narrow passage surrounded by tourists and locals alike. The bustle of those walking by provided him amusement, while he waited for his appointment with a man that he considered old, feeble, and far beyond his prime. He mused whether the ancient Rhodes could even find him.

To his mild surprise, promptly at eleven, Rhodes appeared at his table dressed in a three-piece suit. He carried over his shoulder a tan canvas satchel with a simple flap. It appeared full of something.

"Good morning," he cheerfully piped. "What are you having?" he inquired as he seated himself. He carefully set down his burden next to his calf.

"Expresso," al-Razzuli gestured to his tiny porcelain cup as if explaining this drink for the first time to a child.

Rhodes ignored the slight, hailed a waiter, and ordered himself a mint tea with honey on the side.

*   *   *

While Rhodes faced his personal devil, Ledbetter found herself a seat within the café, but in visual contact with the pair sitting outside. Several hand gestures later, and she had blanketed the pair with a subtle lethargy. Moments later, Ghazi sat down at her table, a nervous bundle. "I hope this works."

As for Fakry, he didn't particularly like the public setting. More used to working in the dark, eleven in the morning represented a bit of a challenge. So he stood in an unused doorway, in its shadow, where he could survey the scene.

*   *   *

The Porters had purposefully put the bazaar on their itinerary as the absolute last thing to experience before catching the red eye back to the States. Hand-in-hand they shared a contented exhaustion that came from seeing everything they came to see: the Pyramids at Giza, Sakkara, the overnight train to Luxor, the Valley of the Kings, the Karnak and Luxor temples, the tombs of the nobles, the train back to Cairo, and of course, several camel rides thrown in for good measure. Frankly, although neither would admit it quite yet, they were beat, their feet hurt, but didn't want the magic to end.

Worming their way through the bazaar's narrow streets and alleys, the couple made their way to a famous café noted for its coffee and mint tea.

CHAPTER 25

Rhodes' mint tea finally arrived, from the neck of its porcelain pitcher funneled out its fragrance like a steam engine's stack, forming about the table a dreamy cloud.

While Rhodes poured himself a cup, he mentioned in passing, "It has come to my attention that you have a great interest in the religious culture of this most ancient land. Is that not so?"

Al-Razzuli looked at the man, sullenly, and grunted his interest.

"I see. I thought so." Rhodes struggled to get out. Ledbetter's spell was clouding his mind too.

"What I have in my satchel are several magical papyri that you might find of interest."

As Rhodes reached over to grasp the satchel's strap, his full head and face intruded into the narrow lane of the alleyway. Placing the open bundle on the table and facing it toward the dark adept, he simply said, "Here, have a look."

Al-Razzuli did, carefully removing one of the papyrus rolls, bound with two reddish threads. Then he noticed an odd movement from within the canvas bag.

But with the papyrus in hand that was quickly ignored.

"Cecil?" a deep, resonant voice asked. "Is that you?"

Blandly looking up toward the source of this extremely ill-timed intrusion, Rhodes saw a tall, black American. The Brit assumed this by the look of him, being quite fit, and his accent. The woman at his side he presumed was his wife.

Once the tall American took one look at al-Razzuli his friendly demeanor instantly changed. Before the Brit knew it, the American had struck the adept four times in the face and head with hammer-like blows, which ruined al-Razzuli's proud nose, blackened both eyes, and cut his left ear. During this all out assault, the American loudly grunted out, "Murderer! Murderer!"

Al-Razzuli, stunned at the sudden and unprovoked attack, reeled with the blows. His telepathic voice screamed "Kill", but nothing happened. Instead the combination of the man's intense rage and something else remarkably familiar had blocked the death shriek. Now feeling his consciousness slipping to a narrow dark tunnel, the adept reached out telekinetically, found a heavy tea tray, and struck his attacker squarely across the temple.

As the big man crumpled before him, out of his foggy peripheral vision, the tan canvas bag again moved. Turning to see what it was, his telekinetic powers again automatically kicked in as he jerked back into the adjoining table to avoid a cobra strike. Seeing this, he psychically crushed its head and spine like a tomato can in a gush of fleshly blood.

Looking now at Rhodes, who was wide-eyed at all the proceedings, al-Razzuli ruthlessly caused a hemorrhage in his brain that instantly killed the man where he sat. Brushing off the dead cobra's body from his lap like so many crumbs, the adept stood, stepped over his attacker and a crying woman, and staggered out of the café with the tan satchel under his arm.

*   *   *

Throughout this entire melee, Fakry had remained motionless in the shadowed false doorway. His aversion to killing in broad daylight had got the best of him. Put bluntly, he had chickened out. When Al-Razzuli's surprise attacker appeared, at first it looked like the tall American would do the job for him. Well, that didn't happen. With the swift passing of his chance to contribute, Fakry made a quick and decisive decision. It was time to move on. Cairo had been a lark, but now he needed another city to call home, somewhere on the Continent with a permanent nightlife. *Perhaps Paris.*

*   *   *

Ghazi and Ledbetter sat in complete shock as the emergency personnel lifted away Rhodes' limp body and the two Americans were taken into custody by the bazaar's security force.

Ledbetter was the first to voice, "Whatever happened to David?"

"He choked," Ghazi surmised with rage. "I wouldn't be surprised if that self-centered blood-sucker split town as well. My money he's headed right now for the Alexandrian airport and some destination on the Continent. Marsha, there's a reason why you can't trust their kind. They're too flaky and self-centered." He paused and realized. "And that was my prize snake!"

"But who was that big guy?" Ledbetter wanted to know.

*　　*　　*

After hours of police interrogation and the intercession of the U.S. Consulate, Jim Porter was finally released, but only because the victim could not be located and Porter therefore could not be formerly charged with assault. The consulate then discovered that Porter was a decorated U.S. Marine officer. After paying a fine of five hundred dollars U.S. in cash, and after signing a *persona non grata* declaration, he promised he would never ever attempt to visit Egypt again. As a further measure, two agents of the consulate escorted him and his wife Nikki through the airport security and waited at the gate with them until they boarded their plane.

Seated in their business class seats, Jim, the knuckles of his hands bandaged and with four stitches in the side of his forehead, looked over to his wife and said, "Honey, this is one trip I think we got more than we bargained for."

CHAPTER 26

Sitting in his hospital chair, al-Razzuli looked like a medieval knight. Nose bandaged, head bandaged, ear padded with gauze, a total stranger had brutally beat him. On reflection, through the fog of the pain-killing sedatives, the adept remembered seeing that tall figure as he escaped from the taxi accident that had claimed Tarek el-Masry. He remembered worrying that "the Egyptian" had made contact with him, perhaps even had transferred his *ka*. Now he had his proof. His assailant had called him a "murderer" while he had pounded his face into pulp. Only Tarek would have recognized Rhodes at the café, because of their long friendship. Rhodes clearly didn't know who the tall American was when he showed up. It all fit. All in all, it had been a strange twist of fate that brought them all together. After a brief vengeful flare of hateful emotion, al-Razzuli allowed it to recede. *Forget it. The man's probably already half a world away.*

Finished commiserating about his current physical state, al-Razzuli returned to the subject of the scrolls from the Djedi tomb, purportedly stored somewhere within the GEM. His sources positively reported that they had been entered into the computerized acquisition system. They had images associated with them. They existed. Now, he wanted them and thought of them as his rightful property.

*   *   *

Reissen decided to drive Sister Josephina to the ultra-modern and glass-bedecked Vienna train station at Favoritenstrasse 51. He didn't have to, but he did as there were several balls in the air that he needed to address.

His tiny red Fiat Abarth made for a snug fit, but it had more than sufficient zip for Vienna's traffic, while having the near preternatural ability to pass through the city's narrower streets.

"Erik," Sister Josephina gently chided, "You didn't have to drive me to the station."

"Least I could do. Besides, you're a good friend. We Viennese pride ourselves on our hospitality." He said with a grin. "Besides, I swear that my office has ears."

"Oh?"

"Just kidding, but if I am going to become a secret agent of the Vatican, don't you think I should start acting like one?"

"Are you sure about this, Erik? Becoming a faculty

member of the Pontifical College is one thing, but swearing your allegiance to The Holy See *and* Pro Deo is a serious career move."

"Sister Josephina, here's what I have in mind. A sort of probationary period, where the powers that be and I can feel each other out. Is that possible?"

"Anything is possible, Erik. The real question is would the 'powers that be' be willing to do so. Personally, I don't think so." She said with a shake of her head. "They possess a very 'all or nothing' mindset."

"So, if I understand you, either commit or not."

"Precisely."

"Hrmph." Reissen grunted as he pulled up the station's curbing.

"Erik." The sister offered. "It is your decision. But if you ask me, you would be a natural. The research opportunities would be plentiful. The funding nearly unlimited. And your latent paranormal abilities would develop rapidly. Think about it."

"'Paranormal abilities'?"

"Yes, Erik. You use them unconsciously every day. It's just that you don't realize it."

She squeezed his forearm, "My friend, I have to go and grab a train. Sleep on it. That's always the best."

While the Austrian wound his way back to the university he chuckled to himself. Now he had another ball in the air to juggle.

THE MAGICIAN'S TOMB

*   *   *

When Reissen returned to his office, he turned on his flat-screen and pulled up the multi-colored 3D-plot of the Djedi excavation. The archaeologist focused in on the structural dimensions that Peters and Frank had so precisely measured. Accessing the calculator function on his smart phone, the archaeologist began scribbling down some figures, and discovered the consistent adherence to whole Egyptian cubit measurements, along with several duplications.

> Burial Shaft: 5 wide by 10 long by 50 cubits deep
>
> First Tomb: 10 square by 5 cubits high
>
> Descending Passage: 3 wide by 5 high by 50 cubits
>
> Golden Tomb: 10 square by 5 cubits high
>
> Man Pit: 3 wide by 4 long by 10 cubits deep

I am not surprised. Djedi was a stickler for consistency, that's his pattern. And if you think about it, a successful magician is someone who practices, over and over, day after day, to perfect a trick. It is just the way their mind works.

That clarified, he next displayed Wald's dense digital imagery of the false door and biographical inscription. Zooming in on the false door, he scoured it looking for clues. Fortunately, Wald had taken multiple views, and at different times of the day. This afforded

Reissen the opportunity to view detail with remarkable clarity—just short of being there. Satisfied, he was ready to write.

CHAPTER 27

That early evening, Inspector Ali Hassan's eyes felt like they were filled with sand. Dog tired and flooded with paperwork on seemingly a daily basis, he stopped and rubbed them hoping for some relief. When he opened them he started, as a well-groomed man was sitting in his office. He looked familiar, but the Egyptian couldn't place him. Oddly, he man's eyes looked blood-shot. After a conversation of about ten minutes, the man left and Hassan got back to his mountain of paperwork. Glancing at his wall clock, he had lost ten minutes and couldn't remember how.

*   *   *

The next day al-Razzuli paid a visit to the conservation department of the Grand Egyptian Museum in Giza. Using his natural charm and gentle telepathic influence as a bureaucratic lubricant, he soon found himself standing outside the office of Dr. Aziza Hassan—Inspector Ali Hassan's older sister.

He knocked on the glass pane of the institutional door and heard an exasperated, "Enter."

Putting on his very best smile, al-Razzuli did, and found sitting behind a cluttered desk a short woman with salt and pepper hair peeking out beneath her head scarf or *hijab*.

Hassan's face was a question mark, "Who are you?"

"That is not entirely important at the moment, Dr. Hassan." Al-Razzuli crooned. "But what is, however, is the location of scrolls from the tomb of Djedi. Please take me to them," he psychically pushed.

Hassan began to object, but the adept pushed harder. "Dr. Hassan. I very much need your assistance."

Hassan's will melted away by the subtly applied assault. She stood. Part of her wanted to resist, but in the end tersely said, "Follow me."

They walked for a good five minutes through sterile and identical hallway after hallway, turning here and there seemingly without logic. Never again would al-Razzuli complain about any hospital's labyrinthine layout. The GEM's operational floors were far worse.

They finally arrived at a locked set of heavy steel double doors stenciled with the words ACQUISITIONS and a sign that firmly stated: "No Unauthorized Personnel Beyond This Point." Hassan's hand floated above the keypad mounted on the wall, stalled, then rapidly typed in a code, and the doors' lock clicked.

Quickly grasping the right hand latch, Hassan depressed it, and opened the door. "Follow me."

Stopping in mid-threshold, Hassan then added, "Stay close. Otherwise you might get lost."

What al-Razzuli beheld was mind-boggling. A vast space opened to him, three stories high, brilliantly illuminated, with walls that he couldn't see. Frankly, he was surprised that he couldn't see the curvature of the horizon. But this vast space was filled with aisle after endless aisle of racking that in most places stood four or more levels high. And everywhere were marked wooden crates, boxes, artifacts wrapped in plastic, and fragments of monumental statuary that only could be moved with a fork lift.

Hassan then turned to al-Razzuli and said, "Please get into this first electric cart. Where we're going is too far to go on foot."

After disconnecting the cart's electrical umbilical cord, winding it up, and placing it on a hook, she took the driver's seat. With a slight screech of the cart's soft rubber tires against the highly polished white flooring, off they went with the adept wondering where.

At Aisle 35, Hassan turned in and whizzed along a broad aisle divided into two lanes with a solid white line for another ten seconds before stopping at Rack 51. Getting out, Hassan led al-Razzuli over to a row of low drawers that dominated the immediate area.

"This is our papyri collection," she announced. "The papyri that you seek are in drawers 23 through 183."

With hands shaking with anticipation, al-Razzuli went randomly to cabinet 17, drawer 93. The bright white label on it stated:

> Location 35.51.17.93. Acquisition Nr. 000459393. Papyrus 6. Neferka Archive. Sakkara, Site Nr. 243. Fourth Dynasty. Austrian Archaeological Mission 2016.

He pulled it open and found it empty except for a small tent card that stated:

SEQUESTERED
Object under Review

"This drawer is empty! The card here says it is under review!"

Hassan testily retorted from the electric cart with her hands on the wheel, "Well, that happens. A papyrus was in it yesterday."

Spinning around, al-Razzuli began opening drawers at a mad rate. Everywhere he looked, he found empty drawers, all with maddening sequestration cards, and in the process, transformed that portion of the neat aisle into a grotesque nightmare of open, nonconforming drawers.

"Where are they?" He demanded with a flush face and clenched fists.

"They were here yesterday," was the dull response.

After a quick probe of her mind, al-Razzuli

desperately realized that she was telling the truth. Hassan literally had taken stock of the collection the day before and handled one of them, but now, where had they gone?

The awesome reality of the situation hit the adept squarely in the face as he spun around on his heel. *They could literally be anywhere in this vast archive.*

*　　*　　*

Dr. Hamid Gohar, member of the International Cultural Studies Society of Cairo, the Supreme Council of Egyptian Antiquities, and the one appointed to oversee the investigation into Inspector Kama's death, looked up at the new file cabinets that had been installed in his office the other day. Unlike the other file cabinets in his already tight office, these had a heavy padlocked bar and strapping mechanism that encircled them along their vertical axis. He was taking no chances. Especially given what had happened to the missing artifact from Djedi's tomb that had disappeared onto the black market. And the news of the failed attempt on al-Razzuli life only added to his heartburn. Add to that, his colleagues at the Vatican Library had already offered their assistance. While much appreciated, Gohar chaffed at their presumption. In his eyes, the scrolls were exclusively an Egyptian matter, actually to be precise, a Hidden Folk matter. And if his instincts were correct, most of these documents were candidates for the Embargo Archive—a place where profane artifacts deleterious to Islamic sensibilities were stored and held back from public display.

CHAPTER 28

For this archaeological season, Reissen did not have to divide his staff. The Austrian could focus solely upon the Ptah Temple and its foundations, the relentless issue of ground water intrusion, and the maintenance of sump pumps. He smiled down along one exposed foundation trench and it felt good. *No booby traps here.*

That did not mean the Djedi site at Sakkara was closed—far from it. At first, Inspector Ali Hassan had questioned the need for any further work, but the archaeologist prevailed, arguing for a final opportunity to wrap up the site with a view on survey accuracy and completeness. Not mentioned was the pregnant issue of the Austrian mission's status regarding their publication rights of the Djedi tomb complex. That, apparently, was still very much mired in bureaucrat limbo.

While the rest of his mission was hard at work in Memphis, Reissen, Wald, and the survey team of Peters and Franks once again stood atop the Sakkaran plateau. Inspector Hassan had assigned them an onsite guard named Ibrahim, as the pressures of his inspectorship prevented his active participation. Reissen, however, thought otherwise. As for Ibrahim, Reissen knew him to be a quiet family man, with a fair disposition, so he purposely included him in the team's morning meeting.

"Today team, we begin by surveying and recording the walls of the so-called Golden Tomb. Why you say? Because we have to record where the gold foil was attached to the walls. That is our last task before our work at this site comes to a close."

Under Ibrahim's direction, the site's armed archaeological guard unlocked the burial shaft's grate, and turned on the power for the lift. At the heavy steel door at the entrance to the First Tomb, Ibrahim opened it using the key that he carried around this neck. Soon afterward the survey team was busy setting up the laser base station within the Golden Tomb. Reissen wanted them to record where on the three walls the beaten gold sheets had been attached with their wedged-shaped golden nails. During all of this industry, Ibrahim stood impassively at the entranceway.

Before the third hour ended, so had the team. The wall attachments had been added to the chamber's plot. At this result, Reissen called for a water break and shooed everyone and their equipment to the surface.

*   *   *

Reissen had arrayed his team at the entrance to the western descending ramp that led to the Djedi false door and biographical inscription. Water bottles were handed out.

"Team, everything that we have found with this tomb has involved ruse, deception, and misdirection."

Peters and Franks nodded in acknowledgement at the observation. Wald looked thoughtful, as if she was searching through an imaginary Rolodex in her mind. Ibrahim looked confused.

"Think about it. Djedi's father Imhotep and his mother Neferka were fabulously successful individuals in their own right. So where are all of their grave goods? What we found were scraps really.

The same goes for Djedi himself. What really have we found? One booby-trapped false coffin, his canopic jars, one chest of personal items, several walking sticks, a cedar wood model of a temple, his remains in a second coffin, and three chests filled with rolls of papyri. This paltry list we found from a contemporary of the Pharaoh Khufu, who reportedly entertained that king with several magical feats."

"What are you suggesting, Erik?" Wald asked.

"Nothing really. This is archaeology. It's a fickle science. The more you dig, the more questions are unearthed. And above all, it never can answer all the questions."

Having drained his water bottle, Reissen sighed, "Okay, everyone. Let's load up the truck. Our work here is complete. Back to Memphis."

CHAPTER 29

The next meeting of the enclave met in the starkly modern conference room of the society's headquarters. Light pastel walls, white Formica conference table, white plastic swivel chairs, and LED indirect lighting. They were there, because the one who occupied both the Senior and First Chairs wished it.

The twenty members seated before al-Razzuli universally wore hateful visages that ranged from barely concealed to outright sneers. He didn't care. What he saw were the old, doddering, and senile. His long term agenda included plans for their removal and replacement with the young, viral, and strong paranormals. Then, this enclave could compete on the world's stage, with the others that al-Razzuli had heard about. But not now, not with this wretched bunch of institution-bound fools.

"We meet today to honor our recent dead: Shaheen and Cornelius Rhodes. Dr. Fakry, it seems, has abandoned us. They will be missed." Al-Razzuli boldly lied. "We must find their replacements. Otherwise, this enclave is in danger of becoming extinct. Don't believe me? Look around and see for yourselves. So, I ask each of you, seek out worthy candidates.

"That is all I have to say. Meeting adjourned." And al-Razzuli got up and left the conference room.

The membership sat in mild shock at the coarse eulogy and harsh brevity of their gathering, coupled with a growing dissatisfaction of being dismissively ordered around by one so young, inexperienced, and brash.

None of the twenty made a move to leave as they glanced back and forth at one another. Call it what you will, they were not taking orders from al-Razzuli any more. In that silence, defiant opinions were expressed. Fully eighty percent of them were accomplished telepaths. The four that were not, made up that deficiency with their empathic skills. Within moments a decision was made. By agreement, the odds of twenty-to-one seemed reasonable, as current conditions were deemed intolerable.

Al-Razzuli, as he sat in the First Chair's office, was unaware of the impending storm. It started with a respectful knock at his door.

"Enter." He offhandedly said from behind his desk, while he concentrated on the screen of his smart phone.

The double oak doors opened wide. Filling the gap stood the enclave's membership arrayed three abreast. Their spokeswoman, a middle-aged Egyptian, who was fond of her lapis lazuli jewelry, emphatically stated aurally and with considerable psychic strength, "You! You who have usurped his enclave's leadership. You have a choice! Leave now or die."

Looking at the throng with a mixture of surprise and amusement, al-Razzuli chose poorly. He reached out with his mind, and in quick succession, mowed down the enclave's first nine, causing dramatic displays of gushing blood and bodily fluids. Their fallen, still twitching bodies clogged the doorway's entrance. The rank smell of death quickly followed.

However, the collective and determined psychic will of the remainder prevailed and took its toll, for among the first nine, eight had been mere empaths. Blood leaked from al-Razzuli's facial orifices. Still he fought on. Gripping the sides of his desk for support, he just managed to claim two more. Smiling at this success, he felt his heart unnaturally stop. Slapping his hands on his chest in a sad attempt at halting the pressure, he lost consciousness.

*　　*　　*

"What should we do with him?" A wheezing voice said. "He persists."

Exile in the Western Desert. Those who remained decreed.

"So be it."

And two of their number hauled off the limp form.

CHAPTER 30

Deep within the walls of Vatican City, down a stone labyrinthine corridor, and behind a heavy wooden door of an official of The Holy See, a frank meeting took place.

"I have reviewed your fitness assessment of Professor Dr. Erik Henrich Reissen. In many respects, it mirrors that submitted by Dr. Sheila Roth. Both of you see much promise in the man." The cleric remarked dressed in the red raiment of a Roman Catholic cardinal. "What I want to know, Sister Busby, is this. Will this man pledge his loyalty to Holy Mother Church?"

Sister Josephina chose her words carefully. "Dr. Reissen is a man of common sense, scientific rigor, and great humanity. When I told him of his paranormal abilities, he looked at me with haunted eyes. He'd suspected, but lacking any outright evidence, had dismissed it out-of-hand—that is until I mentioned it."

"Well said, Sister Josephina. But you didn't answer my question. Can he pledge himself to the Church?"

With a smile, "Cardinal Alberti, why don't *you* ask

him yourself? Or, Your Eminence, are you afraid to do so?"

With barely controlled rage the mercurial cardinal softly murmured, "Sister Busby, do I detect malice in your words?"

"No, Your Eminence. But Dr. Reissen is without question his own man, who holds his own counsel. I wouldn't dream of speaking for him. And frankly, Your Eminence, I am rather surprised that you thought me his emissary."

*   *   *

Sister Josephina stewed in her office at the Gregorian Museum about Reissen's screening interview. She knew for a fact that it had not gone well with the cardinal. But secretly, she didn't care. Cardinal Alberti was just another human resources bureaucrat who understood only square and round holes. Reissen was decidedly neither, and that made him ever so more refreshing and important to the future of The Holy See and in particular, Pro Deo. Heaven forbid that these organizations have a member of the laity in their midst, who possessed a creative, leadership capacity. While Sister Josephina knew that would never be allowed to happen, she could dream, couldn't she?

With that thought fresh in her mind, a knock on the door snapped the good sister back to the here and now.

"Entra." She automatically said without thinking.

A grinning face did—that of Sheila Roth. "How are you partner? Got a minute?"

"For you, always. What's on your mind? Hey! Wait a minute. What are you doing here? You're supposed to be in Egypt."

"I'm just back for the weekend."

"What?"

"Erik has us working back in Memphis, trying to find where the foundation deposits for the Ptah Temple are."

"Really. How's that working out?"

"Interesting, and far less stressful. No booby traps to contend with."

Sister Josephina smiled at that last tidbit. "You don't say."

"Yes," Sheila continued on breathlessly, "Reissen started the ball rolling by brazenly challenging us all to predict the deposit's location down to the meter."

"What are the stakes?"

"Ice cold Cokes." Sheila grinned.

"Did you find anything?"

"Not yet. But we're still digging." As Sheila shook her head in admiration or sheer hero worship, Sister Josephina couldn't tell which. "And that mad Austrian is making it all way too fun!"

CHAPTER 31

He awoke under a new moon in the deep desert. The Milky Way overhead flowed like a molten river of light. Stretched out on his back, al-Razzuli felt like a broken doll, and he was right. Sitting up with a loud groan, his right arm hung at his side, lifeless. The right side of his face mirrored his arm. His left hand idly brushed away a small tan scorpion from his trousers.

Did I suffer a stroke? The adept wondered. When he remembered the confrontation in his office, his suspicion gained traction.

Sitting up, he looked around and saw in the distance the orange glow of a major metropolis. Levering himself up, he managed to shuffle a few steps.

At least I can walk.

As he again took in the brilliant sky, he espied Orion, found its belt, and realized he must be somewhere southwest of Cairo, or at least he hoped so.

Al-Razzuli began his trek toward the orange glow of civilization. As he did, he purposely swung his right arm, hoping to revive it. The appendage remained a dull, silent thing. On he plodded.

Staggering ever forward, he sensed a low rise under his feet as the far horizon began to brighten. Atop the height, he recognized a distant jagged shape against the lightening skyline—the Stepped Pyramid of Sakkara. *I know where I am!* He gasped with relief. *My villa is not far. Just a short taxi ride away—and a hot shower. Then, I will wreck havoc on those treacherous old monsters!*

Another hour later, the adept stopped his shuffling progress west of the pyramid, while he stared into a breath-taking dawn. Ribbons of red and orange streamers of light reached up into the sky. In the distance to his right, a guard shack stood atop a crest. In hopes of finding water, the adept headed for it. Nearing it, something stirred within. Apparently, his scuffling feet had alerted its sleeping guard.

"Who's that?" a groggy voice challenged from the shadows.

"I am al-Razzuli. I am injured. Do you have any water?" The three simplistic, stilted, and slurred statements sounded odd even to the adept's ear. *More stroke damage?*

"What do you think I am wretched looking one—a hospital, a kiosk?" The belligerent voice spat. A rifle muzzle appeared. "Empty your pockets!"

His patience and anger rising, al-Razzuli reached out with his mind to chastise the miscreant and failed miserably.

Finally appearing from his shack, the skinny guard was more child than man. Al-Razzuli didn't move. The guard jabbed his muzzle aggressively in his direction saying, "Give me your money!" The adept remained a statue. The guard advanced within range, and al-Razzuli struck him with a vicious chop of his left hand's edge against the guard's throat.

Falling to his knees and unable to call for help, the adept kicked him, stomped him with his feet, and finally broke his neck with a sickening crunch. Ransacking the shack, al-Razzuli greedily drank the guard's two water bottles and wolfed down a half-eaten candy bar. Refreshed, he emerged, picked up the fallen weapon, checked its loaded status, and marched off feeling invincible toward the bus parking lot next to the pyramid. In the distance he could see that two were already parked there as were two taxis. A ragged smile of victory crossed his face.

As he did, a numb sensation flooded his right arm along with sharp, tingling, electrical pulses. He stopped and ordered his hand to make a fist, and it did, but the exercise was a painful one, causing him to shake off the reaction. *My arm is returning. Perhaps my face will as well.* He vainly hoped.

CHAPTER 32

Gohar clapped his hands together with childlike glee as the technician finished the installation in his office of the small glass hydration cabinet. About the size of a rectangular fish tank, here the papyrologist would begin the gentle process of unrolling papyri. Two axels with handles penetrated the tank to encourage the process. Once sufficiently relaxed, a papyrus would be draped across an acid-free paper backing. Once dried, it would then be permanently mounted between two panes of glass etched with its acquisition number and coordinates.

During this lengthy process, Gohar knew that he would have ample opportunity to examine a document's contents to access whether it should be permanently sequestered or not. Aiding the papyrologist in this content assessment was that most of the Djedi Papyri came with a wooden or ivory label attached to a colored strand of yarn or narrow strip of linen. Remarkably, the labels themselves greatly streamlined Gohar's decision making, allowing the papyrologist to set aside more than fifty rolls for the embargo archive. As for the rest, he would have to carefully unroll them one by one.

*   *   *

Reissen, who sat in Inspector Hassan's office, said, "My friend, it will take decades and an army of papyrologists for the Djedi Papyri to be conserved, read, and published. It will take an army of papyrologists to process them."

"I know."

"And there are more than one hundred and fifty rolls to examine. What a treasure!" the Egyptologist exclaimed.

"Indeed." Inspector Hassan said glumly, which the Austrian easily picked up on.

Facing the Egyptian, Reissen asked directly. "So why the sad face, Mr. Inspector? This is not a find unlike no other."

"Yes, Erik, it is." The man's shoulders sagged.

"So?"

"Within the Supreme Council, there are those who think that this tomb harbors far too many anomalies."

"Does that mean the Austrian archaeological mission will not be allowed to publish the site?"

"A very strong possibility, but I have been working hard to stop that. You and your team have worked too hard to lose such a wonderful opportunity!"

"Thank you, Ali. Your kind words are much appreciated."

*   *   *

Reissen stood atop one of the massive foundation stones of the Ptah Temple. Walking it off, the Austrian guessed its weight as nearly that of a train car and almost as big. With the coughing howl of several sump pumps running, he could see that the day was going to be a productive one in the trenches. That momentary reverie was dashed when someone on the Austrian archaeological mission let out a shout. "Dr. Reissen! Dr. Reissen! I think I found something!"

The archaeologist rushed over to a recently drained area that was under excavation. There an excited and muddy kneed graduate student named Johan pointed down.

"Look!"

Squatting down, Reissen did, and what he saw looked familiar—a fragment of red-fabric pottery with writing on it. Standing up, he said, "Good job, Johan. Now go and find Sheila. She needs to see this."

For whatever reason, the Austrian then turned away from the important find and walked over to a nearby foundation block. Feeling oddly dizzy, the Egyptologist sat down on it, with his hands on knees, and looked back at the trench.

*   *   *

Reissen's vision began with a flash of blinding, disorienting color and a jarring sense of cognitive dislocation. His perceptions seemed sharper—the sky bluer, the air cleaner, the sun's glare more intense. A high-flying hawk screeched overhead. He felt, somehow, younger.

The shallow archaeological trench crisscrossed with flags and survey cords had transformed into an oblong pit. In it nine bound men knelt shoulder-to-shoulder in a row. Their heads arched back in bleak resignation. Rivers of sweat coursed down their bruised faces. Somehow, the Egyptologist instinctively knew they represented Egypt's most hated enemies—the *pdtjw swt* or "peoples of the Nine Bows." By their appearance and clothing he easily identified the Libyan, Nubian, and Asiatic, who were painfully restrained by tying their elbows behind them, causing their ribcages to distend forward, making their breathing difficult. Kneeling did not help.

Behind each of the prisoners stood a bald and clean-shaven *sem*-priest wearing a heavily starched white kilt and sandals. Each held a length of rope. Around the rim of the pit stood sixty bare-footed, bald, and clean-shaven *wab*-priests in their white kilts. Each held out before them a smoking incense bowl that collectively clouded the area with a sweet-smelling fog.

Suddenly, a gap silently formed along the pit's rim that faced the prisoners. The high priest of the god Ptah had arrived. Also bare headed, he wore a white kilt, sandals, a leopard pelt over his shoulders, and was accompanied by a *was*-staff—his symbol of rank and authority.

All looked to the high priest, who with a single gesture of his staff, caused all nine to be strangled to death. Each of their attending *sem*-priests then produced a stone knife, which they used first to cut away the tongues of the sacrificial victims. They were not to speak in the underworld. Then the priests removed their heads, arms, and legs. The quick and clean precision of their dismemberment caused chills to run up and down Reissen's spine. *This clearly was not new to them. Their cuts are too practiced.*

The victim's severed heads were forced into the ground upside-down. In the afterlife, their lot was to forever eat garbage, feces, and worse. The priests flopped their torsos over atop the heads, after having cut away their penises and scrotums. These enemies were not allowed to procreate or have pleasure in the afterlife. Finally, the priests stacked like cord wood the remaining limbs over each victim creating nine horrific piles. Only then did they discard their ceremonial flint knives.

More clouds of incense billowed down into the pit from above and for good reason. The stench of death was intense. The *sem*-priests, now much bloodied, their white kilts stained an awful hue of red, left the pit to purify themselves.

The high priest handed his staff to his assistant, who passed back nine red figurines covered in red hieratic writing. With each figurine, the high priest tore off its head and threw the fragments into the pit. Finished, the high priest turned to retrieve his staff, but he paused, and turned back to look squarely into Reissen's eyes. He grimly nodded, as if to say, "It is done," and then left the edge of the pit. A curious thrill of near-recognition coursed through Reissen like an electrical charge. That face was so familiar. But try as he might, he just couldn't place it.

With the sixty once again formed up around the pit, all now hurled down into it red-fabric bowls covered with red hieratic writing, breaking them utterly. When they were finished, the entire bottom was littered with the broken crockery, which covered the sacrifices. Only then did the sixty turn away from the pit to make their way back to their temple quarters.

For whatever reason, at that moment Reissen looked down at himself and staggered. He saw a tanned chest and strong forearms, a broad gold neck pectoral of the Horus falcon with outstretched wings and talons, and a white kilt and sandals.

Mein Gott! I was there! I was one of them!

*   *   *

"Erik! Erik! Are you alright?" a panicked Sheila asked for the third time as she shook his shoulders. "You look white as a ghost. Johan, get some water. He looks dehydrated! And while you're at it, get Dr. Hampl, too." and off Johan ran.

As the archaeologist emerged from the vision, he shook violently, as if chilled. Then came his response, "Yesss, I, am, fine." He managed to stutter out. Just forming those words was difficult. It was like his mind's transmission was somehow stuck in the wrong gear.

"Erik, are you all right?" the historian persisted as she now knelt on one knee before him. What did you want me to see?"

CHAPTER 33

Al-Razzuli grossly miscalculated his overland route. Instead of taking him south of the Stepped Pyramid, he erroneously took a path that led him around to its northern side. Vexed with his poor topographical judgment and his still shaky legs, he cursed himself and grimly trudged on. But he now carried the guard's stolen AK-47 in his right hand, as that limb had fully returned to its master.

*   *   *

While al-Razzuli struggled on, Hassan and Reissen arrived early at the Djedi excavation. Both were elated with the final results.

"Erik, you and your archaeological mission deserve to publish this site, pure and simple. What an historical treasure-trove it has become!"

The Austrian just stood at the edge of the descending ramp with his head down. "And all because of an inquisitive and observant young boy, Ali. Omar found this site and told his father Habib about it. You cannot forget that."

"Yes, yes, that is true, but who is that?" the inspector said while pointing toward the open desert.

A lone figure, carrying a rifle, moved through the sand and gravel in their general direction. The Austrian squinted and couldn't place him. The Egyptian did as well, but then an ice cold chill ran down his spine.

"Erik, I recognize that face. He is an evil man."

"Evil?" the archaeologist said incredulously.

"Yes, I am certain of that fact."

As they watched, the stranger stopped, raised his rifle, and fired. That was all the Austrian needed to see. "Jump, Ali!"

*   *   *

While Reissen had done his stint as a young man in the Austrian military, never before had someone fired at him with live ammunition. As the nearby sand and bedrock exploded around him and the inspector, jumping for cover afforded by the descending ramp made a lot of sense. But that cover he knew would only be temporary, as whoever was shooting at them would slowly take it away the nearer they approached.

*   *   *

Al-Razzuli was fit to be tied. That weak-minded worm Hassan and someone else were blocking his escape to the bus parking lot. So the adept did what came natural, he fired a salvo at the pair. The recoil of the rifle, however, surprised him, sending the rounds wildly.

No matter. His deranged mind said. *As I get closer, I cannot miss.*

But then again to his surprise, his targets disappeared in the dawn's glare. *Where did they go?*

*   *   *

Hassan hid in the shadow of the descending ramp, hoping that the stranger who had fired his rifle at them would go away. Reissen did not share such a rosy prospect, and he didn't know why. Just that Hassan genuinely feared the man.

"Do you know who that is?" the Austrian whispered.

"No. Just that he is an evil man." The Egyptian answered.

"Ali, why is he evil?"

"I do not know. Just that he is very interested in this tomb."

"Why?"

"He's some sort of a magician. That's all I know."

And that was more than enough for Reissen.

"Okay, Ali, here's the plan. One of us has to run and get help. That means you. Meanwhile, I will distract this madman."

"I have to run?"

"Yes. It's our only chance. Now, get ready. I am going to boost you out of this trench. Then, you run for your life."

"Why don't you go for help?"

"Because I am not the Inspector of Antiquities for Sakkara.

"Now get ready.

"GO!" Reissen grunted as he lifted Hassan clean out of the trench. "Run Ali!"

*　　*　　*

At first, al-Razzuli didn't see Hassan's launch out of the shadow of the descending ramp as the sun shone squarely in his eyes. Only after the Egyptian had broke into a full run, did the adept see him. But even then, the significance of what he was seeing hadn't dawned on his foggy mind. *Who's running away?* His mind asked.

*　　*　　*

Why didn't he fire? Reissen wondered. Then he saw it. *He couldn't. The sun's glare was just too much.* Still hidden by the descending ramp's shadows, Reissen knew that while Hassan was in the clear, he was quickly running out of time.

Then, time ran out. A ragged and bloody figure of a man stood at the ramp's entrance, one hand shading his eyes, trying to make out if anyone lurked in its long shadows. Then, for whatever reason, he began firing wildly into the descending ramp area, barely missing the Austrian, but stitching most of his rounds across Djedi's biographical inscription, his tomb's false door, and curse.

Reissen tried to make himself as small as possible in the face of the hail of bullets. Behind him, the back wall of the grotto's limestone wall seemed to explode after round after round stitched across the delicately carved hieroglyphs and the seated image of the magician Djedi.

What happened next would haunt the Austrian for the rest of his life.

With eyes wide, the Egyptologist saw the man with the rifle plucked from his feet screaming like a madman and hurled bodily against the grotto's damaged back wall with the sickening crunch of broken bone. The gruesome sound reminded the archaeologist of sharply snapping tree branches. First came the plaintive and gurgling screams of pain from the ruined form, then the shrieks of sheer, unadulterated fear.

While lying against one of the descending passage's walls, Reissen blinked in confusion. He thought that he was imagining it. The walls of the descending passage shimmered. Then his perspective cleared. It was the decorative cobra carvings on the two walls that moved, repeatedly hissing, coiling, and striking out at the broken body against the grotto's back wall. With each cobra strike, the pitiful man's back arched grotesquely. His cries of agony pitched higher and higher.

It got worse.

A howl of abject horror echoed forth as hundreds of large black scorpions emerged from the grotto's bedrock floor. Moving as one, their legs and claws creating a chitinous clatter, they swarmed over him. With each sting, the man screamed on and on, which slowly faded into a begging whimper for mercy—a plea for it all to end.

Reissen's mind reached saturated overload. At what he witnessed and heard with his own eyes and ears, it threatened to shut down altogether. Placing his hands over his ears, and shutting his eyes that had seen far too much, the scorpions wriggled their back into the bedrock from which they came, leaving no trace.

But Djedi's curse was not finished.

A swirling, whirling tower of wind filled the grotto's space, bringing with it sand and gravel that pummeled and buried the fallen man, suffocating beneath its weight any final, muffled moans.

The wind died away.

An eerie stillness fell.

Reissen stared at the newly deposited layer of sand and realized he had witnessed Djedi's curse in action. Stretched out along the southern wall of the descending ramp, he trembled as chills of shock ran through his body. Even worse, the remembered image of the crawling grave robber with an outstretched arm, yearning to escape his fate, burned a dark hole in his mind.

But why hadn't they attack me? Reissen wondered. He looked down. Sheila's golden amulet lay visible on his chest. The Eye of Horus had protected him.

The Austrian didn't know how long he laid there, partially buried in the wind-blown sand. His next recollection was of Hassan, who found him, helped him to his feet, and brushed him off.

Next came a bombardment of questions from the local security force, questions that had no reasonable answers. Finally, the Austrian just pointed to the sand-filled floor of the grotto. "Over there you will find the man with the rifle, beneath the sand."

In the end, and throughout the chaos caused by yet another corpse at the site, Reissen managed somehow to right himself. He staggered away from the tomb toward the dig truck with a new-found respect for that which has no rational explanation. But one thing he couldn't walk away from—the ringing, renting screams of a tormented soul.

*   *   *

In the course of any sensitive investigation in and around the ancient monuments, the Supreme Council of

Antiquities requests restraint on the part of the Egyptian authorities. The monuments, considered rightly to be the nation's economic assets, must remain open to tourism. As a consequence, the removal of al-Razzuli's broken body was done swiftly and without fanfare. In close concert, Inspector Hassan took the initiative and had a wooden frame erected sheeted with clear near-bulletproof Lexan to protect the grotto's vandalized back wall.

However, these measures did not affect the medical coroner and its support staff from doing their jobs and asking questions—because they had many. To wit: how could an individual sustain such massive, multiple, compound skeletal injuries, like that of falling off a twenty story building, in the open desert? How could an individual receive so many bites and stings in such measles-like profusion?

Toxicology had a field day. The levels of cobra venom and black scorpion poison found in the individual would kill one hundred men twice over. How was that possible? More importantly, where were these vectors?

But in the end, Radiology and Records won the prize. Radiology discovered that the individual's x-rays and MRI scans consistently came up negative—as in there was no subject under examination. To their chagrin and frustration, only creased impressions could be detected on the white examination sheet. Records threw absolute fits as the shy remains refused to produce an image in either digital or film emulsion formats. In short, the record keepers could not do their jobs. Most certainly Records could not create a file on a dead man without an image.

To all of these curious observations the Supreme Council of Antiquities, through the mediation of Dr. Hamid Gohar, requested an embargo of the medical coroner's office findings and they readily got it.

CHAPTER 34

Before the day ended, Inspector Hassan brought the still shell-shocked Austrian the good news. The Austrian mission had been granted full publication rights on the Djedi tomb. Only several exclusions were necessary and Dr. Gohar would gladly provide further clarification on those. This long overdue news Reissen took with uncommon sobriety, verging on exhaustion.

"Well, my friend," he dully remarked to the inspector, "it looks like I will indeed have to put together a team of papyrologists."

*   *   *

Once a positive identification of the brutalized body was made at the Djedi tomb, The Holy See's contact within the Egyptian archaeological police passed on all the man's particulars. Rather quickly, the organization found the automotive registrations for two brand new Mercedes that had been imported from a dealership in Geneva. That led to the owner's address located outside of Heliopolis. At that point an investigative team sprang into action

Sister Josephina Busby, wearing a black one-piece jump suit and matching sneakers, joined an assault team of five to al-Razzuli's four-acre villa. Her paranormal senses and in-depth knowledge of all things magical made her presence vital.

A white-washed three meter concrete wall enclosed the property. Its upper level was generously covered with a layer of concrete into which jagged and broken glass had been imbedded. Noting this, Sister Busby placed her hand against one of its gate sections and felt nothing threatening. Nodding to proceed, one of her colleagues quickly defeated the gate's lock and swung it wide. They drove through, closed the gate behind them, and proceeded up the circular drive. They parked their borrowed telephone service van so that it blocked any view of the villa's entrance from the gate.

The white-washed villa was built around a central courtyard with tall and heavily laden date palms that spread their canopies wide over the villa's roof, providing some protection from the heat of the sun.

Again Sister Busby felt around the exterior of the villa's double-doored entry. She frowned. Nothing seemed amiss.

"Open the door," she crisply ordered.

They cautiously entered, each with a silenced weapon loaded with hollow-pointed sub-sonic rounds. Sister Busby had her favorite 9mm in her right hand and carried a large leather satchel over her left shoulder.

The sweep of the house revealed much about its owner. Immaculately appointed in marbles and granites, ultra-modern décor, squeaky clean, and dust free, it was the sterile domain of an obsessive male personality. One room, however, attracted Sister Busby.

She still didn't feel any magical threats, but just to make sure, she said to her colleagues, "Okay guys, I want you to steer clear of this room. Understood?"

"Loud and clear." The lead replied.

Standing at the office's threshold, Sister Busby peered in and saw that it was surrounded on all four sides by bookshelves filled with Egyptological titles and paranormal classics. Still, sensing no magical wards, she dared to step in. In its middle, a broad wooden desk stood. Atop it, at its precise center, sat a delicate cedar wood model of an Egyptian temple—the very same one that Sister Busby had seen among the Wald photographs taken in the tomb. Also on the desk lay two papyrus rolls, one bound with blue yarn, the other red. Next to them a marvelous golden amulet of the Eye of Horus was carelessly dropped, its lapis lazuli beads lay in a jumble.

Circling the desk, Sister Busby took in the cedar model's beauty and proportion, but stopped herself from coming into direct contact with the desk and its displayed items.

Decision time!

Putting down her satchel, cautiously, she reached

out with her left hand and finally detected a faint tingling. But it was not from the desk, but rather from the artifacts themselves.

"Interesting," she murmured.

Holstering the sidearm under her left armpit, Sister Busby picked up the cedar container, quickly examined its exterior, bent down, and placed it within her large leather shoulder bag. Into one of its many pockets went the amulet, and into two tubes, the papyri.

Zipping up the satchel while exiting the office, she told the security lead, "Time to go."

"How'd we do?" He asked.

"Got the whole enchilada."

*   *   *

Next on Sister Busby's agenda was a frank visit with Dr. Hamid Gohar. She knew that his office was buried within the administrative section of the Grand Egyptian Museum. While the man did not know it, his day was about to change.

Having changed vehicles and her clothing back into her habit, Sister Busby was dropped off at the staff entrance unarmed and only with a large satchel over her shoulder. Presenting her ID at the checkpoint and telling the security guard of her destination, the satchel went through an x-ray machine and she a magnetometer. When questions were posed about the contents of the leather bag, the fingers of Sister Busby's left hand worked several complex motions.

"I am very sorry, sir," she said in Arabic, "but the contents of this leather bag are for Dr. Gohar's eyes only."

The guard grunted and waved her through. With that sleight of hand complete, on she went through the labyrinth in search of Gohar's office, using her innate feel, and moments later stood before a pleasant woman who was clearly his secretary.

"Good morning," she said pleasantly in English.

Startled by the sudden intrusion seemingly from nowhere, the woman said, "May I assist you?"

"Yes, please, I wish to visit with Dr. Gohar. I have some artifacts for him." Again her left hand worked. "My name is Dr. Busby. I am from the Vatican."

At the word "Vatican" the secretary's eyes widened as she lifted her phone and spoke briefly. "He will be right out, Dr. Bussy. Please take a seat."

"Thank you, very much," the nun gleamed back while ignoring the mispronunciation of her name. As Sister Josephina sat down, she knew the game—the more important the bureaucrat, the longer the wait. But to her complete surprise, the wait lasted maybe thirty seconds, before a short, but fit Egyptian greeted her.

"Please," Gohar said, "come into my office. I apologize for its crampedness. I do not often have visitors."

Now seated, "And for that matter, I am not often visited by a representative from the Vatican. May I ask, who are you?"

"My name is Dr. Josephina Busby. I am an Egyptologist and my specialty is ancient Egyptian religion and magic."

"I see, and my secretary said that you have something for me."

"Indeed I do, Dr. Gohar." Glancing about, "Is there an appropriate surface to make my presentation?"

"Certainly." Gohar said as he stood, rearranged his desk, and laid across it a fine padded linen that he had removed from a drawer. "Will that do?"

"Yes, indeed." Sister Josephina opened the satchel at her feet, put on a pair of muslin gloves, and removed the golden amulet, laying it out before the antiquities official.

"A most handsome artifact. But why are you showing me this?"

"Because, Dr. Gohar, it is only part of a magical package, a magician's kit." Reaching down once again, Sister Josephina produced the two papyri and removed their protective tubes.

"Dr. Gohar, these papyri, one with red yarn, the other with blue, each contain a powerful magical spell. To protect the magician, he or she must wear this amulet."

"How do you know this?"

"I read the papyri. This subject is my specialty."

"I see."

"No, sir, you do not. These papyri have claimed the lives of several Egyptians, including one of your own antiquity officials. His name was Inspector Kama."

This brought a gasp from Gohar.

Sister Josephina, then reached over into her bag of tricks one last time and presented to Gohar the cedar temple model.

The man stood gaping at the artifact. "The lost artifact from the Djedi excavation. Where did you find it?"

Sister Josephina also stood, but then picked up the cedar box, turned it over, and opened its hidden recess. "Dr. Gohar, where I found it is not important. But allow me, sir, to make a suggestion." The nun said as she placed within it the golden amulet and two papyrus rolls. Resealing it, she placed it before him and looked the man directly in the eye. "Dr. Gohar, I strongly suggest that you sequester this magical kit. It has the potential to claim far too many lives."

Gohar blinked and returned to his chair. "Dr. Busby, may I offer you some mint tea?"

Busby, now also sitting, "That would be lovely."

Leaning forward on his elbows the bureaucrat made a telephone call. Finished, he said with a little smile, "Dr. Busby, I do believe we have much in common, and much to discuss."

*   *   *

Sister Josephina's last stop for the day was at the Austrian mission's excavation house in Memphis. She wanted to find its director. After several dead ends, the nun found Reissen sitting in the cool shade of a tarp sorting through a pile of red-fabric pottery fragments. It was a perfectly useful, yet mindless task. She saw that he had just made a join. His face looked serene and intent at the accomplishment.

"Penny for your thoughts." The sister intruded.

"Ah. It's you. I half-expected you'd show up."

"Why?"

"Because you need me to make a decision."

"And?"

Reissen stopped what he was doing, placed the two matching sherds aside, and looked deeply into her eyes. "Josephina, just the other day, in a vision, I saw nine men brutally sacrificed to fill a foundation deposit that only today we are excavating." He said pointing. "The details of the two realities match perfectly."

"What!"

"Yes, my magically-inclined friend, I witnessed the performance of a state-sponsored magical ritual of the darkest kind, all to ensure the security of this temple's precinct." He casually waved about him. "Never before did I believe that such magical clap-trap had meaning beyond pure intimidation. But now I know better."

"How do you know, Erik?" the very frightened nun whispered.

"Because the just other day I saw a man die horribly from dark magic. Have you ever seen something like that sister?"

A negative shake of the head.

"Well, take it from me; the experience truly is the stuff of pure nightmares." Then, "Dark magic truly exists, Josephina." Reissen quietly concluded while tapping his forefinger on the table next to a red pottery fragment inscribed with a curse text.

"And there is more. Sheila last year gave me this to wear." Unbuttoning his shirt, Reissen displayed the golden Eye of Horus around his neck. "And I am convinced that this amulet protected me from that man's fate. So, Josephina, is Sheila a witch?"

A curt nod.

"I thought so."

"Have you thanked her?" the nun countered.

"Not yet."

"Can you tell me about your experience, Erik?"

"I do not want to, but I have to somehow get it off my chest in order to get past it. I have to share it with someone who would understand. That person is you, Josephina. The curse that Djedi inscribed on his tomb is all too real. That man's death proved to me beyond a shadow of a doubt that there are things that should never be known. Dangerous things."

Reissen paused and let his head droop.

"And now there is this foundation deposit. It dwarfs the Mirgissa deposit in all respects. This one," Reissen indicated with a thumb point over his shoulder, "contains not one, but nine dismembered human beings, who were brutally sacrificed. The target focus of the spell was the Nine Bows."

Josephina's hands went to her face in shock and recognition. Next, she reached out and gripped the archaeologist's hands. "Erik, you will get past this. You're strong. Can I help you in any way?" her eyes pleaded.

"Thank you, Josephina. But I prefer to see this through on my own."

"Erik. Have you ever experienced this vision thing ever before?"

After a thoughtful moment, "Yes, yes, I have Josephina. I was a small boy. I used to look for flint tools in the fields and hills around my village in Austria. One day I came across a rude stone circle of what must have been a hut of some kind. In its center was this smoothed stone surrounded by hundreds of stone flakes. Just like the other day, I got really dizzy and so I sat down on one of the foundation stones and faced the central rock. When I looked up, this time it was occupied by a brut of a man, dressed in animal skins. His long and stringy gray hair hung down around a wrinkled and scared face. Across his lap lay a thick animal hide, which protected his legs while he knapped away at the shiny black stone in his hands. I especially remember his heavily callused fingers with tips covered with many white micro-scars. As he worked, he grunted. Then, with a broad smile of satisfaction that lit up his sparkling green eyes, he showed me this perfect black obsidian arrow point, about so long." The Austrian held up his hand with his thumb and forefinger about two inches apart. "Then he said to me, 'take,' and I did. But when I did, I looked down and saw that I too was clothed in animal skins, my feet wrapped warmly as well. Only my heavily tanned forearms were uncovered. Then, a squawking crow roused me from that trance-like stupor. It was sitting on the same smoothed rock that the flint knapper had occupied."

"A black crow you say?" the nun said.

"Yes. A black crow."

"Erik, did you ever share this experience with your parents?"

"No, no I did not. My father and mother held very strong feelings about things that could not be proven."

"Erik, did you know that the Vatican interviewed both of your parents prior to your studies at the Pontifical College?"

"What!"

"Yes, they were indeed interviewed. They both ranked quite high in several paranormal quotients."

"You have to be kidding."

"No, Erik. I am not. In fact their staunch materialism was their practiced camouflage from being detected."

"Detected as what!"

"Extreme paranormal sensitives. Your father was the local veterinarian, was he not?"

A head nod.

"Your mother was a school teacher, yes?"

Another head nod.

"For children with disabilities."

"Yes. Where are you going with all of this, sister?"

"Erik. Your loving parents, bless their memory, were extremely good at what they did because of their hidden skills. Just like you are with archaeology. And with the proper training, and practice, you will be able to turn on and off your hidden skills like a water faucet."

Reissen furrowed his brow in thought. "Has anything ever happened to you like this?"

A wane smile wavered back. "Oh my yes, Erik. Many times. And each one was unforgettable. I will take their every detail to the grave. That is why I am a member of The Holy See and Pro Deo, both to cope, and to make sure that 'dangerous things' do not see the light of day."

"I thought so." The archaeologist sighed. "Josephina, you have such a good soul.

"But to your question, I am not ready, not yet. Not

that I am turning you down. Just that I need more time. I need to heal."

"I understand, Erik. I truly do."

*   *   *

"So how goes the recruitment of Dr. Reissen?" Cardinal Alberti asked.

"Slowly. He is currently dealing with a traumatizing flashback and a grade five event." Sister Josephina reported.

"You have got to be kidding!"

"No, Your Eminence, I am not. Remarkably, he is dealing with these events on his own terms, and without the benefit of any support. All he requested of me was more time. That alone tells me that he is still considering our offer."

"But we want him here in Rome, now!" the cardinal emphasized with the thump of his fist on his chair's armrest.

"Cardinal Alberti. Are you sure your organization wants him? Or, is it more a matter of needing him? I can tell you this. Reissen is his own man. And neither you nor I can change that. His latent paranormal abilities have just begun to surface. So the real question is: once he joins, *if* he joins, can you work with him?"

"Sister Josephina, you well know that is *not* how it works around here." The cardinal puffed.

"Your Eminence, respectfully, perhaps it should."

*　　*　　*

"Sheila, may I have a moment of your time?" the archaeologist asked during the traditional celebratory dinner at the end of the archaeological season.

"What's on your mind, Erik?"

"That special gift you gave me several year's back. It worked. And, I wish to thank you for it."

"Gift?" Sheila said with a scrunched up nose.

"This." Reissen said as he pulled out the golden Eye of Horus from around his neck.

"Oh that! Sister Josephina gave it to me to pass on."

"Oh she did, did she?" The archaeologist slitted his eyes.

"Yeah, we were discussing the tomb, the curse, and everything else, and she came up with that. I've got one too!" Showing off hers. "You never can be prepared enough in this business."

"And what business is that, Sheila?"

Now blushing, "All this paranormal stuff. It's everywhere really, if you know where to look for it."

"I see. Well, Sheila, thank you again. You made me a believer."

CHAPTER 35

The remaining membership of the beaten and battered enclave met for a catered lunch as none of them had any concerns about sunlight. This monthly meeting started on a high note. The new First Chair, Marsha Ledbetter, thought it a grand idea to redecorate the conference room in warm rich woods, billowy cushioned chairs, earth tones, and green plants. The heady scents of lotus and papyrus filled the room, and for that matter, the entire floor. Words like "renewal" and "rebirth" and "self-determination" were bandied about. The membership caught themselves actually smiling and luxuriating in the comfortable surroundings.

"Welcome everyone. Be at ease. It is so good to see you all," the First Chair began. "We have been through a lot recently. We have lost too many souls that were near and dear to us. But they will continue to live on in our memories." Ledbetter then turned to her right and said, "Second Chair, do you have anything to report?"

Ahmed Obadi bowed his balding head slightly in

respectful acknowledgment. His large almond-shaped eyes smiled and long black lashes fluttered. "No, Madam First Chair, we have no anniversaries this month. But next month Dr. Gohar will be celebrating his." He grinned at the man seated at the end of the table.

"Thank you, Second Chair. We all will be looking forward to see what Hamid has up his sleeve for next month's meeting. Speaking of which, Senior Chair, do you have anything to share?"

"Thank you, Madam First Chair," Dr. Gohar began from his seat opposite, "In fact I have much good news to share. First off, seated to my right, we have a guest, Dr. Josephina Busby, from the Vatican. She is both a member of the Roman Catholic clergy and a PhD in Egyptology. I wish to nominate her for consideration to join our humble society. My reasons for doing so will become evident shortly.

Gohar sighed deeply and continued.

"Second, I wish to report that the excavation of the magician Djedi's tomb has successfully come to an end. The Austrian archaeological mission, under the direction of Professor Dr. Erik Reissen, has done a fine job in spite of several considerable obstacles. Bottom line: the many sensitive magical papyri that were recovered have been secured and will not be made known to the public. Our society and the Hidden Folk can now breathe easy."

Gohar coughed into his fist.

"Third, I can report that a former member of our society, a most hateful one who will remain nameless, has succumbed to the dark magic of one of our ancestors—the magician Djedi. Unfortunately, this event was witnessed by Dr. Reissen, the director of the Djedi excavation. I have been assured, however, that Dr. Reissen's new-found knowledge of the existence of practical magic will not spread.

"Finally, I can also report that the missing Djedi artifact has been found and returned to the Grand Egyptian Museum, where it currently resides in the Embargo Archive. This beautifully carved cedar object and its extremely dangerous magical contents were recovered and delivered to me, personally, by Dr. Busby." He indicated with a slight bow.

This revelation caused wide eyes all around the table.

"As a consequence, I am championing Dr. Busby's membership into our society for several reasons. She is an accredited Egyptologist, who specializes in ancient religion and magic, and is employed by the prestigious Gregorian Museum in Vatican City. Further, Dr. Busby is an accomplished paranormal. Additionally, she is a member of the Holy See, the Vatican's primary diplomatic organization. For these reasons, I support Dr. Busby's candidacy."

"Thank you, Senior Chair, for that full report."

Ledbetter then turned to the guest. "Dr. Busby. You have been nominated by none other than the Senior Chair of this society. That, in case you do not know, is quite an endorsement. But before our membership votes on your candidacy, do you have anything that you wish to share with us?"

Sister Josephina shifted in her seat. "Thank you, First Chair, and thank you, Dr. Gohar, for inviting me to visit your society." Busby paused to glance down at her folded and nervously clammy hands.

"Dear members, I am flattered to be considered for membership by your society. There are clear and obvious advantages for someone with my background and abilities to become a member and colleague of your society. It would be quite a feather in my cap. But the biggest advantage is what I can offer *you*. I have been authorized by my superiors to extend a formal offer of *bona fides* between your society and the Vatican."

This caused some stirring, glancing about, and worried looks. Seeing this, the nun shifted into informational lecture mode.

"Such a 'good faith' offer has no limitations or contingencies attached to it. Rather, it is merely a formal document between two parties that establishes diplomatic recognition within a climate of 'good faith'. In many cases, the grant of *bona fides* in diplomatic terms is the first step toward the recognition of a nation's sovereignty."

At finishing her pitch, Busby felt trapped under the steady and piercing gazes of so many paranormals. Remarkably, no one had made an attempt at reading her mind, and that in and of itself spoke volumes.

The First Chair broke the lengthening silence. "Well, Dr. Busby, for one, I'm floored by the Vatican's offer. I'm curious, however, why would the Vatican even want to recognize us? What could they possibly gain from such an arrangement?"

It was a good question and the nun had to think about how to best frame her response. "First Chair, it all comes down to this simple fact. You can never have too many friends. A good example of having friends was our recovery of the missing Djedi artifact. The Vatican suspected that it was exceptionally dangerous. Your society knew it was. We returned it to where we thought it best belonged."

"Are you telling us that the Vatican does not have or collect such dangerous objects?"

"No. I did not say that at all. The Vatican Library alone has its own archive of embargoed manuscripts. The Vatican Museum the same. But the Vatican cannot police the entire planet. It depends upon knowledgeable friends who know right from wrong. In this particular case, an object was stolen from an active excavation, sold on the black market, and then used inappropriately. Our recovery of the artifact and its return to its rightful owners is just good business."

"Most interesting," the First Chair murmured. "However, this good faith offer with the Vatican I am going to table for further thought and discussion. In my mind it represents a very big step for this society, perhaps even a ready avenue for new members. But for now, Dr. Busby, kindly inform your superiors that we need some time to mull it over."

"Fair enough," the nun said.

"Now, as for your membership in this society, does anyone have any questions for Dr. Busby?"

Silence, then the Second Chair asked. "Dr. Busby, Dr. Gohar mentioned that you are a paranormal. May I ask what kind?"

Smiling her best and leaning into the table, the nun said, "A most reasonable question, Second Chair. I can see and understand auras and what affects them. I am a telepath, empath, and sensitive. And, I am a white witch, by *which* I mean, I practice benign magic."

"Thank you, Dr. Busby." The Second Chair smiled. "But I am curious, isn't the practice of witchcraft of any kind against the vows of your order?"

"That's an interesting philosophical and doctrinal question. But to date, what I do and how I do it has not been challenged by Holy Mother Church. Second Chair, contrary to common opinion, the Vatican's thinking on such issues is not mired in some medieval mindset. In fact, you might be shocked at what we openly discuss."

"Such as?" The Second Chair pushed.

"Once your society enters into a *bona fides* relationship with the Vatican, that specific question can be answered. In fact, I and several others actually teach introductory and advanced classes in thaumaturgy, metaphysics, demonology, and the like."

"Are there any other questions for Dr. Busby?" The First Chair asked.

"Hearing none, can I have a show of hands in support of Dr. Busby's candidacy?"

Gohar raised his hand first, and, after a few moments, the vote tallied was unanimous.

"Well then, Dr. Busby." The First Chair beamed. "Congratulations on becoming our newest member!"

CHAPTER 36

By early October Reissen had finished and sent to the publisher his portion of the Djedi excavation publication. Volume one contained an introduction to the Djedi archaeological site, its topographical mapping and survey work performed by Peters and Franks, critical transcriptions, commentary, and translations of the inscriptions, and the position papers of Busby and Roth. Throughout, the clarity of Wald's imagery made the tome come alive. As for the papyri found, fully three-fifths had been embargoed by Dr. Gohar. Even so, that left a decade's work ahead for the team of three papyrologists that Reissen had gathered. As of now, the Austrian set aside sufficient budget for six more volumes, all to be devoted to the papyri.

At the same time, Reissen had handed off his directorship to his departmental colleague, Dr. Gretchen Gunner, who would continue the Temple of Ptah foundation survey. As for himself, he had completed his description and analysis of the grisly sacrificial foundation deposit. Again Wald's imagery played a key role in that dramatic description.

With his immediate responsibilities put to bed, Reissen felt antsy. He needed a new project. Perhaps even a change of venue. He finally admitted to himself that he had put off the Vatican for too long.

In the end, his faithful bright red Fiat Abarth beckoned. Impulsively, Reissen packed a light bag and drove south on the Autobahn through Graz and stayed the night in the dragon-town of Klagenfurt. Just driving through the heavily forested mountains did wonders for Reissen's peace of mind. A heavy foot cleared the carbon from his sports car's motor. His projects behind him, the archaeologist found himself thinking ahead, about what might be.

After spending the night in a convenient hotel, Reissen rose early and made good time as he passed by Venice and Bologna before reaching Florence by mid-afternoon. Because of all the highway construction in and around that City of Lilies, Reissen spent the late afternoon strolling through the streets in search of a satisfying meal and a hotel. Again rising early, the Egyptologist got a quick start on his last leg to Rome—the Eternal City of eternal traffic jams.

*　　*　　*

"Ciao?"

"Suor Giuseppina Busby, per favore." Reissen said into his device.

"Is that you, Erik?" Sister Josephina radiated as she recognized the voice on the other end of the line.

"Yes, it is. Might I stop by around two?"

"You're in Rome!"

"Yes."

"Absolutely! I'll inform security so that you can come directly to my office. See you soon! What a pleasant surprise!"

As soon as Sister Josephina hung up, she called Cardinal Alberti's office.

"Hello, this is Dr. Busby, is His Eminence available?"

"One moment, please." His personal secretary said as the line broke and then began to incessantly buzz.

"Yes, Dr. Busby?" Cardinal Alberti queried.

"Your Eminence, Dr. Reissen is in Rome and will be visiting me at two this afternoon."

"Hmm. That sounds promising. What do you think?"

"I am not sure, Your Eminence. He didn't drive here without a purpose. That's just not Reissen."

"In that case, give me a call if he wishes to speak with me. I will make it a point to be available for the next several hours."

"Thank you, Your Eminence."

*   *   *

The *Musei Vaticani*, or Vatican Museums, is a complex of collections devoted to the world's art and culture. The Gregorian Egyptian Museum housed a top-notch Egyptian collection in addition to other Near Eastern, Assyrian, and Greco-Roman pieces.

Within its highly polished gray granite façade and columns, Sister Josephina waited on pins and needles for her surprise guest to appear. While she had recruited many others in her time, Reissen was complicated. First and foremost, he was a good friend, a brilliant archaeologist capable of making shockingly preternatural decisions, and extremely stubborn when he thought he was in the right. In her mind, all good things.

Still and all, when the knock came on her door, Sister Josephina's heart stuck in her throat. The clock said precisely two o'clock. She stood up from behind her desk and said, *"Entrare."*

Grinning from ear to ear, Reissen did so and filled the sparse office with his energy. Few times before in Sister Josephina's memory had she witnessed such vibrancy. In an unconscious act, she embraced her good friend and actually felt what she had seen—a bright cobalt blue aura.

"Please, Erik, sit. It is so good to see you. You look so healthy, fit, and rested."

"Yes, I do feel good. The drive down really helped. It gave me the time to sort things out."

"You drove from Vienna!"

"Yes. I blame the Fiat. It called to me."

An astonished looked covered the nun's face. *He's ready to commit. I can tell.*

"So, Erik, have you made a decision?"

"Yes I have. I am very interested, but of course, I have some questions as well."

"I see." The nun said, "So do I." She paused. "Erik, would you have any qualms about working with me, as your superior, on a team of specialists?"

"Absolutely not." Came the quick reply.

"That's good. I was hoping that our friendship would not get in the way. By the way, would you like to speak with Cardinal Alberti? He's our human resources manager, so to speak."

"Yes, that would be useful."

Sister Josephina raised her forefinger, reached for the phone, and dialed. After a brief conversation she said, "His Eminence will see you in ten minutes. I will take you to him. Go easy on the man, he's of the clergy." She grinned.

Reissen laughed a relax chuckle that was another tell to the nun of his settled composure, so very different from when she had found him sorting the execration pottery in Memphis.

"So, Erik, we have about five minutes to kill. Tell me of your recent exploits."

*   *   *

The Vatican took nothing for granted as Cardinal Alberti flipped through the thick dossier of one Professor Dr. Erik Gerhard Reissen. Born in a small mountain village of Steinegg, Austria, to Roman Catholic parents with professional occupations, Reissen consistently shined bright through his gymnasium and university days. His graduate work within the Pontifical College had been calculated as one of his professor's had specifically recommended him. Once in Rome, Reissen's academic performance had been deemed very satisfactory as was the Austrian's ability to integrate within the permanent faculty and staff. In short, he held extreme promise and was well liked.

He heard a firm and confident knock on his office door.

"Entrare." The cardinal automatically responded while he closed the man's dossier and pushed it aside.

First impressions were important to Alberti as they communicated so very much. The cardinal, a powerful sensitive, relished such moments, like tasting a new gelato creation. Still, the confident cleric was not quite prepared for Reissen. Upon seeing the man, tall, tan, fit, with shock black hair, and smiling, his psychic presence had hit the sensitive like a ten meter tall tsunami wave, staggering him briefly. Greeting the man, taking both of his hands, Alberti managed to successfully hide his thoughts—but just barely. *Such raw potential*, rang in his mind like the peal of a church bell.

"Please sit, Professor Dr. Reissen. It is indeed a pleasure to finally meet you. Sister Busby has spoken very highly of you."

"Thank you, Your Eminence. How do we begin the process?"

So surprisingly direct. So all business, Alberti thought.

Placing his hand on the thick dossier to his right, Alberti asked, "Professor, are you still a practicing Catholic?"

"No, Your Eminence."

"May I ask why?"

"Certainly. There are many things in this world that the Roman Church does not openly recognize. While I fully understand the reasoning behind that position now, as a young man that wisdom was not made clear."

Direct indeed. Time for business.

"I see professor." Alberti warmed as he leaned into his desk. "Holy Mother Church has many audiences, each of which is capable of coping with only so many pieces of dogma. The finer points are for the few to discuss. However, that which exists *beyond* dogma exists regardless of the teachings of Holy Mother Church. We must deal with such *external* thoughts and deeds with understanding and all due care. This is why Pro Deo was formed in the first place."

"During the Second World War." Reissen interjected, proving to Alberti that the man had done his homework.

"Yes, and no professor. Pro Deo, the organization given that name, was indeed convened during that troubled period and thereafter publically disbanded. Today, it nonetheless persists. However, the organization's origin and mandate can be traced to a time far earlier."

"How can I contribute, Your Eminence."

He wishes to 'contribute.' How refreshing.

"Professor Dr. Reissen, this rather thick file to my right is yours." The cardinal indicated with a tip of his head. "We know who you are. We only suspect what you can become. An individual like yourself will require a certain amount of basic training, which will require practice."

The cardinal paused to take a sip from a water bottle, not because he was thirsty, but to allow his words to settle in. His guest remained mute, attentive.

"As for your contribution, you possess many valuable tools, Professor Dr. Reissen, and we would welcome your presence." The cardinal pitched with open hands.

"Being welcome is one thing, Your Eminence, but I need to know why I should leave my academic post in Vienna. While I am prepared to do so, vague words like 'beyond' and 'external' require clarity."

Direct, and pushy too.

"Professor Dr. Reissen, you would first be trained to join a team who specifically investigates suspected paranormal objects and locations. That is all the specificity that I can offer you at this time."

Reissen nodded. "That is most reasonable, Your Eminence. Where would I be domiciled?"

"Here, in Rome."

"Again, most logical. Would I have an office? An opportunity to undertake research?"

"Indeed, professor, on both counts. However, your future publications' record would be pared back. Much of your research, while requiring a written report, would involve embargoed subjects."

"So, to summarize, you need Indiana Jones."

Frowning at the reference before the light bulb went off, the cardinal finally answered, "Yes and no, professor. I do not think you will need either a whip or fedora, but we do need an archaeologist with an extraordinary sixth sense, which you, sir, have."

"One final question before I sign my life away, Your Eminence". How will I be compensated?"

Again with that direct approach.

"Offhand, I would say extremely well. Direct pay will be double that of your current university post, with the usual benefits, plus a flat in Rome. A parking place for your red Fiat you will have to arrange for." The cardinal finished with a pointed finger.

"When do I begin, Your Eminence?"

"For all practical purposes, you have already have done so, Professor Dr. Reissen. Welcome to the Vatican."

Epilogue

The tale of Djedi the magician appears only in the *Westcar Papyrus*, or *P. Berlin* 3033,[1] a narrative that scholars variously date to between the eighteenth and sixteenth centuries BC.[2] Its content, however, refers back to events during the Fourth Dynasty, a span of some seven centuries. This fact is significant, because it suggests that the magician Djedi's story was well known to the Egyptians,[3] like the frayed page corners of a favorite book.

The *Westcar Papyrus* recounts the many wonders brought before King Khufu (builder of the Great Pyramid) for his amusement. While no archaeological or historical evidence can attest that Djedi ever lived, the magician nonetheless continues to fascinate historians and Egyptologists. As you will see in this abbreviated translation,[4] Djedi was an extremely

---

[1] Verena M. Lepper, *Untersuchungen zu pWestcar. Eine philologische und literaturwissenschaftliche (Neu-)Analyse.* In *Ägyptologische Abhandlungen*, Band 70. Harrassowitz, Wiesbaden 2008, pp. 41–47, 103 & 308–310.

[2] M. Lichtheim, *Ancient Egyptian Literature. A Book of Readings. The Old and Middle Kingdoms*, vol.1, University of California Press 1973, p.215.

[3] Lepper, *pWestcar*, pp. 15–17 and Lichtheim, *Ancient Egyptian Literature*, vol. 1, pp. 215 – 220.

uncommon commoner. His name, incidentally, means "He who endures," an appropriate moniker for someone who reportedly lived one hundred and ten years.

To set the stage, Prince Djedefhor, a son of King Khufu, tells his father about the man.

> There is a commoner named Djedi, living in Djed-Sneferu. He is a simple man, but 110 years old, who eats 500 loaves of bread, a shoulder of beef, and drinks 100 jars of beer every day. He is capable of resurrecting decapitated beings. He also is said to be able to make wild lions so obedient that the animal would follow him with its leash dragging on the ground. In addition, this Djedi has secret knowledge about the sanctuary of Thoth.

Needless to say, his son **Djedefhor's narration intrigued** King Khufu, who orders his son to bring Djedi to the palace. This he does by enticing the old man with delicacies. Standing before the king, Khufu then grills Djedi with many questions.

> The pharaoh asks: "Is it true that you could mend a severed head?"
>
> Djedi says: "Yes, oh sovereign, my lord. May you live, be blessed, and prosperous. I know how to do that."

---

[4] Adapted from William K. Simpson, ed., *The Literature of Ancient Egypt: An Anthology of Stories, Instructions, and Poetry*. Translations by R.O. Faulkner, Edward F. Wente, Jr., and William K. Simpson. New Haven and London: Yale University Press, 1972 and Lictheim, *Ancient Egyptian Literature*, pp. 215-220.

Khufu orders: "Have a prisoner, who is jailed, be brought before me, so that his execution may be enforced."

Djedi refuses: "Do not make a human suffer, oh sovereign, my lord! May you live, be blessed, and prosperous. You see, it is never allowed to do something like that on the noble flock."

At this point in the papyrus, Djedi chooses three animals to prove his magical powers: a goose, some kind of water fowl, and a bull.

He decapitates the goose and places her head at the eastern side of the audience hall, the body at the western side. Then Djedi utters a secret spell and the head of the goose stands up, starting to waddle. Then the body of the goose stands up and waddles, too. Both body-parts move in equal directions, then melt together. The resurrected goose now leaves the hall honking. The same performance is done with a water fowl and a bull. Both animals are brought successfully back to life.

No doubt impressed, now King Khufu wants to know if Djedi has access to the secrets of the god Thoth. This is important, as the king believes that the scrolls of Thoth help him with the construction of his burial—the Great Pyramid.

The king says: "It is said that you know what is inside the sanctuary of Thoth."

Djedi replies: "May you be praised, oh sovereign, my lord! I don't know what is inside, but I know where it can be found."

Khufu asks: "Where?"

Djedi answers: "There is a box of scrolls, made of flint, which is stored in an archive room at Heliopolis."

The king orders: "Fetch that box of scrolls!"

Djedi replies: "May your highness be prosperous and blessed, I am not the one who can bring it to you."

Khufu asks: "Who is the one who can bring it to me?"

Djedi answers: "The eldest of the three children in the womb of Rededjet, he will bring it to you."

The king says: "Who is this Rededjet?"

Dedi replies: "The wife of a minor priest of the god Re. The god has indicated that the eldest of the three shall worship him as a high priest of Heliopolis over the whole realm."

King Khufu now becomes impatient.

Khufu replies: "When will this Rededjet give birth?"

Dedi says: "It will happen during the first month of the planting season, on the fifteenth day."

King Khufu then complains to Djedi about the impassability of the Nile Valley during that season, in which the magician promises him a safe voyage through sufficiently deep water. Upon hearing this, the king stands and decrees,

> "Have Djedi assigned to a place within the palace of my son Djedefhor where he shall live from now on. His daily ration will be 1000 loaves of bread, 100 jars of beer, one neat, and 100 bundles of field garlic." And all things were done as commanded.

So goes the official story of Djedi the magician, but now you know better.

ABOUT THE AUTHOR

For W.J. Cherf this is his first foray into the realm of paranormal archaeology. He suspects that his recent paranormal series, The Adventures of J.J. Stone, might have had something to do with it.

Cherf is no novice to either archaeology or ancient Egypt. My God the man has seen the sun rise from atop the Great Pyramid! His award-winning five-volume time traveling series, The Manuscripts of the Richards' Trust, showcased his credentials with their adventure, intrigue, wonder, and vivid description.

As to why Cherf writes in his retirement years, he says, "I always wanted to write a book without footnotes." This is an oblique reference to his treadmill "publish or perish" days as a professor of ancient history and archaeology.

To find reviews and free chapters to all of his works, not to mention a handy source for the latest news in Egyptology, go to www.wjcherf.com. And if you are so inclined, read his BLOG and comment as necessary.